The Rembrandt Decisions

The Rembrandt Decisions

Anne V. Badgley

Dodd, Mead & Company
New York

Copyright © 1979 by Anne V. Badgley
No part of this book may be reproduced in any form
without permission in writing from the publisher
Printed in the United States of America

1 2 3 4 5 6 7 8 9 10

Library of Congress Cataloging in Publication Data

Badgley, Anne V
    The Rembrandt decisions.
    I. Title.
PZ4.B1417Re [PS3552.A315]   813'.5'4   78-13159
ISBN 0-396-07622-X

Chapter

1

The Director of the National Collection of Graphic Arts was a good deal like the sixty thousand prints under his care. He was precise, grey and white, almost two-dimensional, as though years ago he had been squeezed through remorseless print rollers. Not only was his personality meager, it was also rather juiceless. On occasion, however, the Director became quite deft and he could be clever; it was on one such occasion that he called an assistant curator to his office.

Washington was in full leaf that heavy, hot July day—albeit very languid leaf—and its residents came to work in a frank state of exhaustion. A month of record high temperatures and humidity had reduced everyone to lethargy or bad temper. Everyone but the Director. He was impeccable and immune. He would spring to his feet like crisp lettuce, then sit down at his desk again to consult tidy lists and clear notations.

'Yes, yes, get to the point,' thought the assistant curator with a tired annoyance. She knew the spiel: first the weather, then the growth of the museum to date, then the splendid job that her department was doing, his pleasure in the reputation her work had acquired—it was routine. And then little bits about some New England collector whom no one knew . . .

The small blonde summoned to sit out this recital on the latest *Who's Who in Prints* was looking into the light, and trapped in an air-conditioned draft. She felt that when he finally got to the point she was not going to be in the mood to prepare for a centennial of anyone, or the five-hundredth anniversary of anything, nor would she want to write the notes on next year's exhibition of aquatints. In brief, Mrs. Gordon wanted to be left alone to finish the chiaroscuro prints. The Director, however, kept on. He found his own conversation fascinating.

"We think Mr. Renshaw must be quite old by now, and by his own choice he remains almost unknown. We've heard rumors, naturally, for years that he was buying up prints and drawings." 'Naturally,' she thought. "At first he negotiated his own purchases, and then as he became too much in the public eye he bid through agents. Even then, that was a long time ago, and he's been buying for at least sixty years, which makes him," and the Director hummed softly as he computed, "somewhere in his nineties, I believe. At some point he grew tired of New York and moved up to New England, to an old wooden farmhouse lost in those bushy hills, I suppose."

'I suppose.' she thought.

He pushed an ashtray toward her in a conspiracy of two.

"Will you smoke, Mrs. Gordon?" He opened a silver box with Pollaiuolo's *Ten Fighting Men* engraved on the lid.

2

Catherine Gordon raised her grey eyes and shook her head. And the grey and white man smiled deferentially and kept talking.

"Now," he said with sudden sprightly decision, "Mr. Renshaw has his whole collection with him in New England. It's shocking to hear they're all stored in that ancient farmhouse, don't you agree?" The emphasis was on the word "shocking," not on the word "agree" and he shrugged his shoulders in emotionless despair.

"It'll burn. Eventually all those old wooden places burn. Isolated up there on a cold winter night with an antique thermostat pushed up high, and the furnace vibrating and boiling away . . ."

The Director was known for his long self-conversations. Mrs. Gordon was silently sorry about the furnace, but if he could just state his business instead of wondering out loud, then she could get to lunch before the salads ran out.

". . . or the collection will be burgled. Harry Renshaw must have a hundred windows in that place, we hear. If someone decided to make off with a whole roomful of prints, it would be a simple matter to loosen the century-old putty and walk in through the French doors. Just that. Even the storm windows, I hear, clip on from the outside."

The grey man stopped, tapping his teeth with a pencil.

"Of course, you understand that these are all rumors, Mrs. Gordon, just rumors from an old friend, and, I might add, one who is hoping to get the whole collection left to Harvard."

The assistant curator could scarcely have cared if it all went to Harvard or blew up with the furnace, so long as no one asked her to delay those chiaroscuro prints once more. And although the Director had stopped tapping his teeth and put down the pencil, he had not finished.

"At any rate, we may safely assume as true, I believe,

3

that Mr. Renshaw lives up there now, with an enormous amount of prints and drawings and a small staff of servants. You can probably imagine how the prints fare, all hung over radiators. Probably the ceilings wet down each spring with icicle backup. If the paper doesn't dry out and crack it'll mildew in the summers . . . those specimens that are left intact will be stolen as a matter of course as soon as the collection is better known. Now, Mrs. Gordon, we are most concerned, for some of these specimens are the counterpart of the Windsor, Chatsworth or Vienna collections. Magnificent, superb." He paused then to change the vibration. "We here, as guardians of world art, so to speak, are greatly interested . . ."

The Director was noted for his boa constrictor concerns, especially when said with a corporate "we."

"Now, Mrs. Gordon, you realize that the uncertainties of such a collection are legion . . . legion" the man repeated, fascinated with his chosen word. "Furthermore, it appears that Mr. Renshaw is a singular man, one with decided likes and dislikes." He paused, maybe unable, or perhaps unwilling, to define further. "You are a New Englander, are you not?"

She slowly froze. Partly from that last phrase, and partly from the draft on her shoulder. The boa constrictor slowly tightened the coils, with silent, oily precision. He picked up a small manila file from his desk and cleared his narrow throat.

"Mr. Renshaw has indicated here that he would like someone of sound report—he mentions you in particular— to come and catalogue his holdings, and would be pleased to offer you a substantial compensatory emolument while you were on leave from us, Mrs. Gordon. You might find it most generous."

He let the vision of money sink in while moving the

4

primary objective into second place.

"I think, and I do not feel I am being presumptuous, that Mr. Renshaw might be considering the donation of his collection to us, Mrs. Gordon." He wrinkled his brow, an effort often effective. "Naturally, it would be foresighted on our part to have the collection catalogued and assessed before the donation. . . . Do you see what I mean, Dr. Gordon?" Pause. "I'm sure you do."

Dr. Gordon was sure she did too, and she hated men who asked and answered their own questions. That requiem chant for the Renshaw collection in its little old farmhouse was primarily a love song. A love song in the mouth of a tiger . . . and the chant kept up—

"We could thereby gauge what is superior to our own holdings, and what is inferior. What attributions are shaky, what might be invaluable. After all, Mr. Renshaw may be a merchant prince in steel and fertilizers, but he is not a scholar in our sense of the word. In fact, some of his collection may be very inferior indeed. We can't know until we see it. And through your eyes, we shall have quite an in-depth view of the whole . . ."

The Director was one of those "in-depth" types, quite shallow overall, and he kept going on—

"It might even be possible to spruce it up . . . the collection, I mean. We might be able to improve the conditions of its preservation."

He dropped his voice, as though the hoary Renshaw might hear him, all the way from New England.

"Naturally," he went on, "the whole situation calls for delicacy . . ."

She understood. Whenever one planned to swallow something whole it had best be done as delicately as possible.

". . . delicacy and infinite tact and, I might add, a sense

5

of quiet persuasion," the man continued, examining the idea like a many-sided mouthful. "When Mr. Renshaw mentioned you as a primary possibility we concurred immediately."

Why would Renshaw have mentioned her? Before she had even considered this, the Director beamed; he radiated as he enumerated. "You are, shall we say, above the . . ." and here he paused a split second to think of a tactful adjective, "above the flippant age, and furthermore, your work has been most scholarly. In addition" and he turned the morsel of Renshaw's collection over another inch, "you present a gracious appearance. One that inspires confidence, we think, and one that reflects credit on our young institution." He inclined his head to accept imagined plaudits left and right, before he turned back to her with a lifted eyebrow.

It wasn't true. It couldn't be. There were other people around. There was no particular reason to ask her. No one else had wanted to go, that was all.

"You are at perfect liberty to refuse, of course, Mrs. Gordon. But," and here he threw in the road block, "but we at the Museum thought that in view of your recent widowhood, you might actually welcome a change of scene." And then the sincere approach: "These have been most trying months for you I am sure. Although New England is rather remote, yet," here he placed his fingertips together, "if you think of it in the larger sense, scholars are never remote, no matter how far afield they go. In the broader sense, we are a family, are we not?" He nodded to himself that they were. "But then, on the other hand, we mustn't be too precipitate either, must we? Take time to consider things in perspective, Dr. Gordon. Take time."

He didn't mean it; that much was obvious. The answer must come now, and right now, never mind perspective.

6

He was tapping his teeth with the pencil again, and the consideration should take no longer than two minutes, for he glanced at his watch.

Catherine knew the appropriate answer was "yes" and that it was appropriate right now. If the offer had not been "suitable" and "appropriate" for a young widow in her thirties it would not have been presented, since the whole administration considered themselves such a bloody family of scholars. At this hour the quiet, richly panelled office with its suitable prints and appropriate books (about sixty square feet of the former and three hundred square feet of the latter) gave out a deliberate feeling of finality. Possibly some of the proposed holiness had been unknowingly eliminated by a poor, precipitate interior decorator who had not been given time for perspective. One would never know, but Catherine could infer. After about two minutes, despite a wildly fluctuating pulse, she managed to say quite suitably, "Thank you, I believe I will accept."

That was all. He waited for any further phrases. There were none.

"Splendid! Splendid!" said he, filling the gap with one minute of suitable enthusiasm. "My secretary will give you the complete details."

He stood and she stood. He closed the folder on his desk, and they shook hands.

"We understand each other completely, I am sure, Dr. Gordon."

And sure or not, a month later Catherine walked out of the National Collection of Graphic Arts forever, and what happened to the chiaroscuro prints was not even considered.

It is one thing to be single by choice. One may be brilliant, witty, capable, and quite frank in one's reasons for

7

staying single. But it is something else again to be suddenly recycled by fate . . . to be thrust, reborn, into the world as one half of a bisected couple; incomplete, uncertain, and certainly unwanted. In Washington the unattached, uncertain female of the species is superfluous compared to the unattached, certain male.

In the physical sense, time had dealt serenely with her features, and one could say that it was not too late to be recycled: her angular, fine-boned face was unlined, her figure slim, and tragedy had enhanced all the elegant qualities—her eyes were even larger now. But it was more in the mental sense that Catherine had become the neutered half. The townhouse that had been so quietly joyous, so filled with life last year, had metamorphosed, downward. It was the same, but meaningless. Merely filled with furniture this year, and once that their (hers, now) two young sons had returned to boarding school, the unchanging silence of life's final decision made the hours unendurable. Who filled the evening conversation? . . . the recounting of small items? Where was his wrinkled smile, the questions to be talked about, the epoxy that cemented the door shut, the party invitations, the menus for a buffet dinner; the rumors and the small chat; and a new small car that was highly praised in the *London Times*. . . . Now, in the space of a few months all had changed: the new model was in the garage, but Charles was gone. And after the closets were cleaned, the sewing was done, plants were revived, and the freezer boxes were neatly labeled, everything, but everything attended to, Catherine began to decline.

After two months there were carefully worded suggestions, and she tried again. She threw herself into work with a frenzy, but the frenzy evaporated. The small victories previously of such moment—whether the artist had assimilated new ideas between a second and third state of a

8

plate, whether Jacopo de Barbari had influenced Dürer, or whether it had been the reverse, or the effect that Mannerism had produced on Abraham Bloemart's middle work— Dear God. She faced the appalling fact that people had lived and died without ever having considered the effect of Mannerism on Abraham Bloemart and she also had good reason to doubt the ultimate usefulness of knowing the effect of Mannerism on Bloemart at all. It was seen by everyone at the Museum that neither Renaissance prints nor Mannerist drawings would be manifestly able to pull her out of the depths of partnerless gloom.

So at six months there had been different suggestions, again carefully worded.

"I mean, Catherine, why don't you try hard to gain some weight, and then join Parents without Partners."

"So, try something new. Try the Club Méditerranée. Ride the elevators at the Georgetown Hospital. Maybe you'll meet a partnerless doctor. Buy a dog. You'll meet a man at training sessions. Write up the notes on Salviati and give a paper."

Catherine did give the paper. It was not particularly memorable. The new projection assistant had put the first slides in backward and upside down. The talk was well received however, and a few weeks later, when it was known that Harry Renshaw was seeking Dr. Gordon's help, her name was graciously offered. It just might work, and truthfully, as she had guessed, no one else cared to live in an old farmhouse or be buried in the wilds just as the season was starting. Even Catherine herself, at this particular moment, actually believed it might change the course of her useless existence.

Some of her friends did argue the point:

"Look at things. That man's had seventy years to classify his collection. And most of them are 17th century. So

9

what's struck him so all of a sudden? He mentions you by name? Well, forget it. There must be someone in Washington under ninety that's alive."

"But Catherine, think about it carefully. Your professional reputation. You won't be a northern edition—you'll just be out of print."

"It's not a leave of absence, it's a leave of wits."

"I know." she had said sadly to all and sundry. "But I haven't any other choice that looks better. I'm getting mousier by the minute and I've got to get away."

It was to her credit then that she refused to panic. The choice had been made with only one moment's consideration, and if common sense had been lacking at that moment the only sensible thing now was to keep from mentally pawing the idea over and over lest she change her mind.

So, in a somewhat dazed condition the townhouse was rented to friends, the boys and the school were notified of a temporary change in address, the insurance companies, the milkman, mailman, and a host of responsibilities were attended to, the furniture was put in storage, the plants were given away. In fact, the ease with which one could accept and then uproot, after thirteen years, was quite appalling.

Chapter

2

At eight o'clock one tepid Washington morning in early September, after the boys were settled in boarding school, Mrs. Charles Gordon, the remaining half of Mr. and Mrs. Charles Gordon, filled her thermos with strong, hot coffee, placed two large suitcases in the back seat of the car, and slipped noiselessly and unnoticed into the freeway traffic headed for Baltimore and points north. The rush hour was just passing its peak, and because she was headed out rather than in, the delays were minimal. The car purred out to the Beltway and onto Interstate 95.

From 95 through to the Harbor Tunnel Freeway she drove with a mind absolutely blank . . . past the brewery, past the sign with the long list of prohibitions for those entering the tunnel (one went by them so quickly it was a wonder that explosives, horse-drawn vehicles, self-drawn carts, and pedestrians didn't get sucked in by mistake), and on into the tunnel. If she had become a similar victim,

11

sucked in by mistake, it was also too late, and what lay ahead was only the inexorable progression of uncertain events. In this frame of mind she remained wedged between two diesel trucks, one "Nonflammable" and one "Caution, Flammable" for several miles.

Then the whole of the New Jersey Turnpike to its bitter and acrid end, and the George Washington Bridge. Suddenly Catherine stretched and smiled, for somehow the lower level of the bridge reminded her pleasantly of the Library of Congress with its subterranean steam pipes and its Piranesi dungeonlike regions.

For that one building alone she had moved to Washington fourteen years ago; for its seventy-five million volumes and three hundred miles of shelves, and it had been within that intellectual ghetto, in the Stygian gloom of those unwindowed stacks, that she had met Charles Gordon.

Charles was ten years older, and had rescued her from exhaustion and dehydration when she had exited from the elevator at the wrong level and could no longer find her way to the cafeteria. After remarking that she looked a bit peaked, he had assessed the situation and had then pursued his quarry with such low-keyed intensity that Catherine had fallen desperately in love without feeling trapped either by Charles or by the complexity of the Library. Their marriage had been harmonious; it produced two sons and thirteen years of delight.

During the early years of motherhood she had retired from research to devote her complete energies to the two children, but as they became old enough to cut and paste, the vast untidied fields of Renaissance problems beckoned once again. After much anguish and deliberation, Catherine Gordon shifted her allegiance down the hill to the newest museum, the National Collection of Graphic Arts. The Li-

12

brary, it was true, had been more homey, more comfortable, more old-fashioned and relaxed, but Graphics had higher ceilings, it even had windows, and it had money. Money somehow did make a difference.

And one could say also, as she drove onward, that the difference between Connecticut and Vermont was money. For it seemed that greasy civilization, which had squatted untidily more than two centuries over the southern part of New England had probably decided that the northern states were hardly worth a squat. Nothing this far back had changed since her childhood. Here and there a few unpruned apple trees were holding desultory fruit and last winter's sand was still on the edge of the highway. Traffic was light and troublefree. Like the Museum staff, maybe no one civilized had wanted to come this far north and aside from a rude Jaguar that flicked its lights with imperious disdain as it prepared to pass, the majority of the cars were the same salt-corroded, tired vehicles she had known in her youth. She drove on, sniffing the autumn air. Another fifty miles brought her to a Scenic Point where Vermont sloped steeply down to the Connecticut River, and somewhere across the river in the woods would be the Renshaw farmhouse.

Catherine pulled off into the parking area to enjoy her coffee. It was quiet. At the far end the Jaguar was parked and empty, and the tones of autumn lay everywhere about. Catherine's spirits rose in that sunny spot, and the precipitate decision seemed almost lighthearted and correct. For the first time, the New Hampshire assignment could be thought about with a certain feeling of reality, even though recluse ninety-year-old New Yorkers might be presented to her in all aspects. New England had so many of its own. Cadaverous coots who hid their dollars behind loose bricks and up the flue or Berensons-in-reverse who placed Italian

13

villas in surprising spots, always chosen in full summer or early fall with small regard for the complexities of full winter and early mud. The first type always kept the original grey and green battleship linoleum in front of the kitchen sink, worn right through to the boards by three consecutive wives who dropped from exhaustion, and, in the latter case, it was the Italian cypresses that were hard put to survive. She was confident that she could remain quite detached about either kind.

After the last cup of bitter brew, she felt revived, even quite courageous, and watched the owner of the English car climb back up the steep meadow slope with a pair of binoculars in hand; a foreign bird watcher who slipped into his car and roared off. Catherine sat on in a muffled contentment until a family with four children drove in next to her. They burst out, the children investigating, prying, trying everything in sight—swinging the garbage can lids, trying to lift the cap rocks off the retaining wall, kicking at the loose stones. When they led their pets to relieve themselves on the tires of her car, she left, heading off the parkway and down across the river to look for a gas station and for the Renshaw place. In about ten miles the general character of the trip became much more specific.

While gas was groaning out of an antique red pump, Catherine ventured a question on the Renshaw farm, but none of the men who lounged in the afternoon sun could rightly place the name. The query was then hollered back to the rear of the general store, through the old chicken-wired swinging doors into the gloom of its ancient clutter, and a boy of about twelve appeared. He was juggling two apples and a walnut and was none too eager to stop, but at the end of three unsuccessful tries to integrate the walnut he gave up.

"Yeah. I know where he lives. He's the guy up the

14

Mine Road. My mom says he bought old man Pelham's place. He's old. In fact he's so old that he's stuffed. He's . . ."

"That'll be enough, sonny. The lady ain't pining for details, just directions," said the red-faced man at the pump. He looked at her rather closely as she paid him for the gas.

"That'll be about four miles further, over the hill and a turn to the left. Richard knows the summer folk on account of living up there. If you might be wanting to drop him off he'll show you the right turn. They're not all that well marked."

Richard accepted this ploy to protect the apple and nut bin with reluctance, as the back of the general store was the height of a day's excitement after school. He stuffed the fruit into a shapeless pocket, and climbed in beside her; he kept silent as she drove over the hill. Then he decided to eat one of the apples and, once his mouth was full, offered the information that Mr. Renshaw was old, almost dead as a matter of fact, and rumor had it that just his body and not his brain sat in a big chair at a table . . . and that he was a mummy—stuffed you know. He looked at her for confirmation. Maybe even a prospective victim of sorts, for he knew that being as old as Mr. Renshaw must equate with evil. In fact, while speculating too long on evil, he missed the turn.

"Oops" he swallowed hard, "there's the stop back there, lady. You just back up to the tree and turn in there, and keep goin'. You'll see the house after a while. He's old, lady, real old. My mom says old man Pelham didn't fit in around here too well neither . . ."

Richard got out, gave the apple a big heave at the dusty elm, and walked backwards toward his lane to watch her car drive away to some sort of interesting doom. Catherine

15

waved her thanks and turned her car into the dusty, unmarked road and kept going, a last turn in this inexorable progression.

It was a typical New Hampshire back road, really back, cutting through tree roots, overhung by willowy shrubs, poison ivy banks, dipping into thickety hollows of standing water with straggly hemlocks, and one could almost feel its abandoned, airless character even with the radio at full blast and the windows shut tight against the dust. The road merely proved that this coot would be the battleship linoleum version of New England recluses; the kind who drag about in a dirty bathrobe ordered from Montgomery Ward forty years ago with twenty scrawny cats breeding in a back barn. She knew how the prints and drawings would be—all thrown on damp mattresses on an unheated attic floor, in drunken piles tottering on old apple crates, and lying about over cracked mirrors or bowed in curves inside old wash basins, and stained where last winter's snow had sifted through broken roof slats.

Catherine, however, was made of fairly stern New England stuff herself and made a mental note to write L.L. Bean for some insulated sleepwear. That was all. Eventually she saw the sign.

It was a very small sign: "H. Renshaw." Nothing remarkable about it, except that it was cast of heavy bronze and did not lean drunkenly or show any evidence that it came from Montgomery Ward. After her car turned in through a broad gate, the wide driveway led up a shallow hill, through birch clumps and white pine of immense size, and then wandered with aimless unconcern for the sterner realities of the price of gravel or snow plows through an extended parkland of trees and meadows until it came to rest, as if by surprise, at the vast terrace of a tremendous house. Not that the house itself was many storied or fiercely

16

dominant—there was just so much of it. Its one level flowed on and on in various directions, not by a pioneer addition or subtraction, but in one great coherent mass until it covered the hilltop. Catherine reassessed her thoughts. All right then, she could abandon the linoleum image, but what came in its place?

Without doubt this was still New Hampshire, but the house, the meadows, and the long approach were pulled together in such careless magnificence that only an outsider could have conceived it. She shook her head in an inbred native mistrust of all those fool enough to park houses a block long on the tops of remote hills, miles from county telephone poles and snow plows . . . or who deliberately planted clumps of trees in open land once cleared by unbelievable exertion, or who had enough money to bury their oil tanks out of sight, to place telephone wires underground, to put everything unsightly out of sight. The land itself was in splendid shape only because the farmer himself had sold out, and long ago.

Well. Catherine stopped the car at the broad steps, turned off the engine, and considered. Maybe this was not the house of an old linoleum coot, maybe the Director's own house would burn down before this one did. In fact, if Harvard were indeed tugging and bringing its own mystique to bear on the collection inside, the National Collection had underestimated Renshaw and had sent exactly the wrong person to play tug of war.

There was no sound. The car cooled with a "plink" now and then; that was all. And it was not a very expensive "plink" either. It was, rather, a cheap tinny sound, as if all the important parts were made of plastic—a material that did not fit in with the tremendous terrace above the driveway. There were large tubs of flowers—not thin and exhausted petunias, weakened, weedy after a summer of ne-

17

glect, but fat, healthy specimens, bursting with well-pruned life. A well-paid gardener came with the well-pruned plants. But even more could be inferred from those tubs and pots. There were not so many as to seem garish, and not so few as to appear miserly. It was what one might call a "relaxed" amount, halfway between New England "suitable" and California lush. The Director had never inferred that Mr. Renshaw might know exactly what he was doing. While he was thinking crisply and tapping his teeth, he had left out the main point completely: that this position required a first class public relations man, not a widow, growing mousier by the month.

Catherine continued sitting and looking. Would the knowledgeable, intuitive, expensive Renshaw realize that hers was not a well-thought-out acceptance? That it was actually a flight, a rout, a disorderly dash from nowhere to nowhere?

There was still no sound or movement from the house, and for a second she had the wild impulse to drive madly around the circle and back to Washington. By midnight she could be there. But the moment of panic passed. She opened the car door, walked up the great steps and knocked.

A grey-haired servant opened the door.

"Good day, Madame?" It was a question. She had perhaps lost her way?

"I'm Dr. Gordon, from Washington."

He bent his head in a kindly manner as if she were speaking Sanskrit by mistake. There was a pause. She enlarged the description.

"Mrs. Gordon, from the National Collection. I believe that Mr. Renshaw is expecting me."

The man paused. He looked at her as if a woman, or anyone under seventy had never been seen there before.

18

Then he beckoned her inside and indicated a carved Flemish bench, suitably uncomfortable—no doubt for transients.

"I'll ask Mr. Renshaw, Madame." He turned and disappeared down an immense hall, around the corner, and was gone. Not a sound further. Naturally, there was the possibility that the ninety-two-year-old Renshaw might have forgotten his request. He might have become senile a month ago and incapable of recall—in which case she could drive right back to Washington with justification. But from the uncomfortable bench Catherine could see into two reception rooms, each of which could hold a hundred people with ease. Great oriental rugs lay heavily on the parquet floors, their richness illuminated by huge windows alternating with immense French doors. In size alone, the space was meaningless. The incredible aspect came from the walls, from the Renshaw collection. It ran in riotous profusion, along the front hall into the back hall, into the reception rooms. The prints and drawings were hung at all levels—from the ceiling moldings to below waist height—soon one would have to crawl on hands and knees to see the latest additions. No one, it was rumored, knew the size of Mr. Renshaw's collection, and he himself might have forgotten its actual numbers. No curators had ever been invited, it was said, and nothing was allowed to be published or photographed; only by referring to scattered records of sales and auctions all over the Western world could one perhaps infer which buyers had bought for Renshaw. It was apparent that he had both his collection and his privacy, and the fortune to afford both.

The only other features were tall narrow bookcases that rose at intervals to restrict the flow of art. Even the books appeared to be filled with engravings; probably geographical, botanical, mythological. All had beautiful bindings. And since no one returned, Catherine got up and

19

wandered about, looking at what there was, compared to what the Director had imagined. These were wonderfully preserved prints, beautifully matted, none dry and cracking or foxed with little brown stains, none hung over radiators or under evidence of icicle drips. In fact, only if she had been ill-intentioned would there have been reason for the Director's doubts. A good-sized plucking of the bottom layers and a quick dash down the hill could have been effected, especially with the French doors wide open at the other end.

"Dr. Gordon?" He had arrived so silently that Catherine had had no time to compose a suitable, museum-type phrase, so there was a moment of silence.

One could see where the legends began, for Mr. Renshaw was difficult to determine. He was a shrunken, indistinct thing in a wheelchair, wrapped in an enormous white wool shawl that covered a dark suit. The mummylike wrapping was the same color as his hair and his skin, and when one had separated the three, there was still not much to see. It was as though the substance had evaporated over the years, leaving just a voice and brilliant dark eyes.

Renshaw himself was in no hurry for phrases; he looked at her from top to bottom, lowered his glasses, looked again, and then he slowly extended a parchment-colored hand beyond the confines of the shawl.

"Dr. Gordon? Ah yes. How do you do." The hand was dry and cold, but quite firm. He turned to the butler who was standing in the background. "Lawrence, tell Mrs. Oliphant to prepare tea."

The dark eyes watched the butler disappear and then they turned slowly to her with a strange expression. Catherine looked back at Mr. Renshaw with some unease, hoping that he was not about to pursue and pinch. Her experience with older men had not been extensive. However, all he

20

did was to ask her courteously to sit down, and waved his hand toward a large Queen Anne chair.

She sat.

"You're very young to bury yourself up here," he pointed out and then fell silent. He had not used the word "inexperienced." The statement had been meant as bald fact, not as an accusation, but she felt that an implication was there nevertheless. Mr. Renshaw had probably been close to sixty when she was born, and there was a vague lack of confidence in a grandchild expert. One could not simply answer "But I am thirty-five," for in the eyes of ninety-two it seemed ridiculous. So she said nothing and just looked at him steadily with her grey eyes. Then he continued.

"I'm an old man as you can see, Dr. Gordon. I enjoy my seclusion. People come to me, but I no longer make an effort to get out. One gets cantankerous and used to one's own things." He wheezed slightly, and used short phrases.

There was a pause and again she said nothing. One could hardly agree "Yes, you do get cantankerous" or dare to disagree. The eyes kept studying her face, with reptilian, unblinking assessment.

But who else would Mr. Renshaw have cared to assess at the museum? Certainly not the Director. And certainly not the smooth, tattersall-check boys with their busy assurance and overquick laughter. One older curator did come to mind, but she was cantankerous too, and that combination would have been disastrous. Mr. Renshaw had simply not researched the situation. Maybe the head of the Smithsonian would have suited this place, but he lacked the grand enthusiasm for prints.

A few wasps were walking up and down the big windows, making a dull search for an exit; there must have been a parallel somewhere between the insects and the young curator. Then, without a change in expression, some-

21

how Catherine felt that the issue at hand was resolved. Mr. Renshaw had considered the problem and it was dismissed. Having once and for all expressed his surprise at being offered a lesser creation, his manner changed. It became gentle, as if women were a special order of humans who needed encouragement since they were fundamentally inferior.

"Did you drive from Washington in one day?" he said, to put her at ease.

"Yes. I left this morning. The weather was magnificent." There was little else to add except routes and the traffic count so she stopped. Mr. Renshaw, however, had his purposes. Without much surprise, Catherine found herself being dismissed.

"Then you must be weary after such a long drive. Mrs. Oliphant will have tea ready for you in your apartment." He turned to the butler with a smile. "This is Lawrence. He has chosen to share my retreat . . . for thirty years . . ." The intuitive mummy paused to get more breath. "You know, Dr. Gordon, this is a very simple and isolated life. They must have told you that in Washington." He looked at her again with rather neutral enthusiasm, doubting whether the simple, isolated life would really do. And contrary to her first thoughts, although Mr. Renshaw was rather old and crippled, there was nothing decadent or crippled in his conversation or regard. She obviously held small interest for him: he was used to his own discussions and his own conclusions, and his conclusion about her was just so-so.

"We have cocktails at seven-thirty . . . the south living room," and he waved a wraithlike hand toward the other salon. "Dinner is at eight—informal of course. Right now there are three of us: you, myself . . . and a Scottish friend. Tomorrow I'll show you the collection. We can talk about what you'll do here." As a matter of fact, Catherine had

22

thought it was the reverse, that she might be telling him what she would do here, but before she thought this through, he had turned her over to Lawrence.

"Show Dr. Gordon where you will garage her car, Lawrence. Then show her to her rooms, please."

The last phrase gave off just a bit of an impression that he hoped that she would stay in them, but then Mr. Renshaw added with more grace that he hoped she would use the house and grounds as her very own. At this last, Catherine smiled with equal grace. Mr. Renshaw then wheeled himself off, and Lawrence stepped forward to open the front door and indicate the low silhouette of the garage down the slope.

"The car doors are on the other side, Madame. Mr. Renshaw never cared to see the inside of a garage from the reception rooms, so he had the entries moved. I'll show you your spot."

They walked down the terrace together and down the secondary flight of steps at the far end that led to the remodeled barn. At the far side was a large, black Daimler, maybe used in years past by Renshaw, and next to it was a Jaguar, much like the one in the parking lot this afternoon. The next stall was hers. It was one of several that must have known days of splendid social activity long ago. There was even a second floor, a loft of sorts. Lawrence held the small front door of the garage open for her as they finished the tour.

"I'll put your car away later, Dr. Gordon. We leave the keys on the dashboards here."

That was sensible. Certainly, after earning the first fifty million it must be easier to lose a car once in a while than to rummage about continuously in pockets for car keys. Catherine followed the butler as he took the suitcases out of her car and carried them with care back up the main steps, in the open door, down the central hall, and along a large gallery that ran the length of the rear of the house. At its north end he turned another corner and opened one of the two doors toward the front of the house.

"This is your apartment, Dr. Gordon. I'll place the cases in your bedroom." Lawrence passed in front of her, glancing about each room as if he were checking the maid's work, and then indicated a bell on the wall. "If you want anything further, you may ring. The gentlemen will be expecting you at seven-thirty, Madame."

The butler left her then. He closed the door firmly behind him, and his footsteps became more and more indistinct until they vanished, and the accustomed silence of the isolated house oozed slowly back into every corner. It was an eerie sensation. The inexorable progression suddenly had come to a halt now, like a movie with the sound suddenly broken off or a train stopping in the middle of nowhere and just puffing to itself, in a field of corn stubble.

She sat down in the living room, on the elegant sofa, beside the coffee table in inlaid woods. Someone had brought tea before she arrived and it waited for her attention: the gracious silver service, the pile of tiny cakes decorated in pink, green, and blue fondant frosting, the embroidered napkin, the silver hot water jug and tiny slices of lemon with a fork, a folded newspaper. Outside the window the setting sun reflected itself off the hills to the east.

Catherine poured herself a cup of tea and then picked up the paper, trying to slow down, trying to idle away the time. The *Boston Herald* seemed to carry its international news on the second or third page, in small print; today it was below an advertisement for kidney pills. There was not much: Israeli conflicts, an Arab oil price increase expected, a kidnapping in Italy, and an art theft in Kabul. She read the latter with mild interest:

24

Kabul: Officials at the Kabul museum report the daring theft of eleven priceless 16th century manuscripts valued at well over a million dollars. Guards managed to wound one of the robbers, but the coup was carefully planned, and the men escaped in a government vehicle.

In lightning succession this daring group has pillaged three museums here, with the apparent collaboration of an inside informant each time.

A tight lid of secrecy has been clamped on the affair pending investigation by the police.

She put down the paper. Her feet were cold and her spirits were chill; in a couple of hours an uneasy life began with two elderly men in a quiet house. The collection itself would be no problem; she could call in experts in other areas to help, but Renshaw himself: what would she talk about with Renshaw, not just tonight, but every day, week, month, all winter long?

After a second cup of tea, she ran herself a hot bath in the elegantly fitted bathroom, and after soaking up its warmth for half an hour she slipped between the silk bedsheets, set her alarm for seven, and fell asleep.

25

Chapter

3

To fill the minutes after her sleep, Catherine unpacked slowly, almost reluctant to empty the suitcase. The thick, wooden, satin-smooth hangers that clustered in the closets were relics of a better age—like Mr. Renshaw himself. They issued from a time when life was worthy—created handsome, durable, and meant to be savored; when everything and everyone was chosen with great care, like the leatherbound, gold-tooled books in the reception room, the heavy doors that shut perfectly, just like everything that was in its place and in working order. The only flaw in this room was herself. She was misplaced; not only out of print from the start, but a complete misprint. Once the first, perfect, ancient gentleman was reinforced by a second, both of them shaking their prehistoric heads in grave doubt, the effect would be overwhelming, and she might spend the whole winter shuttling from the prints to a teacup quarantine.

Naturally, she saw why no one else had been fool

enough to volunteer. They had seen, far better than herself, that the whole idea was too equivocal: not only to catalogue someone's collection in businesslike fashion, but to radiate goodwill and tact, all winter long, night and day, hour after hour to an old man with quirks . . . and now two of them.

Certainly Mr. Renshaw had wanted someone distinctly different. And the fact that he was now confronted with an unwanted female, possibly immature, would be closed in with her for the winter, well, it was a poor beginning.

Most probably Renshaw and his friend, clicking their teeth at lunch, had already formed an image—a stellar person, naturally. A Dr. Gordon to liven up the dreary season; a gentleman of course, wise and urbane, sliding with ease from the world of art to cocktails at great estates, speaking only with the upper echelons, coping expertly with protocol, someone knowledgeable about the World Bank, the International Monetary Fund, the state of federal spending, the seasonal expansion and decline of everything, and all of this at the dinner hour each evening, for cocktails before, and loving it.

Not long after this analysis, the voice of the second member could be heard in the gallery talking to the first. For a ninety-year-old his voice carried strongly and well. Too well.

"Harry, I say, whose car is in the garage?" He pronounced "garage" with the accent on the first syllable.

"That's the new curator from Washington."

There was a silence, dumbfounded, or maybe his teeth had slipped.

"A curator? Here? Right now? Harry, you're joking of course." A silence. The voice changed its tone; becoming moderate, restrained: "We agreed, Harry, didn't we, that we couldn't let anyone in at this time. That it was going to have to be carefully controlled from now on?" At this Ren-

28

shaw must have made some gesture. "Then, what's this man doing here? Jesus Christ, Harry, I just arrived. This is my holiday. How long is this freak going to stay?" The last was said in total exasperation.

Renshaw must have been mustering strength.

"All winter, I expect. Maybe longer." It was a soft reply.

There was a groan of dismay. "God, Harry! Curators. They're all a bunch of misfits. Even if you collected paintings they'd be misfits, Harry, but *prints!* Some ass who spends his life looking through a magnifying glass at little lines, who writes delicate notations in margins, who gets in a funk about mildew, who washes his hands before touching . . . pale and shaking after years in darkened rooms to keep his precious parchments out of the light!" The irate man paused, but not for breath. "Where'd you put him?"

"Next to you, Forbes. It's the only apartment left."

"Good grief!" The man lowered his volume to a whisper. "Next door? Why didn't you say so!" He then made an abrupt decision. "I'm going to need a drink, and right now."

To this Mr. Renshaw must have agreed, for both voices retreated back down the gallery and she could hear voice two announcing that he had been coming here for nine years and how could Harry spring this on him with no relief and all the southern apartments ripped up for wiring, and then just mumbles until they turned the corner.

Catherine sat down on her bed with one of the thick, smoothly polished hangers in her hand, feeling even more widowed than usual. Never mind the winter's conversation, the Monetary Fund, the seasonal declines of soybean futures. She would surely arrive back in Washington within the week: unused, unwanted, more uncertain than when she had left, and the Renshaw collection would fly to the Fogg.

29

A black wool dress was the only outfit suitable; she pulled it off the hanger and put it on. She rolled her long blonde hair into a severe French twist and applied makeup with reserve. Somewhere in the house a large grandfather clock sounded the solitary note of doom. A grandfather clock, of course.

She opened her door and set off down the long hall.

As luck would have it, Mr. Renshaw was nowhere in sight. A cheerful fire cast flickers of brightness on the walls and a portable bar was rolled to one side. Three chairs had been nicely arranged for conversation. Three chairs, dear God.

A gentleman in rough tweeds was there by the bar, his back to her, humming softly and mixing himself a drink . . . probably the fourth by now. From the look of his powerful shoulders, the guest was hardly the ancient equivalent of Mr. Renshaw in years, and certainly not his equivalent in manners. Catherine felt some sort of back-to-the-wall survival surge into her blood. Boors one could always cope with.

The man turned around, glass in hand, smooth banalities in reserve; but then he stopped his stirring, put down his glass and stared. She stared right back, she might as well take a good look if this was to be but a one night stand. One night it was, plus one afternoon, for she had seen him climbing back into his car in the freeway parking vista; the amateur bird watcher with expensive toys. He even looked like a hawk with deep-set eyes and intent, arrogant stare.

"Hello." he said, "Are you a guest I haven't met?"

She debated the strong approach, going over and pumping his hand vigorously, or throwing herself carelessly into a chair, one leg dangling and stretching out a hand for a cigarette. Neither appealed so she was left with the small side of the answer.

30

"No." she said.

"Well! If you're not a guest, then you must be permanent." And he left it to her, smiling with secret amusement. He measured the soda carefully, squinting through the glass into a light.

"I'm the curator from Washington." There should have been a fine cutting edge about freaks and misfits, but three cups of coffee and two cups of tea in five hundred miles hadn't left much originality in her and she lost the tactical advantage right there.

"Well, well! Think of that! My names is Forbes, Duncan Forbes." He turned back to the bar and picked up a glass. "Come over here and let me mix you something. Better still, sit down and I'll bring it to you. What'll you have?"

The man spoke with the effortless grace of one who has kept all his relationships two-dimensional and pleasant, with no intention of allowing significance to intrude. A basic burr in his voice was almost unnoticeable, oiled away by expensive schools and expensive friends. The timbre indicated neither the obstinate American nor the overbred Britisher—such a careful compound, this overweaning bird watcher. He waited for her answer and even covered for her silence when she could think of no particular drink that appealed.

"If we haven't got the fixings here, Lawrence can get them from the kitchen. Harry stocks everything: Mexican, Greek, Russian. You name it, we'll have it!"

Catherine debated the wisdom of having anything at all on an empty stomach, but opposite this worldly paragon it would sound too prim and nonalcoholic to say ginger ale and, in addition, she needed the blood sugar before Mr. Renshaw arrived.

Forbes turned about again and surveyed her propor-

31

tions, top to bottom, in a rather too-candid manner, and announced that he would mix her a martini as it was the only American drink that he knew to be potent enough to equalize everyone in the country for one hour. Half was comment and half was insult, but she nodded in vague assent and put her faith in an imminent equalizer. For a few seconds there was just the sound of the hissing and spitting of the fire, little ice and glass noises. Then he came forward with a highball glass filled to the brim.

"There you are, young lady. A bit larger than usual, no doubt, on account of the uncertainties. Two men on a hilltop in the wilds of America are a bit much, I expect."

Perhaps the "bit much" referred to his slurs in the gallery, but he said nothing further and sat down in the second of the three chairs, next to her.

"Cheers," he said, to prompt her demise. The drink would have filled a pitcher, even without ice. He was hoping she would pass out before dinner.

"Harry will be fifteen minutes late. I turned off the electricity this afternoon and I never got back to his clock. Yours must be the wind-up variety." He looked over at her and smiled. "I say. I'm sorry about the curator fuss back there in the gallery. You must have heard. Actually, for a woman, it seems quite natural, after a bit . . ."

After a bit of alcohol. Catherine was fortified by the first sip. "If I'm pale and shaking right now, it certainly isn't from years in darkened rooms."

"You're entitled to be, at any rate, tonight." He rose to pass some smoked oysters on little toasted rounds—not dried out melba, but crisp hand-cut rounds, oozing with lightly browned butter and still warm.

"Tell me" he said, popping three or four in his mouth at once, "Why do you just say 'Dr. C. Gordon' on your papers? I saw them on Harry's desk a while back. In your

32

profession is it better to pretend to be masculine. I mean, don't people find out eventually?"

Banter, but so typically continental. One had to keep explaining oneself, and they never took it with grace, so she just smiled. In Scotland it was probably the Stone Age still, or they hung moose heads.

With great good fortune the slow squeak of Mr. Renshaw's wheelchair rescued her from a tedious turn with the Caledonian bore. Lawrence steered the old man to the fireside, and locked the wheels of the chair. Then, while the butler went to pour out a whiskey, the old man loosened a pole from his chair and hooked it in a ring in the floor. By this means Renshaw pulled himself slowly to his feet, and then, once on his feet, inched his way to the third chair, enveloped as always in his great woolly scarf, and so unsure of his balance that Catherine had the impulse to rush over before he fell into the fire; but Forbes and Lawrence were studied in their unconcern, and Renshaw eventually settled himself to his satisfaction quite unaided. He turned to her as Lawrence brought his whiskey.

"You've both met by now, I'm sure," he wheezed. "I'm late. Forbes; you did this on purpose, no doubt, to meet our new member on your own? Aren't you pleased we have a lady to sit with?" This was a bald prompt, and Forbes bowed with meek grace from his chair.

"Indeed I am pleased. We should have tried one long ago!"

Renshaw smiled. "Forbes patents things, Dr. Gordon. Electrical things. He tries some of his inventions here. You'll find that the power will go off periodically and suddenly . . ." The little man slowed down for lack of breath, and then started up again. "He's rewiring the place, says we can't burn down the guests like we used to. Last year he did the north wing where you are. This year the south, before

33

that he redid the main halls, the print room . . ."

"You're an electrical engineer?" Catherine asked the bird man, trying to hold off commodities reports for a while.

"No. Actually I'm a barrister, a lawyer to you. It just happens that electricity, a hobby, claims most of my time right now." The man called Forbes fell quiet suddenly; he turned his glass around and around in his hands as he watched the fire. Somber lines about his mouth carved his face into a kind of deep relief portrait.

" . . . not all electrical," Mr. Renshaw was saying. "Forbes invented my hook and ring. Before that I was even more of a prisoner. Try sitting for days, Dr. Gordon. It's nice to move without calling for help." His thin hand waved toward other parts of the room. "Watch for these rings. Forbes simply put them where he thought it would be handy. Not handy for others, though. On festive occasions with people wandering about I find it best to have them all removed. Otherwise one sees most astonishing gymnastics from time to time." He chuckled at some remembrance and then went right on to another thought. "Tell me, Forbes, how was Kabul this time?"

The man looked at Mr. Renshaw without expression. "Dusty." That was all he said. So Empire, Catherine thought. So British! To be in Afghanistan and remember only the dust. Probably brought his own tea and marmalade as well.

"I read something about Kabul this afternoon." She tried to hold up her end of the conversation. "A museum robbery . . . manuscripts. That's strange, I find."

"Why, Dr. Gordon?" said Mr. Renshaw. He was quick, for an old man.

"Oh, I don't know. One would think that in a developing country manuscripts wouldn't be so easy to turn over.

34

Transistor radios would have a better chance. I mean, you find works of art as specialized as manuscripts appreciated most in more effete countries—England, France. What chance would a peasant have of peddling a priceless manuscript? He'd have his head cut off in no time."

"What do you think, Forbes?"

"What do I think?" said the man, "I think we should change the 'Doctor Gordon' part." The Scottish guest then roused himself mentally without changing his position. Whether it was the five whiskey and sodas, or an end to speculation about Kabul was not immediately apparent. "Doctor Gordon" he mimicked in a slow way, all the while looking into the fire. "Do they come with names, these curators? Are we to be privileged this winter?"

"Come, come now, Forbes. We've hardly given her a chance." said the little man in the scarf, ignoring much and peering at her from its depths, to see how the balance of power would fall. "You've been talking every minute."

"Catherine." she replied. The giant martini had made some inroads by this time, scattering the little she knew about the stock market, but allowing her the memory of her own name. It would not have mattered much, for Renshaw took "Catherine" into his own hands and threw it out, in a sudden decision.

"Not Catherine," he stated, as if he owned the prerogative. "Call you Kate."

"Good idea, Harry," said the tweed birdman, as if he owned fifty percent of the stock. And before Kate had time to answer, the bookcases on one side slid noiselessly apart, revealing a pleasant interior room of small size.

Renshaw got to his feet and managed a few phrases at the same time. "Not meant to be a secret." he puffed. "Doors are difficult for me. Forbes has put in panels here and there. Other dining room is too big." Lawrence

35

brought up the wheelchair and helped him sit back . . . "too drafty" finished the nonagenarian. "At my age, drafts are difficult."

Lawrence indicated that she was to precede the gentlemen. He seated her on one side of a small table, with the two hosts facing each other on either side of their guest. The panels slid shut behind them.

"I tell Forbes that he can always look out the skylight if he feels penned in. Nothing else to look at here but ourselves."

"Yes indeed. Harry's given me one small area of rest from his collection. It gets to be a bit much, all this print and drawing . . ." said Forbes, smooth now and gathering steam. "I tried to persuade Harry to put a niche in the wall for his one piece of sculpture, just a moment of relief, as it were, but Harry hates sculpture. He'd rather look at plain walls than busts." At this, Mr. Forbes' face twitched ever so slightly as he pondered some further development of his phrase but then, thinking better of it, he smiled instead. Catherine blushed and felt annoyed; he knew that she knew what he thought.

"What sort of sculpture do you have, Mr. Renshaw?" she asked.

"Greek head, I'm afraid." wheezed the man between spoonfuls of hot soup.

"Is that so dreadful?"

"An albatross. Bought it once to help out. Can't get rid of it now without appearing ungrateful. Keep loaning it out . . . Athens . . . Papers written . . . research . . . footnotes . . . For every footnote goes up a thousand in value. Athens resents my having it. Elgin marbles and that sort of thing. Insurance goes up. Liability to everyone." He fixed her with his beady eyes, out of breath, but forming an idea. "What do you know about Greek sculpture?"

36

"Nothing, Mr. Renshaw. Absolutely nothing."

"Just as well," he said, deflating a bit. "Prints less controversial . . ."

"Ah, less controversial, Harry, but so flat!" Forbes couldn't leave well enough alone. "I like sculptural shapes. I like Henry Moore for instance. His reclining women. Tactile: all those hips and holes. What do you think, Kate?"

She didn't flinch. "Solids and voids, I think you mean, Mr. Forbes. Henry Moore is very concerned with positive and negative values."

Renshaw smiled.

As a timid little maid served the courses, the men took over the conversation for themselves. The soup was the preamble to advances and declines on the New York, American, and London Exchanges, and she was grateful to be able to just observe.

Mr. Renshaw was still an anomalous shape. She had a vision of straightening out a piece of cooked spaghetti, trying to define its original length. But at the dinner table his infirmities were not of great moment, and as his fingers deftly moved through the soup course, the rolls, and the wine, his attentive eyes missed nothing. He listened to Forbes and motioned to Lawrence and signalled the maid with an indefinable reactivity of eyes and hands, not completely understood. Duncan Forbes, on the other hand, was too definite, too completely understood. He was one of those total rust-colored Britishers who come on too strong. All ruddy-toned English looked much alike to her, somewhat like healthy vultures, and this man resembled them all, except for his very straight, white teeth, and exceptionally deep tan. His hands looked fortyish, maybe slightly less. They were calm hands, square and blunt, with calm, square and blunt gold cufflinks on the white shirt. Well, who wouldn't be calm with all this spread about every day.

37

Both men were accustomed to being served, she could see that. Renshaw ate in the right-handed fashion; Forbes in the ambidextrous European manner, and neither bothered to establish eye contact with the maid nor even seemed to notice that they were being served. The minute Forbes reached for a cigarette, Lawrence was at his side with a match, and it never interrupted the drop in Bethlehem Steel. However, once the business reports were dealt with, and their primary hunger satisfied, the two men put themselves out to be kind. The Scot spoke up first, perhaps to smooth the edges of previous ragged impressions.

"Harry" he said, "I want you to take note. See how the presence of a woman makes this meal into a truly gracious occasion. You really should have chosen a woman long ago. I always said that this place needed something, and here it is!" He arched his eyebrow at Renshaw.

"Way off the track, Forbes. This place needs nothing. It's just quiet. You're not used to it. If you move around all the time, my place is bound to appear . . . slow."

"Nonsense, Harry. I like being slow. After all, Scotland has its wilds too, but it's a two-sexed wilderness, Harry. Here, it was the perpetual lack—a famine, one might say—" and he glanced at the manna. "Of course, we don't know. In America do experts revert to their type, back in primeval surroundings" He leaned back in his chair and examined a dessert spoon lying above his plate with attention. "I find that a civilization reflects itself in many small aspects. Take, for example, the American "half and half." Now in Scotland when we say cream, we mean Cream! Thick, heavy, smooth, not a pallid chemical substitute. And consequent upon that, in Scotland, when we say women, we mean Women." And he left all the adjectives to regroup themselves.

The new maid in the background giggled at this, and

38

Lawrence indicated his extreme displeasure with her behavior. Catherine hoped that Lawrence might go on to indicate the same to Mr. Forbes.

"Pay no attention, Kate," said Renshaw. "Forbes does pester. That's his amusement when life is slow. The consensus is, I believe, that life was slow, but is now picking up." Renshaw chuckled, and examined some fruit from an immense platter. He took a peach: a juicy, round one, and looked it over as if it were a woman, or cream: thick, heavy, smooth . . .

"Women were a matter of wrong timing for me. When I should have been choosing one . . ." and he put down the peach and picked up a pear that looked more to his taste, "I was quite absorbed in business. By the time I had enough business, women had all been taken up." He handed the pear to the maid for preparation. "I thought about it; I considered it for a long time as a matter of fact. Finally chose the singular estate—more congenial for me." He sat and thought about this for a moment. "Made a good choice," Harry Renshaw concluded. "A lot of my married friends dropped dead."

After the fruit, Lawrence brought in liqueur. The two men went on to explain the household staff by vignette. There was Mrs. Oliphant, a local wizard cook of unknown vintage who had been hired after a whole series of temperamental French chefs. Harry had bribed her, very frankly, with a ten burner stove, four ovens, and then four huge freezers. Apparently all of this plotting had nearly come to naught one summer after an electrical oversight. One of the few situations, it appeared, where Forbes had met his match.

"Believe me," the visitor explained, "that was known as the summer of the great defrost. It happened over a sweltering weekend, due to my carelessness. Everything, if

39

you can imagine it, everything that Mrs. Oliphant had cooked and stored since spring, was gone—an absolute triumph of disaster. The four huge freezers awash, dripping, limp, discolored, or whatever happens to food. Mrs. Oliphant condemned me to eat hamburgers in a hideous little town near here, night after night, until I finished installing an entire special defrost alarm system and an emergency system just for her, and I did it practically on my knees. Even Harry was powerless to help, weren't you, Harry. Next to him, she's by far the most powerful person here. That is, if you're one of those people that has to eat."

Talk passed then to Lawrence who had been with Renshaw for forty-odd years, due to the quality of their association, said the host.

"A purely business relationship." Renshaw nodded to himself. "That's the secret. I never intrude. What he does after hours; what he does with his month off I never ask. He keeps his distance . . . I keep mine. Friendships are wearing. One begins to expect, to presume too much."

Catherine tried to tuck that information away for her own longevity, but she was tiring. There had been so many small facts to tuck away. Forbes was explaining how Lawrence would actually lay down his life for Renshaw at any moment, and Renshaw denied any compassion for that sort of thing.

"I'd rather he didn't. I prefer him alive," said the practical man. "I distrust great, romantic gestures like laying down one's life . . . hardly a business arrangement that is satisfactory to both."

And then there was the gardener, Mr. Turner, the man of the artistic pots and tubs of flowers who had been coming seasonally for thirty years, also keeping his distance, it appeared, and then a long succession of foolish day maids who served, cleaned, and were fired by Lawrence for incompe-

40

tence (today's maid seemed to be about par).

"There we are," said Forbes, "you've heard all about us. How about you, Kate? How long have you been in Washington?"

"Fourteen years," she answered. It was a short statement, too short to be gracious, but all of a sudden, Catherine was too tired to bring it all back, and she would have liked to keep her distance as well. But they had invested time and effort for her, and now without a doubt they wanted pedigrees.

"And what do you do in Washington, when you're not examining endless prints and drawings?" pursued the lawyer, a bit relentless since she had come forth with so little. They were probably wondering about the "Mrs. Charles," and thought that she was messily divorced, or maybe they hoped to hear that she was head of the National Print Club, or that she had written four authoritative books, or that in private life she was the wife of the ex-ambassador to Peru. The day had been so long, and even half of the great martini was draining her of energy. Catherine hesitated, but she saw no reason to bluff or invent, and she told the simple truth.

"I'm not sure what I do when I'm not examining endless prints" she repeated after Forbes, in a tired daze. "Last year I was widowed, and our . . . I mean my two young sons are at boarding school. As yet I just haven't settled into any comfortable pattern, and when I'm through with a day's work, I really don't know . . ." she faltered, and her eyes started to fill with tears under the direct gaze of the two men.

Forbes put down his port; Mr. Renshaw put down his Drambuie. They looked at her with astonishment, without words, and for a brief moment there was a complete silence. Somehow, without even understanding it, she had uttered

41

the right words. In an instant the men sprang to the defense of the beleaguered lady who knew not what to do, and for the first time in a year it seemed that widowhood must have been correct. And indeed it was: a perfect formula, completely acceptable to both gentlemen. A comfortable neuter who offset the dangers they might have faced from any divorced or even yet-maiden lady let loose on the Renshaw domain. In fact it was, for the present estate, the perfect state.

Chapter

4

The first night's sleep was uneven, to say the least, because Catherine had the sensation of being asleep on the edge of a cliff, in a mummy bag—one with its zipper jammed. By the time the fog was lifting in shreds from the eastern meadows she had given up the fight to stay alive and had fallen into an exhausted slumber. The shrilling of the alarm clock could have gone on five minutes before she opened her eyes and groped for it, first on one side and then on the other.

She lay there, slowly coming to life, listening to the heat sizzle gently in the pipes, and looking about in fuzzy admiration at the heavy moldings that ran at the top of the wall. It was a man's apartment, that was clear; the pieces were handsome and ample, neither spindly nor coy. There were no trailing ribbon designs, no *Blue Boy* on the wall with *Pinky* next door or bouquets of dried flowers on unsteady three-legged consoles. Even in the bathroom, she noticed, the same firm attention had been paid to details. The shower head had worked. Kate had always thought one could judge a good deal by plumbing alone, since theirs on Capitol Hill had never worked at all. The townhouse had been redone post war and pre-Gordon, and it had been a minimal effort with a maximum potential for disaster. This shower head worked. It adjusted from fine to coarse without dribbling or squirting odd streams of water at the opposite wall, nor did it all of a sudden fall, disconnected and discouraged at adjustments. She could see the side benefits to the job—if it lasted. Today might be a lighter dress than black, but maybe not much. Renshaw had gone on last night, perhaps to get her mind off Charles. Nonetheless, even in clauses of one breath each, the expectations were too much.

"I don't want academic mush. Don't want to find twenty drawers labelled *"school of so and so."* Don't want ten drawers of *"18th century."*

Catherine felt her stomach begin to tighten up again. However, Forbes was watching her studied composure with great amusement and it would have been too galling to show her true self. She kept her face bland and her hands loose. Renshaw, as the Director had said, had singular ideas, and most of them were about academics, it appeared. Academics like herself.

"Cowards! All of them. If they had strength of their convictions they'd all be millionaires like me. Haven't got the guts. Leave it up to total strangers to make all the investments. Then they move in with their cautious appraisals covering themselves top to bottom with footnotes. Afraid to say something vulnerable . . ."

Failures went into scholarship, said Renshaw. The superior rest, like himself, he implied, went into business, and she took a deep breath and then let it out, little by little; at

44

which point the man Forbes let out a shout of laughter. He must have been watching. Well, if Mr. Renshaw had many more prints than those hanging on the gallery walls he was going to get exactly what he despised: two piles, one by centuries and another "anonymous," and she would be right back in Washington. Not in a week, perhaps, but in a sufficiently short time to be considered damned ineffective. The man Renshaw, though, was the actual one out of touch with reality, and the most real fact of all was that after he had forced her to come to unwarranted decisions on all the prints, the true experts would move in and dismember her with a few genteel shrugs and a polite glance over her head. The real academic mush at the end of it all would be herself: the trial balloon and the human sacrifice.

Catherine rang the bell marked "breakfast" and took a cold shower and dressed. The tray was delivered by some unknown hand in her sitting room, and she ate all of it: oatmeal, muffins, sausages, scrambled eggs, and four cups of coffee. Then she set out once again.

Lawrence had told her that life began at eight in the north living room; the staff assembled there each weekday morning. As she walked in, the little man in the wheelchair was already vigorously ordering his simple life: Lawrence was to get the new maid going, and going right; Turner was to expect the delivery of new bulbs for the west slope and to get them in; Mrs. Oliphant was to lay by a goodly supply of steel cut oats for Mr. Forbes' breakfasts, and then Renshaw looked around for her.

"Yes. Here you are. This is Dr. Gordon." he said. "She's going to work on the collection." He introduced her to the others in short phrases, like the day's duties: a maid, a bulb, a box of oats. "You've met Lawrence; then Mrs. Oliphant here . . ." Renshaw paused, to give her time.

The cook, ample and uncertain, smiled at her and

45

tucked stray hairs back in their bun, and Kate smiled back; a woman who could bring Forbes to his knees was a superior ally. "Turner, here." Renshaw was saying. And Turner, there, grizzled and spare, had a superior look too. Any man who put on other people's storm windows every fall and who took them off every spring was superior, no doubt about it. The world depended on them. Without Turner or Oliphant it would probably wither away—and they knew it. She was then told to be in the north gallery at ten, and the small group was dismissed. The maids must have been too "lesser" to be considered.

Lawrence wheeled Renshaw away; the others straggled off, and she was left in the front room to do as she liked. The sunlight flooded in through the French doors and great windows and Kate wandered about looking, as she had yesterday afternoon. It should have been a staid, serious performance, like the Director's walls. There should have been a print for every three linear feet with a suitable dry factual label for those who put on their glasses and came closer.

But the Renshaw place had no great regard for present effect nor did it have any regard at all for future donations. It was a wild and mad assemblage, packed so tightly together that no label could have decided where it belonged. It was chaos in black and white, personal, intense, hung with regard for Renshaw alone: black chalks, engravings, etchings, woodcuts, mezzotints, charcoals, ink and wash, pencil, red chalks; every size and shape at random, with only the top row as a row, and then just in a line because they were jammed right up against the ceiling, and then flung right down to about two feet from the floor where only a man in a wheelchair, or crawling, could have enjoyed them. Renshaw had no finicky persuasions about the niceties. Here was a graphic brawl: peasants, zoological beasts,

46

gods, goddesses, Virgins, goats, sunrises, angels, pets, evenings, crucifixions, buildings, landscapes, saints in every conceivable agony, drunks, lovers, cherubs, and bodies of all descriptions (headless, run through with spears, cut through by swords, being deposed, dragged, disposed, and dispatched), and artists both great and small, right down to the downright anonymous, unknown centuries even. "Renshaw," she said softly to him, wherever he was, "you marvelous man!"

The trouble all began that morning with a red chalk drawing: a study of women by a fireplace. It hung quite high and stood out by its color. A companion drawing was back in the main hall; she had seen it the day before quite far down on the wall, and since she had two hours with nothing to do except poke about Catherine decided to compare the two.

A ladder. Always, somewhere, when the walls were twelve feet high there was a ladder, usually hidden behind a potted palm. In fact she found the Renshaw ladder behind a potted fig near a big grandfather clock at the other end. She checked to be sure it wouldn't telescope all of a sudden, or maybe fold itself in a clever way just as she was pushing on the wrong lever, with herself folded inside it somehow. These things had been known to happen and she was at pains not to be caught a bit undignified. But this was a straightforward piece of equipment like the owner, and she wheeled it over and climbed up to see the study better. Parmigianino, and a very fine drawing.

Quite simple, actually. All one had to do was unhook the thing to get it down and she climbed higher on the ladder to get a good upward thrust. It came off the first hook, and with a little effort it came up off the second hook, and then Catherine nearly came off the ladder itself, as an

47

ear-splitting noise exploded right over her head . . . a school playground recess bell sort of thing, only this one was indoors, and two feet from her ear. The only thing to do was to hang the thing back again and hope that the alarm would stop, but the hooks wouldn't catch. She was finally reduced to putting the Parmigianino between her knees to steady it safely, and then to cover her ears with her hands to save her eardrums. And it was in this foolish position that she was found by Renshaw, Forbes, and Lawrence, all three of whom came through the big white doors at the other end of the hall to investigate. The "off" switch must have been behind those doors, for after a moment of undisguised astonishment, Lawrence turned back, and the noise stopped then, as suddenly as it had begun.

The reaction, like the market, was mixed.

Renshaw was so amused he had no breath left for words.

The man Forbes was more practical. He took the drawing, put it on the floor with care, and lifted her down, as if she were a child eating an ice cream cone that was dripping all over an expensive sofa. He was also holding her too high above the waist, as if this seignorial right came with the estate. Catherine had in mind to give him a good kick. He set her down, after a long minute, and then remarked on how ladies livened up the place as Harry had said.

"I didn't say it. . . . you did, Forbes." said Renshaw, still short of breath from laughing.

"Did I?" Forbes answered, grinning as she tried to let everything fall back into place without moving. "Well, I'm right."

"Next time, Kate, let Lawrence turn off the alarm first." said Renshaw.

"Yes indeed, Madame." said Lawrence, prim and following the hierarchy.

48

They stood around. Maids were peeking in. Kate was still vibrating. Renshaw consulted a pocket watch that he pulled slowly from somewhere under the woolly scarf, a procedure that took time and settled the situation down.

"I'll see Mrs. Gordon now, Lawrence, since we seem to be here. Put the Toronto call on 'hold'. Is that convenient, Kate?"

She nodded and Lawrence and Forbes walked back toward the south wing together, picking up the broken threads of the morning, while the nonagenarian produced a key.

Part of the collection was in that print room, right where they stood, beyond a panel that slid open like the dining room door. Once Renshaw and Kate were inside, an immense array of dials clicked on in dismay, adjusting themselves to the unfortunate fact that someone was breathing in there. In fact, she thought wryly, all that was needed was a good food vending machine, and life could have gone on forever, sealed and sterilized, clicking on and off. It was a beautiful room.

But Renshaw was brief. She would have liked to sit down with him and open some of the floor to ceiling drawers, and examine their contents, maybe talk a little about policy and what he wanted done first. However, the man was brisk. The Toronto call was hanging on, and this was a business day. Renshaw waved his hands at it all: at the drawers, on three sides of the room. "Prints and drawings" he said. He waved his hand at the bookcases on one side, filled with references she could use. "Books" he said, and finally he gestured to a pad of paper and a pencil that had been placed on a large table to one side of the sky light above, and he said "Write down whatever more you find you want" and then he started to wheel himself back through that sliding door. The new maid, the bulbs for the slope in back, the steel cut oats, and the new curator. Voilà. All done. And now for the Toronto call.

Kate took a quick look at those drawers. If there were fifty prints in each one, between acid-free paper, that would be five hundred to every ten drawers, and—the bare possibility made her wits freeze—perhaps five thousand in ten rows. Five thousand? Five thousand unknown prints and drawings? And she had been loaned out for one winter? Jesus Christ, they must both be mad! The Director and Mr. Renshaw.

It was time to take a stand. "Mr. Renshaw!"

The collector stopped wheeling himself out. He turned the chair around rather than turn his stiff neck. He waited.

"Mr. Renshaw. Most cataloguing, you know, is done by areas . . ."

He listened, unblinking, unmoving.

She swallowed. "Now, I can put some sort of order here; I can separate my own area, and for the others, I'll refer you to good people. For a collection this size it isn't practical for you to have just one person for all this. I'd be wasting your money and my time. The collection is too much for just one curator. Do you see?"

He looked up at her then, and said with finality, "One curator is enough."

The way it was said sounded like her French teacher in school who used to pronounce that 'one egg was *un oeuf*'. It also sounded as if with the alarm this morning, one was even too many, and Mr. Renshaw explained that very point.

"Don't want the house full of people all wandering about bothering Lawrence." He wheeled himself through the door and then turned the wheelchair about once again. "Lock the panel when you're through." That was all he said. The man was cantankerous! Why hire her if he

50

wouldn't listen to advice. It wasn't practical.

"Mr. Renshaw," she said, in a last ditch peep. "It isn't practical."

There was no doubt that Kate was practical, a New England trait as a matter of fact, nowadays involving cans of chicken fat, bacon grease, coffee cans with plastic lids, drawer corners full of twisted stems from bread wrappers, leaf cuttings from African violets—all those saving ways. But Renshaw had been saving money instead, invested at a good yield. His petty income alone came to tens of thousands of daily dollars, also awaiting some clever use. She never could recall in what way he made this small point clear, but he went off to his telephone and Kate was left with the collection, and a pad of paper with a pencil.

Maybe he didn't want his collection catalogued at all. Maybe he just wanted someone to talk to at dinner, like Leonardo and Francis I. Well then he should have gotten himself a Leonardo. To soothe her spirits she started sliding out the drawers. They were handcrafted, and slid so smoothly that one hardly knew they moved. And the contents, even speaking in the broadest of terms, came out like Tutankhamen's tomb. By three o'clock Kate remembered that she was to lock the door but she had forgotten lunch. The key fit in the panel, but it was reluctant.

"Upside down," said Forbes, coming along in a just-fed way, and took it from her to do it right. Kate asked about lunch.

"You haven't eaten? My, you do need a lot of attending to, don't you. Well, come along then, and we'll try to circumvent Lawrence. He can only stand a certain number of upsets in one day."

Forbes led the way back through a series of nether passages to the kitchen. Mrs. Oliphant was there. She was cutting out bread rounds and rolling them on a well-oiled

51

wooden counter. Mrs. Oliphant, dear soul, was not Lawrence.

"That's all right, Mrs. Gordon. I understand," she said, her eyes like raisins in a muffin. "You'll find around here that no one tells anyone anything in time. The first few years," and she glared at Forbes, "are very hit or miss. Now you go sit in the sun on the back terrace there and I'll have the maid bring you something. And you," she poked Forbes with her rolling pin, "you go sit there with her."

"I certainly will, Mrs. Oliphant," he agreed equably. "I'll keep an eye on her fuses."

"Out!" said the cook, but after they were settled, the maid brought him tea and cookies, freshly baked, and then a complete lunch for herself.

"Ah," said the Scot, finishing his tea at one gulp and handing the cup back to the maid before she got away. "More tea, please. A bigger swallow this time."

Kate's chicken pie crust yielded to an exploratory cut, bubbling gently with butter.

Forbes waved a hand back toward the kitchen wing of the house. "Now, you take American houses . . ." and then he popped a brownie in his mouth and ate it without feeling pressured to finish the sentence. He drank more tea. She waited, busy with the chicken pie. In another twenty years the man would be another Renshaw.

"American houses" he continued eventually, "come with termites, develop rot, sag, peeling paint and crumbling insulation. They come with American habits, like overloads, eleven appliances on one old cord, and half of that under a washing machine." He ate another brownie. "American maids" he said then, watching the retreating back of the latest addition, "poke forks into toasters, scissors into plugs, fingers into sockets, drop radios into bathtubs . . ."

52

"Is that what you do here?" she asked, smiling. "Rescue Mr. Renshaw?"

"That's a good part."

"Mr. Renshaw says that you invented his print room."

"Just partly."

"Is that what you do when you're not on holiday? Install electrical things?"

"If necessary."

It was like pulling teeth, one by one, this conversation, once the man's prejudices were finished airing, except that the teeth didn't seem to come out. Instead, he tipped back his chair to a point of dangerous overload, and suggested that they talk about her; for instance, what she did in the print room. He waited, then, for her answer. But she was relaxed. The chicken pie was gorgeous.

"It's a very quiet sort of thing."

"I can imagine that. You enjoy the snail's pace?"

"I don't find it a snail's pace." She sipped her coffee.

"Well you aren't exactly in the middle of a riot, are you?"

She paused before answering, at that point between a lime salad and a roll. "It's quite exciting sometimes."

"In a small, printlike way, I imagine," he said with a shrug, and another cup of tea.

She agreed, feeling friendly about it. "Yes, I suppose it seems rather small."

"So what do people do in these print rooms?" The last words were said with a measure of distrust, as if "curator" were a glossy term, somewhat useless and fitted over a lesser job, like the word custodian or sanitary engineer. Perhaps he meant that a print room was a status symbol, like having a sauna.

"Oh, it's rather cut and dried," she explained, "descriptions and measurements, paper types and watermarks.

Other things too, like facts about its owners, collection stamps, publications where it was mentioned. All the bits and pieces of a print's life."

He listened to this last, turning the teacup in his blunt hands. "And then", he pursued a lawyer's step further, "what does that do for Harry?"

"Do?" It seemed obvious, but some men were dull. "It won't 'do' anything for him except bring some order out of less order. It would support or enhance the reputation of his collection, I'm sure."

Forbes sat his chair back up straight again, and looked at her curiously, one finger tapping the table cloth in an idle way. "But what if he doesn't care to enhance its reputation. What would you consider your purpose to be then?"

She thought about that, and she took a piece of the jellied salad. It fell off the fork and she tried again. "You're right. He probably doesn't care. But most collectors do like to know what they have, and its quality. Then they can donate it, or part of it, or sell it. At least they know where they stand."

Too late. He quietly picked up the last explanations, and put them in place, like the last missing pieces of a puzzle.

"I see." Then, a moment later: "Washington wants his collection." And, a moment later . . ."You're the first wedge, are you?"

The man was not idling in neutral any more; he had shifted into reverse. The accusation was direct; rather rude, in fact, considering the social relationships.

"I didn't apply." she countered. "I was asked to come."

The rust-colored eyes considered it. "So then, let's say that Harry doesn't want to donate his prints. Let's even suppose that he just likes his pictures, period. What's an

54

expert going to give him that he hasn't got already?"

She shrugged. "Organization. Maybe the pleasure of knowing that his print is better than the one in Vienna. He may have some very fine impressions hidden away that he doesn't even realize."

"Or, then again, he may have quite a few that are less good than the ones in Vienna?"

She finished the roll. Let him wait. "I very much doubt that there are many inferior ones. After all, Mr. Renshaw has been looking at prints and drawings longer than I've been alive." Time then to change the subject. "Did you and Mr. Renshaw meet through a mutual interest in prints?"

"Prints?" he said, looking distressed. "My goodness no. We met in spite of them, I'm sure." He offered her a cigarette from his case: a gold box, with gold-tipped ovals arranged in a nice row. She took one.

"What kind are these?"

"Ours."

"Do you manufacture cigarettes?" Pulling teeth again.

He lit hers and his. "No. We give them whiskey; they give us cigarettes. Scottish barter, like your Indians."

"You make whiskey?"

"I don't, if that's what you mean. The family does." He changed the subject back again then, and leaned forward to make his point—or was he trying to keep it all private.

"I'll be frank, Mrs. Gordon. Harry never needed a curator before. He was happy just as things were, all these years." The man looked at her as if she had propositioned Renshaw herself. "Once in a while people do wander up here, you know, just from hearing rumors about his collection. They think they're coming to some Italian villa in the hills above Florence and expect Kenneth Clarks all over. All they meet are Harry and myself."

55

"I'm sure you see to that" she said, annoyed with the insinuations. He expected her to draw some moral, no doubt, from his verbal jottings.

He paid no attention, and went on, examining the tip of his cigarette as if it were a new shape he had never seen before.

"You know," he said, "lot's of do-gooders try to get at Harry. Doing good to themselves, in the main—alumni, museum directors, nonprofit people, nonprofit organizations, all with profit angles in their bosoms, I find . . ." Then he looked up. "Harry's an old man. He's been like a father to me, you might say, and no one, absolutely no one, is going to get at him, angling for anything at all, not while I'm here. Nor is anyone going to make stuffy pronouncements about his collection. Not while he's alive, at any rate. Up until now, you see, he's never given a damn about what others thought. He's happy that way. You understand?"

Then the St. Bernard put another brownie in his mouth as if the gesture made the lunch into a gracious tea party, and he swallowed yet another cup of tea that the maid had brought. She stood up, to cut the whole thing short.

"You spoke about American houses and their shortcomings, Mr. Forbes. Are you sure the fault isn't with Scottish electricians, overheating the connections?"

He grinned, and rose to his feet.

"Don't bother," she said, "I can find my way." And she left through the kitchen, thanking Mrs. Oliphant.

At the print room she got the key in right this time, but it was small comfort. By one she was damned if she did, and by the other she was damned if she didn't. Did the men ever get together on their thoughts?

That evening at the cocktail hour she saw that they had indeed. Over the Rembrandts one could see the resemblance.

56

Renshaw asked her what she thought about his Rembrandts. Had she seen them in the hall? Yes she had; at least, the *Hundred Guilder Print, Christ Preaching,* the *Agony in the Garden,* and the first and fourth states of the *Three Crosses.* Probably there were many others. Rembrandt was Renshaw's passion, especially his biblical scenes, all of them dramatic, all of them scenes where half was buried in murk and darkness, with the other half pushing forward to be noticed. Kate would have preferred Rembrandt in his clearer, more uncluttered landscape moods, or not at all, really, but he had put the question to her.

He noticed her reserve. He asked her, then, plain out, and the redheaded bloodhound was watching.

"Well, if you truly ask me" she said, "Rembrandt isn't my type. In fact, I'm the only person in the world who," she was going to say 'hates' but then she changed her mind, "who doesn't care for him. It's a purely personal thing of course. I don't even quite know why. I think it's because in his religious prints he bludgeons. Even when he's quiet he's at it . . . his way of producing drama, I suppose. It's all propaganda. He lights up just what he wants us to see—his conclusion only. The rest he leaves purposefully vague: messy corners, twilight zones, to keep us from wandering." Thank God Lawrence had produced a strong martini. She went on—a fatal mistake. "I prefer the Renaissance." she said breathing happily. "It's clear, right to the horizon. Such a delight and a breadth of spirit . . . One is free to look, to pick, to choose."

Forbes picked and chose—an argument. "That's not freedom. Wandering about with a thousand facts of equal clarity. That's just browsing. Cows can do that, you know, just pop-eyed helplessness. That's not enough. You've got to come to some conclusions in the world. Rembrandt did."

"He needn't make my conclusions for me," she said, gaining strength. "Give me all the facts and I'll make up my

57

own mind. Maybe Rembrandt's conclusion, maybe not."

"On all these questions? Nonsense." said Forbes. "Waiting to get all the information would be interminable. I say, 'Get a good man and respect his conclusions.' Harry here, for instance, Rembrandt there."

"Rembrandt and I," said Renshaw in a purposeful, pontifical way, "we think alike. That's why I like him. We're the next step after all those choices. We select, we conclude, we push those decisions."

"I doubt if the person who's being pushed feels quite as enthusiastic."

"Quite wrong, Kate." Renshaw turned to Lawrence for a refill, probably indicating that he was going to stick with this problem for an hour. "Best thing in the world not to have too many choices. Best thing to see what needs doing; do it. That's why I don't have too many Renaissance prints; confuse the issue."

She had wondered about that. The curator of 17th century prints would have been a better choice.

"Quite right, Harry." Forbes was saying. He had been mixing himself a second scotch and soda and he turned back now. "I think the same way myself."

Smooth and unassailable, the two men. They had solidified their ranks and there was no putting a dent in them anywhere. Having disposed of the Renaissance, they spoke about a small company that showed promise. Five years back its debt, as a percentage of capital, had been thirty-two percent. Now it was down to twenty-five, and an obvious conclusion and decision were to be drawn: buy.

58

Chapter

5

It was an exceptionally fine autumn, but an exceptionally poor one would have made little difference in the Renshaw place. There was an ageless quality about it, and by the end of the first week she was expected to have absorbed both her new name and the timeless way things "were." It was assumed she would fit in, learning everything by osmosis maybe. And as Mrs. Oliphant had said, no one ever actually laid down what was what, but those things that were mouthed rather casually, the way the British say things, mumbling them in a deadpan, expressionless way—those turned out to be ironclad.

As Renshaw had explained the first day, life was simple. What he should have added was that it was medieval. The hierarchy was permanent and absolute, and she was neither upstairs nor downstairs, but somewhere in limbo, responsible to everyone. The only social rule was presence at the evening hour, but even this was not carefully pointed out as extending from cocktails to Drambuie, and one night she was twenty minutes late. After all, it was twenty minutes out of her drinking time, not out of Forbes', but there he was at the front door, waiting for her and in a fuss.

"Where've you been?"

"Out!" she said breathlessly, after a run through some fallen apple leaf piles then through the gate and up the drive: a completely irrational thing. "Running!"

"Running!" said Forbes, disdainful.

Renshaw was happy to see her back. He half raised himself out of his chair. "Not running from kidnappers I hope. We were getting ready to hand out vast sums . . . ransom . . ." he wheezed, and then he settled back with his drink.

She slipped into her chair, breathless still. "Thank you, Mr. Renshaw. Being kidnapped at my age would be so flattering."

Forbes was in it as usual. "No it wouldn't, foolish girl. They'd be after Harry's money, that's all."

Renshaw tried to balance things. "What conclusions did you come to on the Salviati drawing?" It was one they had looked over this morning.

"I think it's a sketch for the San Marcello al Corso 'Nativity'. There are frightfully interesting problems connected with that series, you know, mainly due to the lack of definitive documentation."

Forbes groaned. She ignored him.

"You see, Vasari doesn't even mention them; Cheney dates them 1557 to 59, Venturi would have them in the previous decade, at the end of the Medici tapestries you know; whereas Freedberg, on the other hand would place them in 1560, after his French trip. It's an interesting point, and certainly requires a lot of thought."

"A lot of thought!" said Forbes, anguished. "Why

60

don't you simply say 'between birth and death'. That already narrows it down, and then you can put your mind to something practical. Imagine five people spending their time trying to figure out where Salviati was and what he was doing from 1557 to 1560? And all this for someone who lived four centuries ago and has never been heard of since?"

"Just because you aren't in this ball game doesn't mean it doesn't exist, Forbes," she said.

He smiled. "Case dismissed, for lack of evidence."

She could hear them chattering in Washington. 'Come on, Catherine. You mean after all these days you haven't got it made yet? Why the Director expects the donation by Wednesday.' And she would shrug and tell them that in a medieval world one could not expect an opening of the portcullis until the bodyguard was won over, and that's the way things stood.

Aside from this necessity of appearing exactly at seven-thirty—for it seemed they suffered fools badly—the three kept to themselves. Forbes seemed to pull wires and cables and various other things out of the walls all day long, amusing himself in the meantime by calling out insults in general to people in particular: shortcomings of Americans in general, Mrs. Oliphant in particular.

"Lawrence!" he would call in a voice that reached to the kitchen, print room, wherever, "when will Mrs. Oliphant learn that I don't want a tiny amount of tea in a tiny Wedgewood cup. I need a decent amount, several times a day, with one mug that holds enough for a decent swallow. Even your inmates in the penitentiary get a better size." And the very next noon, a large stoneware teapot with an enormous mug would be carried proudly aloft by stolid Lawrence, and Forbes would turn to something else: the oatmeal (served with cream instead of butter), scones (too

61

dark on the bottom), American architecture (characterless), American roads (potholes) or the postal system (anyone's bag if they had a sign saying 'frequent stops'). When the mood struck him he would work in the garage with bits of electrical things, trying this and that, and starting all over again quite cheerfully when all the fuses blew. He would emerge then, wiping his hands free of oil or whatever it was with rags, and reset and check things. She wondered where rags came from up here. One could hardly imagine tearing up Mr. Renshaw's old shirts, or the silk sheets. Probably rich people went out and bought rags.

Renshaw conducted his affairs from rooms on the south side. Forbes would drop in there at mid-morning, and the smell of good cigars and the sound of men's discreet laughter would drift toward the print room through the white doors.

Kate kept to the print room until the middle of the day when she would grab a sweater or a coat and take a long walk. There were country roads that twisted for miles through abandoned orchards and down into fens and forgotten brooks. Then she would return and eat lunch. After lunch she would work until evening. It varied. She could also drive off for an hour. On the map, there was Croydon Flat (pop. 1–1000), Croyden itself (pop. 1–1000), Cornish Flat (pop. 1–1000). The map maker must have been relaxed. As she drove through these places she looked to see if they were near pop. '1'. Sometimes it seemed less. Not Trafalgar Square at any rate.

Ordinarily, by the end of each day the social hour should have been anticipated by all, since the days were spent in rather solitary cocoons. Renshaw certainly intended cocktails to be social, and he put himself out to be the supreme example of a fine host, with the slight limitations of paternalism. Indeed, the two men never asked her

62

opinion on any domains of weakness. It was not only a gallant gesture but sensible as well. Her area was the collection, the humanities, and items of general interest; vague catchalls for the untidied seconds of masculine conversation. By this very deference, however, the pecking order was subtly imposed. Renshaw, for all his years, was still mentally agile and on top. Forbes emerged as a powerful guest, not to be pried apart, and Kate, for the Director's sake alone, came out as a jellyfish somewhere at the bottom, neither free to dispose of Forbes as he should have been disposed of at once, nor free to enjoy the collection with its owner. The Scot was always in the way, making arrogant remarks as if he had hired her right alongside of Harry Renshaw. All of them, including Lawrence, had to be handled just right, or the whole thing would blow up and go to Harvard, and Forbes was eternally there waiting to light the gunpowder.

Each evening, Renshaw would place himself very carefully in his chair and inquire about her day with his prints. She would summarize briefly, with Forbes listening in with hawklike concentration, afraid that she would spill out some frightful news no doubt. Some days it was quite exciting good news; exciting, that was, as Forbes had said, in a small, printlike way. Renshaw's print would be better than its counterpart at the British Museum, or she had discovered duplicates in the drawers that they arranged to compare and to sell the inferior of the two. Rarely were his selections inferior, just as she had said to his friend. It was a matter of tiny comparisons. Renshaw enjoyed her, and her stock remained high with him.

His stock remained high with her too. The man was quite without equal. He could recall a lot of his displayed collection. He could push himself along the gallery and rattle off favorites and lesser favorites; dates, prices, sales,

63

auctions. And he had anecdotes in profusion.

Forbes, on the other hand, refused to play. Whether the print had been cropped and cut down, whether the inking was uneven, whether the paper was foxed or had been torn or folded, the legitimacy of attributions and so forth. All this just made him nervous.

"Who cares?" he would say, sublimely ignorant. "There's only one important question to me and that's if *I* like it." It was a good barbaric attitude, but dated back to about 900 B.C., and one night she decided to set him straight.

" 'Liking' is an emotional word," she started in. "It's unintelligent in a collection like this. The print is good when it still shows clearly what was in the artist's mind. You have to be above emotions here."

It was like waving a red flag at a bull, and the words "unintelligent" and "emotions" were singularly unhappy choices. She laid herself wide open.

"I'm a simple man," he said, flexing his hands with the simple, dull, gold-crested ring. It was so simple when one was simply rich. He went on stating his plain little likes. "So why get in such a fuss? Why be so complicated? Why don't you say that art should give pleasure." He sighed, sorrowing. "I suppose you've gone beyond pleasure."

"That's just another one of your words." she said. " 'Pleasure' and 'liking' aren't the point. While Mr. Renshaw was 'liking' Whistler's *River,* it went up from ninety to two thousand, and that was actually a rather small jump in the art field. I haven't seen any recent figures, but it's worth probably much more now. If you can clear away your subjective values, you become a better bidder."

The time to have kept her mouth shut with simple people was before the discussion began. Scots were still hanging antlers on their walls. He would do better in a

64

museum if he never got beyond the postcards. But the man had an ultimate purpose. In spite of grumbling about her uninteresting theories, he would remember quite carefully what she said, and then just for fun he would suddenly regurgitate whole statements she had previously made and get her confused because they were badly out of context, but hard to refute.

"Nonsense," he said that night, getting himself another drink and settling back in his chair. "Art is still pleasure, even nowadays, and I daresay that pleasure is still emotional, even for dry intellects like yours. You haven't come full circle yet, that's all." He smiled into his glass.

Harry Renshaw was conferring with Lawrence, and Forbes took advantage of the extra time, playing it all back with a new twist.

"Why don't you try exchanging that overworked mind of yours some night for something more pleasurable. Just for emotional comparison, let's say. So you can look back over the years and decide which holds its value better, Salviati, or someone less than four centuries old. You might find that there's another side of life you hadn't thought of." He kept a deadpan face. "It wouldn't, of course, preclude the other. You could keep a low profile."

By low profile the man probably meant horizontal, and it was all so outright. She was a sitting duck, for the minute Lawrence left, Forbes continued smoothly on another track.

"Let's give her some American Tel and Tel to hang, Harry. They're nicely engraved. They go up in value. They're even clear, right to the back, like the Renaissance, and everything is explained, right on the front. And they're all the same. We won't have to hear about minute differences, and she won't even have to extract conclusions, just collect a 7 percent yield."

Renshaw enjoyed these evenings. They livened up the

65

long days, and he never allowed the pestering to continue. He tried to preserve the niceties. He would simply change the subject, breaking in if necessary, and Forbes would stop. But then, if one thought that over for a minute it was clearly no compliment: Forbes would otherwise win. With the Director's words hanging over her, it was a foregone conclusion.

This particular night the host rummaged around, trying to find a postcard in a pocket under the shawl. Forbes got the message and he stopped badgering. Renshaw rummaged again, and finally pulled it out.

"Mabel and John coming."

"Good enough!" The dour Scot produced a real smile for once. "I haven't seen them since years back, in Scotland was it? Or Greece?" He drained the second whiskey. "Careful now, Harry. John must be about ready to keel over, and Mabel will start in on you."

"Always liked Mabel, too. But not that much. On their way back, coming next week."

"There's a story about Scotland, as a matter of fact. Yesterday's *London Times*."

Lawrence motioned that dinner was served, and they moved into the dining room. The first maid that Kate had seen was gone, and in her place a new one was being launched. In the time it took for all the instructions to be repeated a second time, Forbes started in on a Celtic cross.

"Happened right near the intersection before you turn for my place . . . a small circle of land in a roundabout. You probably don't recall it."

"Indeed I do, Forbes. By the time we got that far we were looking pretty hard for that turn."

"Well, according to the *Times* it was stolen. Damned heavy things, you know. But the difference was that here, the thing was replaced. A perfectly good replica, and no

66

one noticed, apparently, until some time later.

"And then how did they find out?" She was interested.

"A drunk. Fell over the low railing and right into it. Made a dent in it with his head. He wasn't so drunk as to miss that. And when his story was checked, they found a foam plastic and sand mixture. Not good enough to go on forever, you know, but good enough to play for time. Quite a respectable copy it was."

The maid passed the rolls after the soup, and Forbes went on with details. Apparently the town council had been forewarned by quasi-official letters concerning a free government treating of all stone monuments against petrol fumes. The maid got the next course straight, and brought the dishes in the proper order. Forbes helped himself, giving the new maid a good up and down look, and then went on.

"Of course months passed, like all government proposals. And when a lorry pulled up one stormy day and two men were seen examining the cross, no one wanted to go out in the pouring rain to watch and nothing more was heard. Taking photos of course, and measurements. Damned clever group. Bold. Spent a year probably, making up that dummy."

"Were they caught?" Renshaw waved off the maid with some irritation when she tried to serve the potatoes twice.

"Too smart. Must be a regular rage of workshops these days, especially in northern Italy. Whole altarpieces, apparently."

"Whole altarpieces what?" Kate asked.

"Why, substituted of course," said the superior being. "While they've been having an average of one major theft a day for years, now they've lost count because the frauds aren't discovered right away."

67

"I can't see," said the collector, "advantages in that. Months to paint good paintings. At today's wages profits must be low."

"American style. Paint by number, probably. Who looks at those things anyhow?"

Kate declined the invitation, and he went on.

"The priest doesn't. He's busy with the mass. The devout don't. Now that they participate there's no time for looking around. Not the American tourists who get twenty churches a day shoved at them. The thieves then. They keep the good altarpieces for resale after the legal time limit has expired . . . fifteen years I think it is. Or they cut it up if the painting isn't good: a group of angels here, crucifixion there, two landscapes out of the sides, and the replacement is glossier and in better repair." He lifted his glass. "Good men, these . . . spread it around."

"Oh come on, Forbes, never mind the 'good men' routine. Over here we're all tired of the anti-hero. These men are crooks, nothing more."

"Not 'nothing more'. Maybe they are more. Consider that maybe they started out as experts." he said.

"Nonsense. The progression doesn't go from professional to crook. It goes from little crook to big crook, from bad man to worse man."

"Wrong again. Good men *are* crooks, sometimes. My theory is," and he chose some Brie and crackers, "that good men go into crime because crime is interesting and life is not. Games. Games, Harry, to pass the time."

"But good men do find life interesting," she interjected.

He laughed, if his dry disillusion could be called laughter when it made a sound. "A pious platitude from the academic world."

"Well, no one would believe your theory."

68

"No one would believe your intentions Kate, if I told them that you wedged the front door open with an empty cigarette package the other day. Hordes of enterprising crooks could have swarmed in, to say nothing of flies."

It was true. She had forgotten a sweater outside. The key was way back in her room, and Lawrence thought she was witless anyhow, so it had been a quick trick to save time. Only it hadn't saved time, for the sweater had been left much further down the hill than she thought, and she had to ring for Lawrence in the end—the very thing she had tried to avoid.

"You must have been the one who took the wedge out. Nothing was missing, I presume."

Renshaw was calm. He was hardly bothered about the surge in Catholic counterfeits, in Scottish counterfeits. "As long as there are thirty thousand churches in Italy with no alarm systems—as Forbes tells me there are—I can't get too worried here. Let me know when the supply of churches runs out." He considered a cigar and then passed them to Forbes.

Forbes rolled his gently and cut off the end with a pocket knife. "You're archaic, Harry: out of date. This isn't a progressive disease: paintings now, prints later. It's a department store: prints, paintings, sculpture, mosaics. When the value of art thefts go over four billion, as they have, you can be sure they employ their own researchers."

And so it went night after night: But unlike the men in Washington, who verbally unleashed all their social connections and heavy social artillery during the first few minutes, neither Renshaw nor Forbes ever talked of personal things, of sisters, parents, dogs, cats, schools, hobbies—all the trivia that make up a three-dimensional lifetime. Harry Renshaw kept his distance, and Duncan Forbes kept his. Their anecdotes were removed to Scotland, Europe, the

69

Middle East and their references remote. It was like reading the Sears Catalogue or the telephone book—interesting on the whole but one couldn't find the connection. Not that one expected an encounter group, but it could have been less like sitting on a subway. Renshaw had said that Forbes was due back in the Middle East in a couple of weeks, but whether he went there to peddle his whiskey to Moslems, or whether he sold shag rugs to Afghans was never asked or volunteered. Questions were made to seem in poor taste, that was all. They owned her, but it was not a mutual agreement.

For a few autumn days, when the dry grasses and the hot pine needles gave out an intoxicating smell, and when the sky was a deeper blue than the milky mixture over Washington, Kate thought she had things under control: the envoy-extraordinaire, juggling prints, Renshaw and Forbes like Richard's performance at the gas pumps, and all with that infinite tact and patience required. But then the atmosphere suddenly shifted, and she realized that there was a deliberate campaign to unseat her, to undermine, to shake her loose.

Chapter

6

As Renshaw had said, it was a simple life. It was indeed. In actuality there were just three of them up there, and if one person was off his feed the whole atmosphere became difficult. One person right now was off his feed, and it was suddenly as if the Early Renaissance had evolved right through the High Renaissance, and they were in the middle of some Mannerist confusion that she no longer understood.

Part of the blame belonged to a decision she had taken to cross reference the collection—the walls with the drawers. Renshaw, as a matter of aesthetics, disliked labels. He thought they looked like chickenpox; they disturbed the walls, they disturbed the continuity of the frames, they disturbed him. So the labels, with numbers only, for Renshaw knew his hung collection, had been stuck on the backs of the frames, invisible to the spectator. But there was no sense to a catalogued collection if there were no reference

71

points. It meant that for every card she made one could not find the print except by remembering or searching. It slowed down comparisons, it was inefficient, and she resolved, as a businesslike approach, to spend a few minutes a day making a chart of the walls, and noting the labels on the back, putting order in the system. Renshaw had told her, of course, to start in with the print room drawers, but this was a parallel venture she felt was important, and it would have gone completely unnoticed and unblamed if it hadn't been for Lawrence. She had been asking him to turn off the alarm once a day. Then she would lift up the frames trying to get some label numbers identified and onto the chart. The upper ones were difficult because she had to go up and down the ladder, moving it along, and Lawrence had heard Renshaw say to leave the walls and give the drawers first priority. Lawrence knew that she was not supposed to be working on this part of the collection at all and that he was being disturbed for something not even sanctioned. After a few days he became rather restive. Not that he said anything outright, but his jaw tightened, his head retreated into his collar; he became obdurate. It was the way he inflected what he said. If he waited for her to be finished then she was nervous, and if he didn't wait then she had to call him out to turn on the alarm again, and that was worse. Consequently, Lawrence made three out of three, all stubborn.

But after a week of nerves, Kate discovered, just by chance as she almost lost her balance one day, that if she put a pencil over the hooks on the wall and held them firmly down, one could flip up the frame just far enough to see a label and no alarm sounded at all. It took a bit of fiddling to get the pencil in just the right balance, but it was a personal triumph of the first order. No more Lawrence.

The morning she discovered a second *St. Michael* by

72

Schongauer in a drawer she knew that she had seen it before on the walls, and after she thought a bit, it placed itself down the back gallery, and through the double doors and to the left. It was a large print, quite noticeable, and it hung alone there, across from a mahogany door—probably Mr. Renshaw's rooms. Kate took a pencil and went off to check on the number. But once she was beyond the end door, she hesitated. It was virtually unknown territory; one almost needed an invitation. The print hung there all right, in a doom of quiet that was even quieter than the rest of the house. However, this took only a short, brisk moment, and she slipped the pencil across the two hooks, and when it was firmly pushed down she flipped the frame.

There was an immediate scream of indignation from an alarm that stuck out in full view down the hall. She should have seen it before—and it was as loud as the first. Kate grabbed the pencil back, and stood there, trying not to cover her ears, waiting for punishment and the usual. One could scarcely be nonchalant; the noise was frightful.

Forbes, of course. He materialized from nowhere.

"Where's Lawrence? Why didn't he turn it off?" He opened the mahogany door, reached in somewhere, and the alarm stopped. The echo went on.

It was hard to be casual. Mr. Renshaw and the ubiquitous Lawrence next, naturally.

"I'm sorry," she said. "I was just getting a number for the *St. Michael* because we have a duplicate in the print room."

Renshaw explained it all again, very gently.

"Ask Lawrence to turn off the alarms first, Kate."

She looked from Lawrence to Renshaw. "I didn't think I needed to. I found a way to get around them . . . for just checking labels, that is."

"What?" The testy Scot.

73

There was no way of backing down, and she explained about the pencil and the reason for coordinating things in a businesslike way.

Renshaw spoke first, dear man. "This is a new set of alarms, Kate. They work on a different principle. I doubt if the pencils work here." He was beginning to laugh but Forbes was not.

"Not only that, my dear lady, but they're only good for one pull: pencils, fingers, here, everywhere. So, then, if it won't interrupt your businesslike approach, you can sit down and make out a chart of everything you've pulled apart so far. You might as well take *St. Michael* with you— I won't get back to fit it today." He was annoyed as hell.

"I guess you'd better do what he suggests, Kate." Renshaw was cordial, but firm.

Forbes called to Lawrence as he was wheeling the little man back to his apartment.

"Turn them off for now, Lawrence, and flip the switch for the southwest rooms as well. One of the maids is liable to get into trouble, the circuits are open, the way I've left it."

"Yes sir. I'll see to it." As if Lawrence felt that he was indeed dependable even if Kate was not. Everyone so busy mending her broken fences. Suddenly, the three men were plain maddening in their comfortable solidarity, their decisions, their efficiency, leaving her to feel as if her crime were slowly staining the whole of North America crimson.

Forbes held the double doors. "Between you and the maids there isn't much to choose."

"No one's asking you to choose!"

"Why didn't you call Lawrence. You've probably loosened every wire in the collection."

"Because he disapproves of my checking the walls, that's why."

74

"Well, who gives a damn if he does disapprove? All you Americans worry so about being loved. It's a national psychosis! My God, why don't you just ring for him and tell him what to do. That's what he's paid for."

They reached the door of the print room. She fumbled for her key, and it dropped on the floor. He picked it up and unlocked the door. It was small comfort to be able to hand him the chart she had already made up.

"And the ladder. Where's that?"

"Behind the clock."

He paused, halfway out the door. "Why didn't you do the whole thing right, on one particular day and get Lawrence to help you make this out."

Always there were bright-eyed specialists in someone else's business, coming in after the fact and throwing their weight around, showing others how to delegate authority. He could figure it out himself, this juggling act, and she shut the door, quietly and firmly, in his face.

On the whole, each week in life is composed of seven days, but from that point on, the week seemed to have thirty of them, all precarious. Of the three people present, Harry alone remained serene. He lived on a high plateau, some sort of Zeus or Apollo, and he watched what went on for quite a while, doing nothing.

One unhappy evening the cocktails began with dates— dates of famous artists. Truthfully, numbers and dates had never been Kate's strong point, and after the defense of her thesis she had tossed them all out of her head. One could always look them up for special reasons. So when Forbes asked her casually when Michelangelo had lived, she lit a cigarette and threw the match into the fire. She replied, "15th and 16th centuries." She was in exactly that sort of mood, but he pestered further. She knew that there were

75

sixties and seventies in it, and had she been less annoyed by the whole week it would have been simple to figure out that Michelangelo had not lived a hundred and ten years.

Forbes let it pass with a raised eyebrow but the next night she then left some stupid 18th century artist a century behind, and the red-headed buzzard lifted his eyebrows again, and spent the entire dinner hour on specific rises in book values, per share, during the last five years. Whether his purpose had been to discredit her in Renshaw's eyes or to clear up some remote question in his own mind was not apparent at the time, but it clarified the morning of the day the Housemans were scheduled to arrive. Harry had given the staff their instructions at eight.

Kate got hold of Lawrence early and asked him to turn off the south gallery alarm. She turned off her mind and just told him what to do. Kate had made some notations to the effect that Harry should sell the Schöngauer print, and why, and she carried it back to the south wing. It was as she approached those mahogany doors once more that she heard Forbes on the other side. And like the first day, his voice carried.

"Harry, for God's sake! I point out the obvious gap in our control and you won't listen."

Renshaw's voice was gentle and decided. "She has my unqualified approval, Forbes. That's it."

"That can't be 'it'. Harry. Listen to the facts as they are: There's nothing, absolutely nothing she hasn't found out simply by stumbling around except the recorded message at the police department. For Christ's sake, where was she the very first morning? On top of the first set of alarms. And later, the first week, where was she then? All bright-eyed and running through the leaves? I'll bet. She was running through the gate alarm, remember? Lawrence turned it off and we laughed about it then. And, before that, where was

76

she? Leaving cigarette packages in the front door, to see if that was bugged, and now she's pulling the new system right off the wall. Listen Harry, we had it licked until she arrived. How many prints did you lose before we got the systems installed? They're practically perfect, now." There was a pause. The man must have lit a quick cigarette to control his annoyance. "But, I've reached a new conclusion, Harry. They've regrouped, whoever they are. Now that the alarms are in, they've got a more sophisticated approach. Bolder. They're sending us our better half now aren't they —a half with grey eyes, and a thin, sort of tubercular appeal. And she's found out all they need to know. No risk on their part. Look, Harry, at least let's face the possibility that she's been planted. Once I go, they can move in with the whole place mapped."

Renshaw must have made an impatient gesture, because then Forbes tried a new slant.

"All right, it isn't proved, but what situation is more classic than this? Older men are being duped every day by blondes. How could we have missed it? They send up someone who's read a few things. I mean, after a couple of books on prints I could talk for a few minutes each night. We don't ask her to say much, you know. Look, Harry, she's in Italian Renaissance, isn't she? And she doesn't even have Michelangelo pinned down? Doesn't that make you uneasy? And the widow bit, all prim, done up in a chastity belt, the husband dead so conveniently—if there ever was a husband. Christ, Harry, for all we know the National Collection has never heard of anyone with her name! Why did you ever think of getting your collection prettied up anyhow? It was all right the way it was."

It was not clear what Renshaw answered, and Forbes had further suggestions: "Call them up and ask them, or send Pinkerton's. I'll hold her down until we hear."

She never knew what was said in answer to that; it must have made Forbes angry for he threw open the door and ran right into her.

"Well, well," was all he said. For a minute she thought he would pick her up and throw her through Renshaw's door, but then he stepped aside and walked on, calling back over his shoulder to get that *St. Michael* done right this time.

She hung it right. There was only one way to hang it anyhow. All that talk just to impress Renshaw. Kate walked back to the print room and slammed the panel into the wall. The dials jumped and began purifying, ventilating, humidifying and heating, all at once. Kate sat down, riffling through the cards, aimless now, put-upon, feeling inadequate and just plain mad. Renshaw had made his decision today and it had fallen toward her side, but what his answer would be after a few more sessions with the Big Chested Huff was very moot. Especially if there should actually be a robbery after Forbes left. The process was a slow erosion, a little bit here, then there, and eventually it would have an effect. It would be too silly to rush into Renshaw right now, proclaiming her purity—too melodramatic, unsuitable. Let Forbes make an ass of himself if he wished. Hanging on, just hanging on until that ill-fated bird migrated next week was the only solution. Hanging on without one final explosion that would rock the whole collection to Harvard.

Kate rang for Lawrence. She told him to reset the alarm and asked him to have Mrs. Oliphant prepare a bag lunch. When the maid delivered it, she left for a long walk.

John and Mabel arrived later that same day. Four-thirtish. Kate heard the car drive up as she returned, a sedate sound on the gravel, followed by profuse greetings in the hall. After a moment there were sounds of a car being put away in the garage, and then all was quiet again. The

78

Housemans must have retired to rest somewhere in the south wing near Renshaw.

Cocktails had been set for seven-thirty as usual and, like the first night, Kate rested up for this particular on-slaught. She dressed in the black dress again, and then she changed, thinking that Forbes might assume she was trying to play the broken widow bit; she wore a brown knit suit instead, and put on heavy modern earrings, just to be sure not to look pitiful and tubercular. Seven-thirty came and she waited an extra ten minutes, to be sure that she and Forbes would not be caught there alone by themselves.

How late was "late" turned out to be flexible, this one particular evening, for when Kate walked into the south living room Duncan Forbes sat alone looking into the fire, deep in some ridiculous thought. Lawrence had not yet wheeled in the bar, and the host and the Housemans must still be in the south wing. It would have been too cowardly to peek in and then walk off so she entered and sat down.

After an insulting delay of a second or two the man sprang to his feet.

"Ah, Mrs. Gordon," he said, unctuous, and ready to invent platitudes. "Excuse me. I didn't notice you . . ."

"Oh shut up," she said.

They were saved from any further polite exchanges by Mabel and John. They had arrived without Harry.

A shriek. "John! Look! Here's that handsome Scottish widower we met years ago! Duncan! Duncan Forbes! Dear Duncan, how are you?"

The bird watcher sprang to his feet at the first gasp and went over to greet Mabel. Kate stood too.

"Hello Mabel!" said Forbes.

Mabel gave him a big hug. She was short, and her squeeze caught Forbes right around the middle. Kate saw him stiffen, then, ever so slowly, disengage himself and put

79

his arm around her shoulder. Mabel was speaking—in exclamatory sentences:

"Aren't you goodlooking still, Duncan Forbes! You even improve, just like your whiskey! By the way," and Mabel looked about for the bar, "where is the whiskey? If Harry's gone on the wagon I'm leaving. Hasn't Lawrence brought it yet? That archaic system of his. Why don't you get married again, Duncan? Those boys of yours must be in college by now."

Forbes smiled but in the light from the fire she saw that his face was suddenly pale under his tan, pale and covered with sweat. He turned to Kate and introduced her as a matter of form—even better, as a tactical diversion.

This was Mabel, a big-bosomed specimen preserved from the flapper days. She was motherly, covered in confused layers of jewels and chiffon, and a curly mop of hair best described as some form of nest. Beneath the nest there was a rising and falling warble of words—a formidable woman with a direct attack that reduced pompous men to nothing in short order. She had dealt with medieval men in summary fashion for years, and she was old enough and rich enough and loud enough to overwhelm every sacred male in sight. Forbes had once said that Mabel had the drive of Pope Julius the Second and the endurance of a Land Rover, and Kate believed it now.

"My dear" said Mabel, coming over to her with gestures of anguish. "How do you manage with these cranky old men? So you're the one who's rescuing the moldy prints. I'll bet it's a thankless job! You hate being way up here, I'm sure. Harry has such confidence in you. He can't stop talking about what a difference you've made already."

Forbes said nothing to concur. He looked aimless, with no expression.

'Boor you were, and boor you remain,' Kate thought

80

with indignation, but if Mabel noticed the silence she gave no sign. It had been said before once, at dinner, that Mabel had the dollars, and John had the sense, but after a few minutes Kate decided that it was not that way at all. Mabel ran on—

"Won't you do them good, breaking up their eternal stock market reports every night. I know! I used to say to John—didn't I, John—that the one thing Harry Renshaw needed to keep him from getting too set in his ways was a woman. What good are all these polished floors and rugs if all men do is sit and talk business, business every minute. They might as well sit in a bar. My dear," and she leaned over toward Kate, "when they visit me I never let them say anything!"

"You're quite right there, Mabel," said Forbes, all smiles now, and recovering his tan.

"Do you come here often, Duncan? Have you adopted America?"

"Harry's adopted me, rather. I spend my holidays here. Change of pace."

Harry arrived just then, apologizing for his late appearance and for the condition of the guest room in the south wing.

"With the new wiring, room's almost demolished. Nothing else available now. Kate in north wing, with Forbes."

"That's cosy of you, Harry. And where's the whiskey? Is that in the north wing, too?"

Lawrence arrived with the bar, and Mabel cheered up even further. It was rumored that she had three kidneys, an abnormality that allowed her to drink everyone else under the table and still keep talking in her right mind. Furthermore, John and Mabel had been comfortably used to one another for over forty years, and the

81

longevity of this union gave Mabel an impeccable perch from which to peck.

"How did you ever find a woman to come way up here, Harry? I'll bet you two were hanging out the windows the day she came."

Forbes said nothing. Renshaw filled in.

"Didn't know Kate," he said, matter of factly. "Forbes a bit gloomy, in dread anticipation of some brash, talky expert."

'Like himself.' she thought.

Harry went on, trying to make up for the morning's deficiencies, no doubt. He must have heard that she had heard.

"Kate turned out to be beyond our wildest expectations."

"She certainly has," said Forbes, with complete composure, "our wildest—" and then he stopped, right there. The sudden silence made Mabel look up, but John Houseman then was only too pleased to find an opening.

"Do you still keep your North Highland place, Forbes?"

"Yes, I do, John. I keep it open all year with a small staff. My sons get up there quite often."

'I can see them now,' she thought bitterly, 'sitting in the Great Hall, shooting at rats.'

"Well you can show it to Kate this spring." Mabel plunged in, overlapping his sons. "Harry says he's sending her to the Sotheby sale, and you two can go on from there."

"What?" said Kate.

"She is?" said Forbes with genuine surprise.

"She is." announced Harry, with finality.

Kate looked over, surreptitiously, to see if Forbes' composure was still complete, but Lawrence was calling him to the telephone and he excused himself and left.

82

Mabel kept on looking after him. "Harry! I don't know when I've seen Duncan looking so well again. After his wife, Catherine, died . . . let's see, it was the year after the Hallowe'en party we gave seven years ago?"

John was beginning to let his mind wander, but he remembered that it was ten. One word was all he was allowed.

"Ten? Was it ten? You mean to say that Forbes hasn't aged one bit and we've all grown wrinkled? Well, anyhow, where was I? Oh, yes, I was telling Kate about Duncan's wife. You've heard the whole story I'm sure."

Kate shook her head.

"You haven't? Doesn't surprise me one bit! Houseful of men. Never give one goddamn detail do they! Well, I'll tell you then. Years back it was, this lovely girl, Catherine, died in childbirth, baby girl died too. They had two boys already. Duncan became a madman, so I'm told. An absolute madman, for months. He took his sons out of school, gave up his law practice in Edinburgh . . . the best criminal lawyer in Scotland, and he moved up to his hundred room pile of rocks there in the Highlands, became a horrid Heathcliff. Wouldn't come to a party anywhere. Didn't even answer his mail. Then we heard that he had taken to drink. That's when Harry took him in hand, wasn't it, Harry?" Harry said nothing; he had no chance anyhow. "Then we heard that he had stopped drinking and had taken to inventing electrical things. And then, after quite a spell more, he must have come to his senses, because of his boys, I guess. He put them back in school, but he never would move back to Edinburgh, hasn't settled down since. Every year it's somewhere else he's at. He needs a new wife —that's what—"

'He needs a doctor,' Kate thought. 'Cure him of liver flukes'—

Mabel took a long swallow on her second drink, or was it the third? Lawrence stayed by her side, probably according to Harry's instructions, or by long habit.

"Always more of those inventions now. He's quite sought after, isn't he, Harry? I suppose Harry has told you all of this anyhow."

Harry was a bit nonplussed and said that no, he hadn't thought of it.

"I knew it!" said Mabel. "Kate, you'll never get anything out of that twosome except the Dow Jones averages. They're like gargoyles—mouths open, don't say anything. You'll have to bring a book to dinner. Why Duncan can't invent something practical like a robot bedmaker . . . always burglar alarms. Can't he do anything normal?"

John allowed that one hot and cold running chambermaid was worth several robots, if that one was normal. And Lawrence announced dinner. The Scot had not yet returned, but Mabel decided his fate, normal or not.

"After the Sotheby sales, we'll have a spring houseparty," said Mabel. "Out on the island. I have it all here, springing into my head!"

Harry prepared to wheel himself into the dining room and Mabel jumped up to accompany him, still talking. It was only the quick action of Lawrence that kept Mabel from tripping over Harry's rings. Lawrence guided her arm in a rather decisive manner and steered her around the treacherous spot.

"Harry! Someone's going to kill himself one of these days!" Mabel complained to her host. "Thank you, Lawrence. Without you where would I be?"

"Sprawling on the floor probably," wheezed Renshaw. "Anyone who has four drinks before dinner is bound to end up on the floor."

"Harry, you haven't changed a bit." Mabel said

fondly. "You're the only one who can criticize and still make it sound like love!"

John offered Kate an arm.

". . . and we'll get the Worths, the Mittners, the Grahams, the Stolzes." Mabel had recouped.

"Thank God I'm not coming!" gasped Renshaw.

"And Duncan can get leave and fly in from wherever he is." By the time the soup was served, Mabel had arranged her rambling thoughts in a deadly, systematic order, and the guest list grew sporadically. "And the Pershings can get over from Cairo, and the Browns, and Georges Lisas of course."

"Who?" muttered Forbes. He came in from the other side, late for the soup. "I've heard that name somewhere before."

"Of course you have, Duncan. It's that charming Greek whom we met a few years back. He visits us once in a while to see Julia. You remember Julia, our niece? She fell madly in love with him. Let's see . . ." Mabel tried to remember the unfortunate man's present standing. "I think he's running second now, don't you, John?"

John hadn't thought about it.

The prime antagonist slipped into the empty seat beside Kate, but instead of helping himself from the soup tureen, he took out a little book and wrote "Georges Lisas" in it, then put it back in an inner pocket. The scribbles were not lost on Mabel.

"I hope you aren't writing to remind yourself not to come, Duncan. Be sure and send down some cases of Scotch. If Kate's there, Duncan will come," she announced to the company at large. "I can see that right now. Why, he can hardly keep his eyes off her."

'You're right,' Kate thought. 'He's afraid I'll steal the silver.'

85

Mabel was forced then to stop talking and eat. There was an astonishing silence, but she recovered while the dishes were cleared.

"You still have Mrs. Oliphant, don't you, Harry. This soup is divine. I can tell her touch."

"Yes I do have her, Mabel, intend to keep her too. No stratagem of yours could work on Mrs. Oliphant. I can see through them all."

"Well I can see through your stratagems too, Harry Renshaw. I can see through them all."

John hushed her then, for he wanted the evening market report.

"Harry!" said Mabel. "Is this antique smoke signal still going on? Year after year? Can't you just read a newspaper and keep quiet?"

John told her to be quiet instead, and asked Forbes to start with the London Exchange. Forbes smiled at Mabel in lieu of apology and began, and Mabel sank back in her chair admitting mock defeat.

At the first decent chance, which was port and liqueurs, Kate said goodnight. Harry smiled warmly; Mabel rose to give her a big hug and to remind her about the spring party; John Houseman and Forbes got to their feet. Houseman shook her hand; Forbes acknowledged with a brief nod.

No matter. Tuesday night was Kate's night to call her boys, and she settled herself happily in her living room to hear all about the "B" teams and the small ups and downs of school life. But, this particular night when she picked up the phone, the line was dead. She clicked, hung up, tried again. No tone, no hum, nothing. Forbes had used his cocktail hour to good advantage. She considered different angles of response, but the only other telephones were in private apartments, and Renshaw was busy with his guests. She didn't want to ask. If she made a fuss it would be

86

unseemly; people would scurry to help. If she used a phone in someone else's apartment it would be awkward. Kate decided to let it ride. Why not: the pest's days were happily down to two and little more could happen in forty-eight hours.

Chapter

7

The next morning a thick fog muffled the hill. Kate could see it through the curtains, so cold and wet and heavy that even the birds were late. It was coming in with the dawn, for she could remember sounds of the Houseman's car leaving around five.

Right now everyone must have gone back to sleep, and she rolled over to snuggle out the remembrance of the past day and to block out anticipation of the day ahead. It loomed like a dentist appointment for four o'clock: not quite soon enough to be finished with—one just waited about all day under a cloud.

Mabel, bless her, had put the male nest back into proper perspective. She herself should have been able to handle it all along just like that. And Harry also had helped with the Sotheby suggestion, even if she was the last to know.

The clock said six, but sleep was ridiculous. Kate got

up and stumbled over to the window to shut out the fog and then took a shower. At the start the noise seemed to come from the hot water pipes. She was the first one in that wing to use them this morning; maybe air had found its way into the system as it sometimes did when she was a child and her father had to bleed the lines. After she turned off the shower and stepped out, the noise continued, and she could hear Forbes come alive next door with a string of interesting expletives. He probably had connected the wrong wires and they were about to explode. Abruptly, the noise stopped.

She put on a robe, wrapped a towel about her wet head, and opened the door to the hall. Forbes was peering out too, wearing just a towel about his loins. Above the towel on one side she could see a fresh bandage, very white across his tan, a do-it-yourself effort, using miles of adhesive tape. That would explain the way he winced last night when Mabel had hugged him, although what could come open right there she had no idea. Maybe his liver had burst, from overindulgence. Whatever it was, he was bursting with vigorous epithets this morning, and since the hall was not filling with smoke he nodded to her, minimally, and closed his door.

'I'm not hanging onto a drawing this time.' she thought and turned the hair dryer to high so she wouldn't be dragged out and executed with a wet head. The way things stood it would have been her head, right or wrong, and not a stranger's. She heard Forbes slam his door and she checked her desk, just to make sure the print room key was still hanging on its knob. Thank God for that too: the burglar wasn't going to be caught in the print room.

After her hair was dry she twisted it into a tight bun to point up a nontubercular vigor, dressed in a wool tunic and slacks, and went out to see what was happening. Maybe

90

Forbes had caught some poor unfortunate by now and was methodically hacking him up in an ancient Scottish rite.

Actually, not much was happening. The hall was ghostly and quiet, from the white fog outside. Lawrence was in the reception room, fully dressed as always. He must have been born dressed. One could invariably tell the degree of disaster from the amount his neck emerged from his collar, and today it was just medium. Not so much as when she had pulled off the Schongauer. Mr. Renshaw was there too, with some sort of nightshirt and bathrobe combination and the wool shawl. He saw her and nodded, but kept on talking with Lawrence.

"No one disturbed the print room . . ." he wheezed, "nor the walls far as I could tell. Forbes is checking more closely. False alarm."

"There are no false alarms," boomed the man from some other part of the halls. From down in the valley one could hear the wail of a police siren. There was no mistake about that either. Its sound kept everyone hypnotized as it came toward them, louder and louder in the fog until the car emerged all muddy and not nearly so impressive as its noise, spewing gravel all over the terrace steps. Two patrolmen jumped out and ran up to the door. Lawrence opened it, unperturbed, and they more or less tumbled in.

"The message shooah came loud and cleah" one said. "Damn neah jumped out of ouah skins." The other looked out the window. "No cah came back down the hill and the Squaw rud's shut, so he must still be somewheya." They looked this way and that, hopeful, as though the culprit might be standing on the rug just waiting to be tied up.

"Nobody" said the Scot with disdain as he came down the hall, "nobody will still be here after all that noise. And what makes you gentlemen think he's in a 'cah'?" Forbes looked out of the door onto the front. "Where's Turner?"

91

"He went to the garage to get his gun, sir." Lawrence kept track of everyone.

"Good. Tell him to cover the south. These men will search the back meadow and I'll take the north." Such gall he had, but the police seemed easily led, docile even. "I think the collection came through splendidly, Harry."

"Thank you, Forbes. Thanks to you each time."

It was an atmosphere of much masculine competence again. What could be more satisfying now than for everyone to beat the bushes and shoot someone—anyone—in the fields. It completed such a primal cycle. Everyone could then retire for scones and coffee.

In fact, Mrs. Oliphant came out of her nether regions to announce that breakfast was ready. Nothing had stopped the popovers, but now that they were almost at their pop she had to see for herself. Her short, sturdy figure strained eagerly to observe the chase, but Lawrence shook his head. Mr. Renshaw thanked her with grave dignity for sticking with the eatables, and then invited Kate to breakfast with him by a French door in the north room.

"We can watch 'the action' as they say!" said the ancient child. He would have gone out shooting too.

Lawrence set up a small table. The atmosphere was festive: the fog, hot coffee, the popovers in their linen napkins, fresh butter curls, strawberry jam, eggs with parsley. Like nobles, they were, bringing their picnics to a hill overlooking the battle. Renshaw even announced that because he found himself eating with a young lady while in his nightshirt she should call him "Harry" from that moment on. She spread the napkin in her lap.

"Thank you, Harry, I will."

While they ate and made polite conversation, the fog thickened and lifted off the hill, leaving clouds below and blue sky above and the usual view. No bodies, no hunters.

92

"May I smoke?"

"Please do, Kate."

Before she had found a match—for Lawrence was off to replenish the coffee—the Red Chested Screech walked in from the back gallery. He was dressed in a business suit and carried a briefcase, just like any commuter.

'You never covered your section at all.' she thought. 'There wouldn't have been time.' He'd been beating the bushes in her apartment without doubt, pulling things apart, looking through everything. It was a downright shame that she hadn't set the scene: gin bottle under the bed, fat rolls of greasy dollar bills tucked in her underwear, matches with "Love from Cosa Nostra" printed in purple. Unimaginative clod.

He looked briefly at her unlit cigarette and ignored it.

"I'll be back tonight, I think," he said to Harry and left, shutting the front door with a careful but not careless "thunk" just to show that he was only annoyed with part of the party. The next moment they saw the Jaguar swerve past the police cruiser and scatter another four inches of gravel onto the steps.

Kate wanted to ask about this particular alarm; if that one rang in the police station or if someone had telephoned, but suddenly Mr. Renshaw looked yellow, tired, in the foggy brightness. After a minute more of quiet conversation, she thanked him and excused herself.

There was no point in rushing back to check her room. Either Forbes had turned everything upside down or he had not, so why have a stroke. She dawdled instead, looking at her favorites in the west gallery.

One of the labels had fallen off during the night, and lay at the edge of the parquet. It was number 38, and by chance Kate remembered that it was the Parmigianino she had seen the first day. The one that was too high to reach.

93

But now the ladder stood by and she had a pencil in her bun. No one was looking, so she climbed up fast, pushed the pencil down on the hooks and stuck the label on in a second. Then she let the frame down again, descended the ladder and pushed it behind the potted plants. There was no reason why simply putting back a label should bring on such a furtive appearance, no reason at all.

'And all because' she muttered angrily to herself as she went back to her apartment, 'the events of the past days are designed to make me lose my grip. And that all because a rooster is pecking out some order of merit for himself.'

Nothing had been touched. Nothing except the telephone: it worked now, naturally. Perhaps nothing had been wrong at all. Perhaps the telephone company was dead last night. Could be she was becoming paranoid. She drove off to Boston (pop. 1,000,000 and over) leaving Lawrence a note that she would not be back for lunch.

It was late afternoon when Kate returned, maybe metamorphosed, maybe not. Calm, anyhow, with hair two shades blonder and some new clothes to match. Mrs. Oliphant made her a cup of tea, and she sat down in the kitchen with her to talk over the morning's doings. Lawrence joined them to add his theories, and even Turner had a beer on his way to the back compost heap. Everyone was so genial, so calm. In fact, this was what it might be like every day, when the Scot . . . was not. She felt a silky satisfaction that lasted her until mid-evening. The feeling was even better in the print room where she checked the label number. She had been right; number 38 was the Parmigianino.

Before there was time to think about this, Turner asked her about the crate of books that had arrived at noon. He put them down by the print room door.

"I'll unpack these right now, Turner." And as the man

94

left to get a crowbar from the garage, she could hear the Jaguar roaring back on the driveway, scattering another four inches of stones, across the grass this time. Its smoking hot hood was probably being gently eased into the stall—if it hadn't squashed Turner beforehand—where it would cool with an expensive and disdainful "plink" just like its owner.

But its owner had cooled down already. For some reason, the man came along the back gallery relaxed and smiling. He put down his briefcase. He sprang to help her pull books out of the plastic bubble wrap. Forbes must be one of those perennial *enfant terrible* types; if anger had been to no avail, he would now try simply oozing charm, or use the sincere approach, or have sulks, or try first-craven-then-sullen—anything at all to get attention.

"I've been hoping to see you," he began, on his knees beside the crate—as if he'd had to look all day—"Lawrence just told me that Mrs. Oliphant had to leave suddenly to see a sick relative. She left dinner ready, of course, but I thought maybe you and I . . . maybe you'd care to go out to dinner with me. You know Harry is served well enough by Lawrence, but three of us might be a bit much for him to handle without her. There's a very decent inn about an hour from here." His voice trailed off, and the way it was phrased, he had left no loophole—that is, no loophole if she was compassionate. But she looked him right in the eye and said no thanks, she'd really rather stay here and be a bit much for Lawrence. She threw him the print room key and left. He could put down the books he was holding wherever he wanted. Two grown people. It was ridiculous, but there was no sense in graciously adapting to outrageous changes in posture.

And at the cocktail hour Kate arrived late in a new long Irish wool and silk outfit, a frightfully expensive thing she

95

wore mainly to show Forbes what the place would be like after he left. After the lower hierarchy had moved up one notch.

At her entry, Harry put down his glass and put on his glasses. He made appreciative noises, and even Forbes stared. He put down his whiskey.

"You've decided to be a 'bit much' too?" she said. She accepted the martini he made for her and then went to sit with Harry. Hitherto Harry had filled all the conversational gaps that came along, but with the events of the past two days, Kate decided to go on strike. She said nothing. Forbes came over and stood by the fireplace, leaning against the mantel with its carved festoons and cherubs and stirred his drink. She still said nothing. Harry smiled quietly and said nothing either.

It must be said that in the pinch Forbes came through. He raised his glass to her with a disarming smile.

"Kate. Apologies are in order. From me to you and in front of Harry. I've been guilty of a complete misjudgment. Accept my penance now, please do."

She gave a sigh of boredom. "The certificates of virtue are handed out with the telephone wiring?"

He tried again. "I've already told Harry all of it just now since I've come back. I've been a precipitate boor. I'm terribly sorry, Kate. Would you—"

"Never mind," she said, cutting him off. "As you continually intimate, you're in the homeland of boors. There are so many of us I suspect you weren't even noticed. And I could have told you, of course, what you must have gone to great extremes to find out. If you ever listen to anyone but yourself . . ."

Had her past history been exceptional, colorful, tinged with excitement and equivocal experiences, she might have felt uneasy, but as it was the day must have yielded facts of

96

the most tedious sort, unenlivened by any sudden distinctions.

"You're deliberately obscuring the real issue, Kate. You've got to see yourself as an outsider like myself sees you." He was winsome, appealing even. "You know Harry's been having trouble with thefts. We don't know who. On and off, no pattern. So, while your application is in the works there's a quiet span . . ."

"Before that, too, Forbes. You're cutting it too fine. Forbes's alarm stopped almost all of it . . ." said Harry.

"That doesn't mean conclusively that it's the alarm. Maybe he, or they, are regrouping. The alarms are just making things tight enough so they have to think of a new angle. So then, let's think this through as any normal person would."

"Normal?" she said. "Are you bragging or complaining?"

He let it by. "So, if Harry sends to a government agency for help, and here I'm thinking of the National Collection of Graphic whatever it is, as a kind of agency. . . . Well, if Harry asks for expertise, what do you suppose is the form and shape that expertise arrives in? I know what happens in Scotland when we ask for expert help, and it isn't slim and blonde and all ready to hitch up for the second go around."

"Why don't you do all this glib penance somewhere alone. Make a tape and I'll listen when I'm feeling strong."

Even Harry was surprised. "Is this going to be an apology, Forbes?"

Forbes was one jump ahead of everyone. "It's a documentation, Harry. The very thing that Kate understands; all the footnotes of my thoughts! It's a compliment! Why, even Mabel thought we'd ordered Kate up especially. After all, as I was going to say, by the time an expert is seasoned, if

97

she's any good she's been snapped up, hasn't she? So they send out some lump. I mean competent, naturally, but stuttering or uninteresting to the point of disaster. At least that's been my luck, and if that's what they send me, think who'll volunteer to go up to the wilds with a ninety-two-year old crank like you, Harry."

"Forbes," she said, "your little speech just proves that all the gorillas aren't yet in the zoo."

The man smiled. "Look at things as they are," and he looked at her as things were in the classic Italian fashion: no clothes. "After all, Kate's skinny, but nothing that couldn't be improved. So, the first day she's pulling one of the alarm systems, then she tests the gate alarm one evening, then she's pulling the newest system right out of the wall—all this just by chance, naturally."

"Naturally," Kate agreed.

"And then, the great predicament of Michelangelo. Ah yes. If the lady couldn't fit him into his niche, there should of course be a reasonable doubt. After all, anyone can read, these days. And last night, as we know, someone turned off the alarm to the main collection and it was just Mabel and John's early departure that botched a big job—perhaps. We don't know that yet. The gate alarm was the only one tripped." He turned to her. "You can see, Katy, that at this point something had to be nailed down, for your sake too. Documentation, either yes or no. You'd approve of that yourself now, wouldn't you? Conclusions. Harry would approve. So there you are."

"Beg pardon, sir." Lawrence, maybe for the first time in his life, became more than a fixture. He volunteered a footnote. "I'm afraid it was a misunderstanding—the alarm to the main collection. Turner was starting to put on the storms in the north gallery and two of them stuck so badly that he turned off the alarm for fear the pounding would

98

make all the pictures jump and set off an alarm immediately. We agreed that since we were there it would be all right to turn it off. Turner must have thought I would reset it and I was under the assumption he would, and I'm afraid, sir, that with the Houseman's arrival I failed to check. It was a bad oversight, sir."

"Turner told me that in the garage this morning, Lawrence. Thanks. But you can see how it looked. In previous years, I know Harry would have gone to Washington himself to make sure of Kate, to verify that he wasn't being assigned a lemon. But he's staying home this year. If I had known, I would have gone down myself. Then again I thought that maybe there *was* another Gordon down there, completely unaware of an imposter, or maybe the whole correspondence had been faked. Several interesting possibilities came to mind."

"The most interesting possibility that comes to mine," said Kate, putting down her glass with a grand gesture, "is that if I had swept in here like Mabel and said what I thought it would have cleared the air."

"If you had been another Mabel, my child, you wouldn't have lasted one week. Isn't that right, Harry!"

Harry's face broke into an ancient smile. "Probably right . . . I was barely able," he wheezed, "to get Mabel off me onto John two generations back. I was vigorous then. One weekend of her . . . quite enough. John has remarkable staying power."

"Kate's quite durable too, really," added Forbes, making further judgments that were none of his business.

Lawrence announced Mrs. Oliphant's improvised dinner, and it put an end to speculations. Forbes seated her with unaccustomed care, but the weekend market review went on as usual, with particular emphasis on a new precipitator at American Smelting and Refining that had

99

absorbed the profits for the quarter.

Kate let her mind wander back to the 38 label. They were quite durable really, those labels. They never just fell off. And why that particular one, one she had mentioned as being interesting the first morning—none of the others had lost their labels. In fact, the only way a label would come off was by being handled quite severely, as when stuffing the whole drawing into a briefcase or between some layers that might rake it off. If that had happened, the person must have been careless, hurried enough to ignore a falling label or not to notice. And the reason for the hurry, possibly, was that Mabel and John had gotten up at four A.M. Three hours ahead of the household schedule. Turner had turned off the alarm with Lawrence's approval, and whoever it was must have known the alarm was off. The alarm had started up because that drawing perhaps had been disturbed? Really pulled at? Or just disturbed by the hammering? It was inconceivable that labels would come off just because panes of glass were being replaced. Understandable that maybe the maid had not cleaned the back gallery because of the fuss earlier—an oversight that was not corrected later on.

Harry was asking if she would like some rare or well done roast. She interrupted her train of thought long enough to answer "Yes, thank you," which made him ask the question a second time, and then she got it right. He thought she was brooding over the compliments thrown around earlier, perhaps, and smiled warmly. She gave him a broad smile back, just to show that she was quite unaffected. The whole idea of the label was just too silly. After all, as Forbes had said, nothing was missing, so why give it any thought.

After the market report, the men set out with determination to be good hosts, just as on the first evening. They were witty, anecdotal, complimentary, but Kate was still

100

vague. If the second alarm was the gate—the one she had accidentally set off without even knowing one afternoon—had he, or they, gotten away through that gate?

Harry misinterpreted her vague replies; he thought she was depressed about being the stuttering stone or whatever Forbes had mentioned, and at the liqueur he tried to fix things up. He got ready to leave.

"Tomorrow, Kate, we'll get together to look over the questionable ones, poor quality prints, fakes; see what we should do . . ."

As soon as the words were out she watched Forbes' face turn dark like an approaching storm, and if Harry had thought he was mending fences, perhaps he was mending his own and knocking down hers.

"Mabel and John upset my schedule this morning. Retiring early tonight, I think. Forbes, I'll see you at breakfast. Good night, both of you." He had Lawrence wheel him out of the dining room first, for once, and she and Forbes were left alone together.

It was a good deal more togetherness than she needed. The man was starting in already.

"Kate, I told you before . . ."

"If you'll excuse me, I have work to catch up on now," she interrupted. "The maids can clear."

"Certainly." He rose. It was almost eerie—so British, so well-bred even when they were cross. She left, but the man was right with her. And once inside the print room he chose an empty spot on the wall and lounged against it, lighting a cigarette and smoking, waiting. Harry would have had a fit—a smoker in the print room—but she figured that since Forbes had installed the controls, the controls would take care of anything he did.

She put away the card she had pulled this morning, checking it a last time against the chart.

101

"Testing your memory?" he said, waiting for the right moment to fuss.

"A label number," she answered, still preoccupied with the why of it. "A label that I found on the floor in the north gallery this morning. It was from the Parmigianino I was looking at the first day . . ."

"Yes. I recall that."

Naturally he recalled. Thanks to him probably everyone recalled it.

"I remembered the number but I just wanted to make sure. It's odd to find a label just lying on the floor. They don't come off, really."

He was unimpressed. He picked up a pile of drawings, the unknowns, the questionables. "Maybe Lawrence comes by every morning and sweeps up labels. Did you ask him? What are these in this pile?" His last night. The last sermon.

She stalled. "I didn't get the chance to ask Lawrence. Things were too confused."

He put down the pile, temporarily. "Much more to the point, by the way, is whether you asked Lawrence to turn off the alarm when you checked. Did you do that?"

No point in cheating. "No, I didn't."

"Ah! Things were 'too confused,' I suppose. You stuck it back with your pencil method." He ground out his cigarette on the bottom of his shoe until it was cold. "Point one: these alarms are not a slot machine. They're destined for one pull; that's what I told you. This is my last day and you still seem to miss the point—you seem to want to miss it, week after week." He was building up steam.

She stuck to her importances, in order. "More important, it seems to me, is how the label got to the floor in the first place. Only an act like trying to stuff a drawing into a sack or a box could rip that label off. Not replacing window panes as Lawrence said."

102

"Nothing was missing. Why would a burglar hang it back up? Maybe he decided he didn't like it! I think that for now you can leave your sensitivities in your apartment where they belong. Lawrence probably sweeps up labels every day. And point two, and I've told you this before as well, is that I don't want Harry harrassed by your 'authenticities'." He picked up the pile of drawings once more. "Harry is the one to be looked after, not his collection."

She seemed to pay no attention. "The Director in Washington said this was one of the worst protected collections in the world. He had heard that even the storm windows clipped on from the outside. Anyone could get in, any night and pull drawings right off the wall . . ."

Forbes snorted. "Your Director! I saw your Director. You can relay the information back to him that the storm windows do not screw on from the outside. That was one of the first things I had Harry change. An American wooden house is a disaster to begin with. Any fool can come along with a chain saw and cut a hole right out of the wall." He glared at the wall, as if some circular blade were coming through right then. "But other than that, *you,* my dear, are the greatest disaster Harry could have. Point one is that pulling on a drawing will invalidate the alarm system, and point two is that I know you're going to start pruning and fussing away at the collection the minute I leave. This pile here for instance . . ."

Her shoulders sagged. All right. One last humility and he was gone. Tomorrow morning would bring some peace.

"There aren't many," she explained. "That one on top is maybe a fake Raphael. Maybe, just maybe. I'll have to get a better opinion than mine."

"It's too messy?" He was sarcastic.

"It's too clean . . . for Raphael," she said.

"Why?"

103

"Why? Because a lot of his drawings were studies—explorations—very private sorts of tentative drawings. Scribbled, blotted, with other drawings on the same sheet, some pricked for transfer. This one looks too pretty to be true. I don't know. As I said, it's just a guess. He paid for it as a Raphael. I'll have to see what he wants done."

"I told you the very first week. I was very explicit. If he paid for a Raphael, then see that he has one. You know what I want done."

"What *you* want done. You?" The word 'explicit' had pushed it all over the edge. "Forbes, I don't give a damn what you want done."

"If you don't give a damn, then I'll *tell* you what you're going to do. I'll tell you once *again*. If the prints look wrong in a raking light, don't *look* at them in a raking light. If the Raphael looks too clean, put it away and don't look at it at all. If the labels fall off every goddamn print, then sweep them up and keep your mouth shut. Do you understand?"

"We went over this before and I said that I didn't ask to come; I was asked. Period. This is my print room, and now you get out."

Forbes picked up the whole pile of questionables and threw them in the wastebasket where they slithered and finally came to rest.

"If there's one thing worse than a ninny, it's a self-righteous academic."

She took the print room key off its hook and turned at the door. "You want me to cheat, don't you. Cheat Harry of the dignity of knowledge, honest knowledge. Feed him Cream of Wheat, mealy things, pre-digested half truths. And you know what will happen. Someone else will come in and tell him the truth. That not only did I not serve him honestly, but that he was a fool to hire me. Frankly, I refuse.

104

He's going to hear it just as it is. And you, Forbes, can go to hell."

She threw the key at him and walked out, going back to her rooms fast, and slamming her door. He could turn off the light and lock the door of the print room himself. He knew how: after all, he had installed everything.

But it only took a second. The man knew his installations too well, and then he was through her door. He came in, furious, grabbed her by the shoulders and tightened his hands until she thought her joints would separate.

"Listen," he said. "I don't give a damn if *all* the drawings are fakes—if they all turn out to be Xeroxed! Harry's last months are going to be good ones. He's got to be confident and powerful, just like he's always been. I'm not about to see him worn down by some half-assed female, fussing about fakes, fussing about inferior prints, worrying over mistakes. If half the stuff is no good, forget it. Do the other half. I can't stay on to protect him from you, and nobody's going to slip doubts and problems in now where there weren't any before. You're not going to ruin him for a bloody set of principles!"

"No bloody set of principles ever ruined anyone," she answered, and to punctuate her thought gave him a good hard kick in the shins and pushed him off.

It took maybe a second. Then he reached for her so fast that it was as if she had been slammed against a wall. After his mouth came down on hers it was more like being dropped into a five thousand foot airpocket, and then being swept under a gigantic wave on a Pacific beach—a chemical reaction that must have been percolating since the very first evening when she walked into the living room for cocktails, or the second night, or the third.

And when they finally slept, it was already into the early hours of the morning, and by the time Kate awoke he was gone.

105

Chapter

8

The Renshaw estate was practical. It took perfunctory notice of the comings and goings, and then life closed back over the gaps. The weather had turned cold after Forbes' departure, and if Kate seemed silent, distraught, and thin, the household blamed the weather; on that particular summit, the wind accounted for much.

Renshaw had never left anything in his life to complete chance, and this applied also to the elements. The French doors were fastened shut and puttied. Storm windows were hung, screwing on from the inside. Supplies arrived from Boston: mop heads, even, lest the dust pile up inside like the snow outdoors, candles and matches for ice storms, food for freezers. Over the past thirty years disasters had been studied and tabulated, and now they were like a ship to be marooned in the ice off Baffin Island, albeit marooned with a certain ease.

The routine remained. But when the finely focussed

days of fall had ended, with the acrid smell of burning leaves and the warm sunshines just a memory, and in their place the grey, damp hours with heavy air, and drafts and sullen chills that settled in the pockets of the meadows, the routine became a cosy thing. Early darks, and lights coming on, hissing of cheerful heats, and hot cups of coffee from perpetual percolators in the kitchen slowly salved the raw edges of Duncan Forbes' departure, and Kate was happy with smaller things.

Dinner was the same ceremonious event, and Harry was appreciative. He was gallant and attentive, but nothing interrupted the sacred report. It now came by telephone, and Lawrence would bring in earphones after the soup. Harry would put them on like sacrificial vestments and would listen, interjecting commands.

"Go ahead on that, Mr. Klein," or "Sell." Once she heard the demise of a man who had given him poor advice. "All right, then, raise his salary and fire him." It seemed that there were signal honors before the guillotine.

About twice a week there was a Forbes report. Nothing personal—postcards, with large, decisive writing, just three words to a side. Once an envelope with a clipping and a note scrawled on it to the effect that pretty soon Kate could relax. This brought a smile to Harry's face as he showed it to her. A *Caritas* by Salviati, one of several, had been stolen in northern Italy, and Forbes hoped they would soon all be gone.

Harry missed Forbes and his frank, aggravating ways. Kate stabilized, after feeling like a yoyo for days, and Renshaw stroked his chin more than once, wondering not so much whether the simple life would do, but wondering why it did.

Shortly after the first sleet storm Lawrence issued an invitation at the print room door. Mr. Renshaw would be pleased if she would take tea in his apartment after lunch.

Kate had never attempted to put herself in the place of Forbes as a friend. She had kept to the print room, unwilling to push herself forward, as a matter of good taste. But with the onset of cold weather, Renshaw weakened. His breathing was worse and, to save energy, he kept to his bed during the day. He had done the same the year before, but he found it confining.

"I'll be delighted," Kate had said to Lawrence, and the butler's stolid face relaxed, just once.

For a minute after he left there was a small, fierce feeling of triumph, as the inner sanctum swung open, but the feeling was quickly tempered by the fact that, had a better person been available, she would have been ignored, as she had been all fall. Even so, the quick anticipation when she presented herself at the south hall was much like the feeling on the first day. Lawrence showed her in, through a private entry with several doors, and into a large austere bedroom filled to overflowing with all sorts of impediments to a gracious tea.

Renshaw was in a large bed surrounded by tables, clearly temporary improvisations that satisfied no one: tables with rolling wheels, tables that slid over beds, tables that had cubbyholes, or telephones, or bookcases, or filing cabinets, and then great, unhandy piles of legal size papers all threatening to slither. One could see that this was never going to breed a cosy interchange. It was meant to breed business and tea was thereby a pretext.

This particular day, Renshaw was galled to the extreme. He was dressed in a brocade dressing gown, with the woolly scarf hampering the clear, decisive movements so dear to his nature.

"Hurry up, Lawrence. Pour the tea. Keep the calls on hold."

109

Lawrence, poor man, did his best, winding his turtlelike way among the telephone cords and the reports whose covers stuck out over the edges of the tables inviting a crash at every turn. Harry glared at the inconvenience of it all.

"Doctor told me last year to move to Florida in the winter." He shook his head. "Got rid of him." Lawrence was kicking a telephone cord under the bed. "Got rid of one fool. Another one now."

She thought he meant the butler, but Renshaw smiled suddenly and she saw he meant himself, in a gentle sort of way.

"Have myself, to put up with."

Kate murmured something polite about his health; something that should not have been mentioned, and he started chittering like an angry raccoon.

"Don't want to be asked one more time. Is that clear?" and he looked down at some notes in his lap, putting an end to niceties in general. Kate took the cup that Lawrence brought; she sat sipping and waiting.

The man put on his glasses and looked over. "Now, get down to facts. Think I recall, last summer your Director implied to me that if you came here, all . . . of this," and he waved his hand at the walls, "all of this might go down there. Was that implied?" He peered at her over his frames. The room was filled with the sound of his gentle asthmatic huffle and the colors of the red lights on the telephones on the tables, obedient in various holding patterns, some fast and some slow. Renshaw's black eyes looked at her steadily.

"The Director mentioned it." Kate looked back at him just as steadily, in some sort of holding pattern too, maybe just holding her breath. The best she could have hoped for was that the subject would never come up.

110

"Expected so." he was saying. "Given it some thought."

Well, it had probably all been decided or he wouldn't bring it up, so she decided to breathe normally rather than turn blue.

"I had only two considerations in mind," the collector started, and she knew the game was over.

"The first was that one bomb would get all the collections: the National Gallery, the Phillips, the Freer, the Hirschorn, the Renwick, yours . . . everything, including mine, if it was there. Second, was that overgrown amounts are never well managed."

He simply stopped at that point. He didn't look for discussion. Discussion took a lot of his breath, and she was not called in to talk things over; she was being informed. After a moment Kate nodded. He was right of course, on both counts. If one lived in Washington one had either to come to grips with the bomb or move away. He was also right about his collection: it would be merged; it would be rounded; it would be given signal honors and then little axes here and there. The essence of his fierce enjoyments would be diluted, and Harry's personality would disappear. Renshaw was right, in every way. And for her too, whether the man ever knew it or not, it would buy time, just in case the pile that Forbes had thrown out turned into what he feared. They could be all copies now, all fakes, all Xeroxes, and her little champion would be safe.

But if she was relieved on the one hand, she was defeated on the other. She hadn't been able to swing it, that was all. Perhaps it had been the Director's long shot, perhaps not, but Kate knew how his gaze flicked lightly over the heads of failures; those persons became gracefully and smoothly nonexistent from that moment on. And in July she had seen the man's mind already embracing this addition;

111

how he had been licking at the edges like Winnie-the-Pooh at his honey pots.

Renshaw, however, was not the Director. He was not an insensitive man. "I've placed you in a difficult position, haven't I. That is, if you really wanted to go back. I had hoped you'd want to stay." For once in his life Renshaw looked flustered and inadequate. In fact he looked like a child holding a cat that it had drowned by mistake while trying to improve it. The sight of the man, so kindly and so concerned, made her break into a big smile. Like the fog that had lifted in an instant the other day, the clouds through which she had been fighting life suddenly billowed, and Kate began to laugh: first quietly, and then more openly, and soon almost hysterically. Renshaw himself joined in, laughing soundlessly, in a conspiracy of two.

"Harry," she said, embarrassed by the tears in her eyes. "It's such a sense of relief: your collection staying here. In September, you know, I was really running away." And although she was still laughing, the admission was close to tears.

Renshaw looked at her fixedly. "Knew that," he said, back to his usual terse self. "Called the Director last week. Told him what your answer would be." And then his own face broke into a thousand parchment folds, and he laughed the hardest and the longest: the drowned cat had come back to life.

He handed her a letter and Kate steadied herself. The man was a thousand miles ahead of them all, and he had told the truth. She knew the color of the vellum. The Director, of course. She could visualize him now, putting his bloodless fingertips together, expressing the corporate regret of the National Collection that the Renshaw Collection had not been passed to them. He would add, of course, the hope that they, there in Washington, might be of "value" to the

112

"fledgling effort," and he would smile a deprecatory smile as he dictated. He would be thinking that one new collection was opened in the United States every week, cluttering up the country with weak research facilities and diluting serious efforts. What the man would refuse to recall was that his first words had summarized Harry Renshaw completely: "a singular man, of very fixed ideas."

She handed back the letter, unopened. "I know what he said, Harry. I know it all by heart." She got up to go.

"I asked him," said Renshaw, "three weeks ago to send back my Rembrandts. Afraid he might hold them as hostage to get you back." Harry held out his hand; they shook on it. A pact of two.

It was only much later in the day she remembered that three weeks back had been the day of the Houseman's visit. The very lowest ebb, she had thought at the time, but apparently nothing of the sort.

The following day Lawrence was again asked to invite Kate to tea. The next visit, however, was a cheerful one.

Harry lost no time in pulling out his two reborn Rembrandts: the first and seventh states of *Christ Presented to the People.* Lucas van Leyden had done a similar print: Christ on a parapet in the center of a city setting, a mob all about. Rembrandt had brought the scene closer, pushing again.

"Aren't these beauties!" Harry exclaimed. "Aren't they magnificent?" They were laid out before him on the bed.

"They're superb impressions, Harry."

"Come on, Kate, can't you come to terms with him here? They're clear; they're not messy in the corners; they're filled with detail." He waited. The game wasn't quite as cat and mouse as with Forbes, but he waited, almost as vulpine. He baited the trap more firmly. "After all, even at the seventh correction it's still clear right to the back!"

113

"Ah, Harry, Rembrandt hasn't changed! Neither have I. Neither have you! He's still got me in prison, except the prison is more clear. If he had made thirteen states he'd be right back to his steel wool, believe me. See the intensities coming in, darkening the side buildings; the clarity of the architecture is gone. The building is too squat; the front drops us into the dungeon; he's sacrificed everything to push, to load the dice. I like my Renaissance."

"But he's done all this on purpose, Kate. He wasn't afraid to change it around. Anything that would suit his purpose he tried."

"I'm not the type to be pushed. The seventeenth century and I don't get along, Harry." She laughed. "You know, you and Forbes are just alike. You like only what you like: opinionated, both of you!"

"Oh?" he said. "Thank you. I take that as a compliment."

Harry said no more about his Rembrandts. He had Turner hang them across the room where he could see them from his bed.

A few days later Harry had a new idea.

"What would you think, Kate, if I asked you to fly out to Castellorizo, the Housemans, you know, to pick up the head and bring it back."

Kate put down her cup and saucer, and thought. That was no question; it merely had an interrogative pronoun at the start. Harry never asked; he pronounced, so the plan must be already in the works. Kate was beginning to get a feel for these things. Quirks. Renshaw was gentle, but he brooked no tangents. Renshaw was not Forbes either, to whom she could reply that she'd rather stay home and be a bother to Lawrence. The only excuse now would be gangrene of all four limbs and a sore throat to boot. Certainly Harry left her no way of saying she'd rather stay and finish

114

his Prosper Scavezzi's prints. She took a breath.

"When would you like me to leave?" The only answer.

Renshaw smiled as if she'd made a brilliant chess maneuver out of Capablanca versus Lasker, 1921. "I'd like to see the head again. See what you think too."

"Harry," she answered, "I don't think at all when it comes to Fourth Century heads. Why don't you send out an expert from the Fogg Museum." She could stay home with Scavezzi.

"Boston office," he answered putting his glasses on, putting her devious tactics off, "made arrangements." He read a memo on his lap table: "TWA, New York-Athens. Castellorizo by private charter. Few days rest. Back. Leave day after tomorrow . . . that suit you?"

Like the Director and his "time to consider," the question was purely rhetorical.

"That will be fine, Harry. I'll be glad to go."

The man gave her a tender smile.

At dinner the next evening Harry asked how things were progressing. All was fine, meaning that she had given herself a shampoo. He nodded with another tender smile. And were there any questions? A bit too broad, that phrase, somewhat like "How was your trip to Europe?" Broad enough to forestall an answer, and she shook her head. Satisfied then, Renshaw relaxed and talked about a point concerning an anonymous Milanese engraver who had copied parts of Leonardo. Harry was witty and relaxed; he told anecdotes. No further mention was made of the trip. As they took a Drambuie, Harry handed her an envelope. Sealed.

"Don't open it . . . already done. Discussions are a waste. My energy better spent on other things. Appreciate this trip. Good night." Lawrence wheeled him off.

115

The next day Kate saw him for a minute to say good-bye. He waved off her protests about the bank deposit with a peremptory gesture. Both the check and her departure seemed to concern him no longer, and he turned to the call from Hamburg.

Chapter 9

Boston was not far: two hours, maybe two and a half, and Lawrence himself solved the conversation problem. He opened the rear door of the Daimler, helped her in, then put himself at the wheel and slid the glass partition between them firmly shut.

It didn't matter really. The sky was low and lowering still further, and it was nice to think about nothing. As they approached Boston, an oily, rush-hour murk came licking out to greet them, and there was nothing of interest that moved except cars. She had been at Renshaw's for so long that even cars were now faintly interesting.

Lawrence parked the Daimler right in front of the terminal entrance, in the yellow-banded "no parking" zone. After helping her out, he just left the car there, keys in the ignition, engine running, and called a porter to remove the bags. Kate was impressed.

"How delicious! They can always buy another," and

117

she allowed herself to be swept into the terminal with this grand approach to life. The reservations were waiting of course, and as Lawrence handed the packet to her she could hear the flight being called. He was pleased and still pompous; pleased with his well-oiled car, pleased with the well-oiled machinery of the Boston office and pleased with his own timing.

"There you are, Mrs. Gordon. Your bags will be picked up in Athens by the charter. You'll be met, of course. Have a pleasant trip." He tipped his hat and inclined his head ever so slightly—not because of her, but because he was the Renshaw man present at the moment. Then he turned and went back to the Renshaw car.

She opened the packet as she walked along checking the flights. The Boston office had sent her via New York, and first class all the way! But, later on, after working her way through champagne, lobster, French pastries, and Antiguan coffee, she decided that flying was still not the most comfortable way to spend a night. The engines whined, first at one level, then at another, and whatever level they were looking for they never found. She finally dozed off just as breakfast was served, and then slept soundly until Greece was putting its paws into the sea below. The rocky spines of the mountains were just as she had seen them once before, with Charles. Before she could get really upset they landed.

A man met her there, and it took another hour until the small float plane touched down and taxied to the dock of Castellorizo. If the land had flattened out around Athens in an open gesture of welcome, on Castellorizo it did not. Instead it fell into the sea in some fit of total abandon, leaving the town with its two streets and its docks to hang on as best it could. The superimposed rows of houses, balconied and whitewashed, blinked solemnly out to sea like owls.

A crowd of boys surrounded her on the dock. "Tour,

118

lady?" "Shine shoes, lady?" "Rooms, lady?" Anyone standing alone on a dock in a raspberry-colored suit was fair game.

"Allez!" said the long-legged goddess who gave them all a whack on their rears, and then stuck out a brown paw. "I'm Julia." Her handshake was warm and calloused, her voice the same. "You're Kate, of course! Isn't it lucky that Harry sent you out by plane. The ferry from Rhodes is so rough that one throws up for hours."

She couldn't be anyone's offspring but Mabel's. Julia was Mabel, fifty years younger, breathless with talk. "We're so glad you're here! Mabel's waiting for some lamb from the butcher so she stayed up on top. Do you want a carriage ride? Ride a mule? Are you feeling strong enough to walk?" Her tawny hair blew around in the breeze like her words.

"I'd love to walk," Kate answered. "I've been sitting for hours, and First Class is pretty dull."

"Well, you won't find it dull up there. All of us—and Duncan Forbes too. He flew in today, says he knows you. He's sick. He took one look at all of us and disappeared. I haven't been able to pull him out since he got here. Says he's got 'Bombay Tummy' "

Julia looked about on the dock for a porter, and then pointed to the two suiter and Kate's square case and then again to the top of the hill. A man nodded.

"Do you want to give him your coat too? It's going to be warm in the sun. That's a beautiful matching outfit. The next time I'm in Rome, I'll look for one too."

Her recording played on; Kate's was stuck way back at 'Duncan Forbes too; he flew in today,' which kept repeating itself. Unreal, like the unblinking sunlight. When she collected her wits Julia was onto the subject of Castellorizo itself.

"I've done everything there is to do. After you leave

119

I'll go to Rome. My tan isn't getting any darker now. I've tried all the cafés. One has cheezies stapled in plastic on a cardboard, and the other has a waiter with hepatitis. You take your choice."

They walked up the road; it turned into a ramp that wound around the steep hill behind the cafes with cheezies and yellow waiters.

"I don't think Duncan Forbes has hepatitis," declared Julia, scientific. "He has bubonic plague. Swollen glands under his arm—as big as oranges—I felt them. Then I looked it up in a medical book Mabel and John keep in their study. "Armpits and groin . . ." She nodded. "I don't know about the groin. It isn't polite to stare. Anyhow," and Julia gave a happy sigh of relief, having disposed of the plague by enumerating the symptoms, "there's Georges too." She stopped. "He's indescribable, Kate. He's mature, he's concerned, he's strong, he relates, he's gentle, only . . ." and she scratched her tousled head and threw her hair on a different side.

"Only what?"

"Only, he's so intellectual! He keeps feeding me, force-feeding actually, Homer, Herodotus. For instance, last night at dinner, mind you, it was the Persian Wars, Books One, Two, Three—all of it. We heard how the Scythians came along after the Cimmerians, or was it the other way. How many men the Persians had lined up, every tribe from Ethiopia to the Black Sea. I swear, Georges must think I'm interested. And here's where *you* could help, Kate. I mean, you could point out some other possibilities. Even if you're neutral?"

Julia turned suddenly with a radiant smile. "He's got class, Kate! How many men do you know that have class? Nowadays." The avalanche of words stopped for breath and Kate grinned.

120

"Not many!" She let the breeze tug at her hair. "Actually, don't you think that all of Herodotus should be counted as a plus? It's a compliment from a man with class. Georges could be steered later, perhaps, to subjects that are a trifle more pertinent."

"I asked Duncan to help, but he just said gloomily that by the time I'm forty Georges will be on his second set of false teeth. I'm counting on you, Kate. Mabel believes Duncan, you know, and I need a counterbalance. Between Mabel and John and Duncan, Georges won't stand a chance to get me."

The road became quite steep at this point and there wasn't that much breath for sorting out strategems. So Julia stopped to pluck some grass and chew on it.

"Maybe you could lean toward Georges? Do you think forty is too old, Kate? I mean, I think a little advance is a good thing, don't you? You don't get many sensible men at age twenty. They're not even interesting until they're thirty-five, I find."

Julia's finds were probably well researched, and Kate asked what Georges did. For a living, she meant.

"Do? He reads history. Georges has so much money he doesn't need to do anything. He comes and goes. I don't know if he 'does' anything. He has it made."

"Well, most people do something even if they do have it made," said Kate, wondering what Forbes did.

Julia didn't really care. Life was desperate right now, but it was more interesting that way, and she caught sight of a form coming over the brow of the hill.

"Here he comes!" she squealed. "See what you think, and tell me tonight," and she scampered off to meet her Greek.

Kate watched the action, like a silent film, and in a few moments Julia came back down the slope with Georges

Lisas, patting him as though she had won him at a bazaar. He kept his arm about Julia as he extended his hand to Kate.

"Is this 'the' Kate that I'm meeting?" Georges smiled. He had all his teeth. "We're delighted to have you in Greece! How was the trip?"

Unlike Julia, Georges waited to hear her answer. He was even interested—one of those Greeks with whom one had instant rapport. Maybe it was just imagination that gave him the faintly Hellenistic look of a tortured Meander, or even a little like a Rembrandt self portrait or, more likely still, the look of a Basset hound in distress. His forehead, under a mane of dark silvered hair was permanently wrinkled in sympathy, but his eyes smiled. Julia again patted him happily.

"I'm so glad you two've met. Georges, I'll have you know, is the most wanted man in Greece. Aren't you, Georges!"

"Well, my dear, that's a very ambiguous phrase. It depends on how you mean 'wanted.'" The English was flawless, more British than Forbes, although that man spoke 'American' deliberately, she was sure, in order to crankily separate himself from England.

"Wanted? Why you're the essential ingredient! You make the unwanted feel wanted, the wanted feel admired, the older people feel young, the young people feel suave, the . . ."

"Julia," interrupted Georges, "is like getting tangled in flypaper. Run along child and let me show Kate the view. It's not quite a 'rosy-fingered dawn,' but it has interesting historical points. Now, from this side you can see . . ."

Georges never got to that side. Julia shrieked instead, just like Mabel, "Oh God! He's at it again! Homer, you'll get today. I've had Homer! The saffron dawns and Hector and Achilles, all the men run through with spears. I'm going

122

to go see Mabel. I can't stand it one more time." And she scrambled off the ramp onto some vertical shortcut and disappeared over the top.

"My!" said Georges, taking Kate's arm to help her over a hummocky part where the cobbles had given way. "I hope she's reached her growth." That was all he said.

They climbed in a companionable silence. Kate stopped once to exclaim, and then they climbed some more.

"I didn't know there *were* quiet Americans. Smoke?"

"Thanks. I'd love one while I take a long look from here."

Georges took off his windbreaker and folded it for her to sit on. The grass was prickly. She sat down and he lit her cigarette, cupping his hands against the breeze. He settled down beside her to watch a fishing boat coming in. The sun was warm.

"How was your trip, Kate?"

"Oh, smooth, but tiring just the same. I get tired sitting, I guess."

"I think so too. It takes three days to get over these flights and no one takes three days, so one is tired all along." He didn't push her for details; he didn't push the view. "But, I think you are quiet by nature."

She smiled and rubbed the back of her neck to loosen the sat-up-all-night feeling. "Maybe."

"Well, don't let anyone change you. A quiet woman is one beyond peer."

"Thank you." She laughed. "It's never been a particular asset. One is either classed as timid or colorless or academic."

"Not in that suit I'm sure." The raspberry color stood out in the sun and against the winter grass. She tried to think of a suitable equivalent and decided that it was the alarm in Harry's silent house. "I work alone so I get out of the habit

123

of talking, except at the dinner hour."

"What do you do?"

"Right now, I'm cataloguing a collection of prints, in a quite remote part of New England."

"That's interesting."

"I think it is."

"Mabel says you're coming to pick up Mr. Renshaw's head."

"Oh, you know about Mr. Renshaw?"

"Just from passing conversation. You can stay a few days I gather. When you're rested I'd like to show you the island. I have a villa below here on the other side."

"Oh."

"Forbes says you're an art historian. Do you like to go on digs? Or do just archeologists do that?"

"Unfortunately there isn't much digging in my field unless you want to crawl around the foundations of churches to see what the supports look like. I've never found anything in my life."

"That's fine! Marvelous! You can start finding things tomorrow!" He stubbed out his cigarette. "I uncovered the foundations of a small temple last year here. No one was even interested in it, not the Greek government or even the people around here, so I bought the land. From time to time I look around; pieces all over, you know, but I'm going to start a serious study now, doing it right, setting up a grid and all that. You can come out and start me off."

"That's unbelievable! You'd think the islanders would keep it for themselves. To develop, you know."

"Too poor. Archeology runs on the rich, I'm afraid."

"You're probably right."

He stood up and gave her a hand. "Well, I'm going to be *persona non grata* with the Americans if I don't get you up there. Maybe tomorrow you'll come and have a look?

Nothing stupendous to see of course, just remains on a terrace—I uncovered one base. The columns probably rolled into the sea . . .''

Georges saw the ring on her hand as he helped her up. "You're married! I'm sorry that your husband can't be here as well.''

"I'm a widow. He died last year." She said it quite calmly now, for some reason, but Georges was shocked and leapt to make amends.

"Oh, I'm so frightfully sorry! Believe me. What a dreadful thing for me to say. I should have seen the ring is on the other hand for Americans."

"We were in Greece together once. There's that, anyhow."

"My dear lady! What a painful visit. Do you have some family?''

"Two sons."

"Ah!" His face lit up with hope. "This summer, you bring them to me. I shall teach them boating. We have a marvelous sea. I have a small yacht below, and no children at all, unhappily. I shall teach the boys boating, and you and I will dig. How would that be?''

It was impossible not to respond, Georges was too eager, but she kept it in check.

"I'd love to see the little temple before I leave."

"I've been trying to interest Julia, but the responsive chord isn't there."

"Julia has other responsive chords," she said, happy to shift Georges back to Julia.

"She is totally unlike any girl I know." He looked at her for confirmation.

"Absolutely! I find her delightful, and very intelligent. Quite unique."

He picked up his windbreaker and slung it over his

125

shoulder. "Come. Mabel will be wondering where I'm keeping you. We'll talk about next summer when you've rested. Boys need uncles, you know." He smiled again, reassuringly, and they walked over the crest of the hill. From the top one saw the Houseman's place. It lay beyond a low, whitewashed wall that, as Georges explained wryly, protected the rest of the Castellorizo from Mabel. Goats were tethered there, and beyond them there was a group of five or six stone cottages that sat low and heavy in a circle, a Stonehenge of sorts.

"Mabel used to let the goats just roam about, in what she called her 'Greek' period. I think this ended when they roamed in and ate half of an oriental rug. It's too bad the wind is cool right now. In the spring we sit outside. Are you hungry?" He felt the side of her face with his hand. "Are you cold?"

Before Kate could consider it Mabel came running out.

"My dear! Here you finally are!" and she gave her a hug like Mother Earth and then let her go to look at her.

"You're white. No, maybe you're not. It's probably all the rest of us. We look like peasants. All that Boston winter ahead of you. What a long trip and then walking up that hill. I'd never walk. It's too exhausting in the wind. Takes your breath away. Come in and sit down for a minute, or would you like to clean up first? Your cottage is over there, next to Duncan's. He arrived here all of a sudden today. Isn't that nice? Come in anyhow and sit down and let's talk. John's napping. The cook sent back the lamb and I'm waiting for the butcher. They simply butcher everything to pieces here. Are you cold? I think you are!" Mabel pushed her inside the main cottage. It was one big living room filled with deep chairs and a dining room table. A fire was flickering feebly at the end, and a figure was asleep there, its back

126

to them, stretched out on a chair and ottoman.

"Everyone will be in to say 'hello' eventually. This is where we all congregate. I'm dying to hear about everything. Harry said you were only staying two or three days. He's keeping you awfully close to him, isn't he. Don't you ever get a day off?"

"That's the American way of life, Mabel." The familiar, arrogant voice, from the depth of a deep chair. "They run themselves to death like sheep over a cliff."

"Duncan? Is that you? Kate's cold. She's white."

"She was always white," he answered. He spoke from the prone position, not moving. "Hello Kate. Are you cold?"

Mabel wanted her way. "The wind was chill. Kate walked up with Georges. Get her a whiskey, Duncan. That'll put some color in her cheeks."

Georges looked in through the door. "I think Kate might like to try a glass of hot goat's milk; that certainly hits the spot."

She toyed with various answers but Forbes was more articulate.

"Splendid idea!" he said, thinking it through. "You bring the milk, and I'll bring the mop—just in case the spot it hits is the wrong one."

"What she needs is a big whiskey," said Mabel. "All these stupid men with their feeble ideas. They talk and talk and don't get anywhere. I've asked the cook to bring you some sandwiches and some hot coffee, Kate. They're probably in your cottage right now. Duncan will bring you the whiskey, won't you Duncan. How's Harry?"

"He's fine, Mabel. We've had cold weather since you left and he's been a bit bothered by it. He spends most days in bed, but then he's up again for dinner. He sends his best to both of you."

127

"Oh, I do love Harry! I almost married him once, you know, instead of John. We'll have to fly over the minute New Hampshire warms up. God knows when that is. I guess you've met everyone here. Duncan is under the weather as you can see—probably under the table as well —aren't you Duncan?" There was no particular answer. "You and Georges have met, haven't you. And Julia, wherever she is."

"Yes. She's a darling."

"Now, let's see . . ." Mabel was pulling various threads together. "Duncan will bring you some whiskey. Georges will bring you some goat's milk; I know him. The coffee and sandwiches are there—Mercy, you're so thin."

"From the amount of food Kate packs away, I don't think we're dealing with malnutrition as much as with a huge tapeworm," countered the voice from the fireplace. "Cheer up, Kate. Goat's milk is guaranteed to please. You drink it and then either you like it or you get it back." Forbes got up, finally, from the deep chair and came over. He was dressed in old army khakis, and he walked with a slightly tired gait. But his voice was the same, and his eyes picked her up again and lifted her five thousand feet and she floated there, half paralyzed.

Julia came in. "Here you are, Duncan! I've been trying to find you," she groped. "I'm half blinded by the light outside. Come and play while Georges gets Herodotus off his chest. It's being delivered with the goat's milk. I can tell. You can entertain me instead. Teach me some wrestling maneuvers, a new grip." She came up behind him and grabbed him by the neck. "Mmm, you're muscled," she murmured.

Forbes disengaged Julia's arms gently and pulled her around in front of him.

"Sweetheart," he said, "if you haven't become a

128

confirmed nympho by the time I get back you can come to Scotland and meet one of my sons. He's your age, and just as determined." He looked over her head at Kate. "Katy and I will sit back and watch the wrestling. But right now, young lady, I'm tired."

Julia bowed to the inevitable. She poured herself a sherry from the decanter on a side table, and got in a last lick. "You weren't too tired a year ago, Duncan! Wow! Remember? You said that before anyone went to roll in the ruins with me someone should take me in hand, and that you were . . ."

"Julia!" Forbes cut her short. "You're taking a bunch of phrases out of context."

"Quite right, Forbes." Georges came in with the hot goat's milk and put it on the table. "Julia, sit down and be quiet for once."

"Georges! Here you are. Oh, I love masterful men," she breathed, unabashed. She pushed Georges into a chair and sank slowly on top of him. "All right. Let's be quiet together, just you and I—or is it you and 'me'? Whatever. And don't upset my sherry!" she ended up squealing, and Georges was immobilized under it all.

"My dear Julia!" Forbes took Kate's arm, and passing by Julia he ruffled her hair as he passed, "this year no one needs to teach you anything. Come on, Kate, I'll take the goat's milk."

"Don't drink it! Pour it into a plant. Give it to a goat!"

Kate smiled at Georges. "I'll do no such thing. Thank you, Georges."

"My pleasure."

Mabel stuck her head in the door. "Just to check with Kate before she naps, in case you do nap, Kate. I'm about to call a few friends now that you're here. Harry did me out of a really big splash, but we'll have a little one just for you.

129

A few people who live around here . . ."

"I've met them! Refuse, Kate! Forget it! Mabel, why can't we keep Kate just to ourselves now for a couple of days?"

Georges stood up and dumped the speaker unceremoniously. "Come, come, Julia! No one asks a twenty-year-old what mature people enjoy. Now run along and play."

Forbes answered for her. "Kate won't be here that long, Mabel. She's going out tomorrow morning. Sorry."

"She is?" Mabel deflated.

"No, I'm not. There's some misunderstanding somewhere. I've got a couple of days, I'm sure. I'll check it out. It's in my bag. I'd love to meet your friends, Mabel. By tomorrow night I should be quite alive."

"By tomorrow night, sweetheart you're going to be back in Boston."

With the warning note in Forbes' voice, Mabel put off the decision. "You two take a look at the itinerary and come to some sort of conclusion. I'll be in the kitchen house." She left, calling the cook about the lamb.

Kate and Forbes went across the patio and Forbes opened the door to her cottage. The cottage had just the one big room, with rough plaster walls and heavy woven linens, heavy furniture. Big pots of flowers sat about on strong tables. Good for Mabel. For some reason Kate had been afraid that she might be the china dog type, or the endless petit point; or favor a kind of Greco-Chinese Chippendale. Mabel, however fool her talk, was no fool. Kate's suitcases were on the fireplace ledge and there was coffee with sandwiches. Forbes put the goat's milk down. In spite of the plague, he seemed to move in rather fast.

"God I'm glad to see you." He started taking the clips out of her hair.

130

After a moment she came up for breath. "Mabel's waiting."

"So am I."

"Mabel's waiting out there. This just isn't suitable, Duncan, right now. Operate on my level for a minute."

"All levels . . ." he said, holding on. "Let's give Mabel a rest."

"Be serious, Duncan." She pushed him off and went to look in her nightcase at the Boston envelope. "Here it is—I have two more nights after this, whatever day we are. Let's see, '5' means November, and this is—"

"The date doesn't matter. Sorry. I had to reschedule you."

"You had to reschedule *me?*" She moved further off and poured herself some coffee. "Well, reinstate me please. You made a mistake."

"Katy. We don't have much time. I had to do it this way. I know Harry sent you to get the head, but the head has to stay here and you have to go back. Please don't ask me any more. We haven't much time."

His conclusions were not her conclusions. She went back to the crux of the argument. "The head? You have nothing to do with the head. Nothing. Harry went to a lot of trouble to set this up."

He shook his head. "Harry didn't go to any trouble at all. The Boston office went to all the trouble and they're paid to do just that."

"But that isn't the point. Only Harry can change my plans. If I had picked up the head in Athens you wouldn't even have been there and the problem would never have come up."

"I'd have been there."

"Well then for some reason I'm not getting your facts. I know my own." She picked up the telephone and held it

131

out to him. "Would you speak to the operator for me and I'll get through to Harry." Then she put the telephone back down. "No. I can't do that." She drank the coffee and walked about the room, and then she turned back. Forbes took the goat's milk and poured it down the sink in the bathroom.

"I can't listen to you, even if you are his good friend, Forbes. He sent me off with orders; they're spelled out right here. You know how he feels about people fussing over his conclusions. Once Harry makes up his mind that's it." She handed him the itinerary. "And furthermore, for some reason he gave me a huge bonus to do just this."

Forbes looked up at this, and she felt she had to apologize and explain. "I don't know why. I never should have made even tacit acceptance of that money, but he had forestalled every argument. There was no check; it was just a receipt for money he had already put in my account and the time schedule was so tight I couldn't go down and pull it out and write another check and push it back at him." She looked confused. "Somehow it was all handled so that I couldn't refuse—either the money or the plan to come here —I had suggested sending someone from the Fogg, someone in 4th century sculpture. Well, he just didn't want to have to start talking with another outsider, I guess." Kate sat down on the bed, ate a sandwich and finished talking with her mouth full. "So, you see, there's nothing I can do, even if you feel desperate about something. Besides," and she got up to collect another sandwich, "I'd like a couple of days in the sun."

"So would I," he answered, putting down the glass. "But right now there's been too much interest in that head. People are hanging around here. You go, get out of the way. Harry expected me to take care of you, and I'm doing just that."

132

"Harry couldn't have 'expected' anything. He hardly knew that I was coming; he hardly knew himself three days ago."

"False assumption."

"I barely had time to shampoo and pack."

"You're assuming that when Harry told you it had just entered his mind."

"Well, give or take a bit."

"Long ago," said Forbes. He was staring out of the window, and the last had been said with such a quiet note, completely unlike his arrogance, his overweaning bossiness. He stood there, hands in his pockets, a look of exhaustion on his face. Once before she had seen that when he was staring at the fire, the first night at Harry's. The way people had looked when Charles died. Her throat tightened . . . and she stopped the repartee that echoed in empty air.

"Tell me," she said.

"Harry's dead."

She saw Forbes watching her—a frozen moment when the only moving thing was the rest of the water that had been used to flush the goat's milk down the sink. It gurgled in a pipe somewhere under the cottage, and outside one could hear a goat bleating, and the soft sighing of air through a crack in the window.

"He died last night," Forbes' voice faltered.

Either the night had been too short, or the day was too long. Any moment she would wake up and still be on the plane, with mask demonstrations, movies, 'the seat belt sign has just been turned off; you may now move about the cabin,' and she could adjust the pillow and go back to sleep. But words she had heard were still there, floating in the air like the afternoon sun streaming in the cottage window, still there . . .

"I just left him," she said.

133

"I know."

"He was fine—a little tired, that was all."

"I don't know many details. Lawrence was very upset."

Through the open window they could hear Julia laughing.

"He was ninety-two, Kate. That's pretty old. He did everything he ever wanted to. That's some sort of record, isn't it? He was still at the top. How many men are at the top at ninety-two?"

She said nothing.

"You wouldn't have wanted him to drift downward, getting senile, beaten finally. You've got to think of this as a kind of privilege, Kate." He'd had hours to think up platitudes. She wanted to cry that death was no privilege, ever, for Charles or for Harry, but her voice chose other words.

"Mabel and John don't know?"

"No."

"Why not?"

"I want you back before the news breaks. I asked Lawrence to delay the public announcement as long as possible." So damn efficient. She felt dull, novocained all over.

"Why? I'm sure he's made a will. Everything in order."

"Just to tidy up loose ends, that's all."

She sat for a while, and then she got up. It was an effort, and she went to the bathroom and washed her face, rolled her hair.

"All right," she said, dull still, "I guess I should go back. Maybe they'll need me."

"Good girl." Hearty now. The plague was a thing of the past.

She opened her suitcase. "When do I leave?"

134

"Tomorrow morning."

"All right." She stared at the suitcase, couldn't remember why she opened it, and then she turned. "But I am taking the head. For Harry."

"For Harry! Kate, for Christ's sake, what have we been talking about?" The man was unintuitive, insensitive.

"About Harry." She stared off into space. "Just leave me alone. This is my private part of the contract—between Harry and myself—You can go peddle your whiskey or whatever you do. I don't want Harry to feel abandoned, that's all."

"Harry won't feel a thing. He's dead."

"Don't be so *crude.*" She turned on him. "That sort of answer just makes you into a clod. And starting to make love when you knew Harry had died. My God, Forbes!"

"I didn't want to tell you. I knew it would end like this."

"Well, what do you think?"

"I think in compartments."

"Well I don't. I'm a totality. I think you're blunt, brutal, insensitive. You're . . . you've just got the feelings of a peasant."

He bowed. "And you're the princess! That's just what they're counting on. Some romantic princess, wafting back to change Harry into a human form again, carrying the head like a chalice."

"I'm not a bit romantic! I'm finishing a contract for which I've been paid."

She saw Julia coming up the path over the meadows. He went on scolding.

"They're waiting just for this, for you to carry a million dollar head home to Harry's grave. When will this opportunity ever come again? The Boston office is full of emergencies. The owner of the head is gone, no one has time to

135

check on a piece of sculpture they've never even seen. You're handing it to them! You're a fool."

"To 'them'? Who are 'they'? You were all upset about burglars way back in New Hampshire, the safest state in the union. You saw burglars behind every wall. You'd be the one man wearing overshoes in a restaurant in Claremont— so sure that they'd be stolen if you left them under the coat rack. You're paranoid, that's all. And if you're so worried about head snatchers, you can hole up here with your Bombay Tummy and drink yourself into a stupor. When I get back I'll send you a secret signal: "Tummy Okay. Stop."

"Well then, think of your sons."

"Listen, the Capitoline Museum has hundreds of heads, all genuine, all lined up. You can't even get anyone to go in and take a look, and their doors are wide open! Harry has the papers to this one. Anyone who wanted it could have stolen it for years. And I am thinking of my sons. I'm not going to chicken out on Harry's last request."

He tried a different tack. "All right, let's assume you hang on. You get off the plane; they take the head and dump you. You're found—eventually—it's winter time and you won't decompose. Hands turned black from the ropes, skirt over your head, messed up. Bladder and rectum, you know—they relax. Nothing attractive about a woman in that state . . . and Harry still won't have his head."

She gave him such a look of contempt that he laughed.

"Ah! You're going to hold off these men! With what? Your virtue?" He laughed again, and lay down on the bed, loosening his tie and making himself comfortable. "Listen, my sweet, by today's standards your physical attributes— well, they're magnetic to me, but they're past the prime outside. You're not marketable; Julia, maybe, but you?" He shrugged his shoulders against the pillow and took out a last cigarette from a Turkish box. "You'd be tossed aside," and

136

to make a parallel he crumpled the box and threw it across the room into the wastebasket. She wished that his aim had missed, but it didn't. "Even if they could get two for the price of one—the head *and* you, they wouldn't take you." He lit the cigarette and put the match into the goat's milk glass where it sizzled out on the bottom.

"Well, thanks a lot. Don't waste your time on such a dismal Miss Prim. Try Julia. She's teetering between you and Georges anyhow. You can knock on any door . . ."

Julia was at Forbes' cottage next door, knocking. "Are you there Duncan? I need help with my bike. It came apart at the wheel on the path to the monastery." She listened for a minute, and after there was no answer she went off, kicking stones in the path.

Kate yanked open her suitcase. "If I'm going to fight all the way home tomorrow, I'll need some sleep today. So, if you'll just leave." She pulled out a robe.

He didn't get up. He just stayed there, relaxed, having made his point.

"Frankly, I'd like to hang around, watch you sleep." Cheerful even.

"Look, Forbes, there's a time and a place. Right now . . ."

"Right now you've got the time and we've got the place."

He got up and came over and put his hands around her throat. "Admit it, Katy. That last night at Harry's."

"You think *that's* what's on my mind after everything you've just said? Harry's dead!"

His hands were heavy and warm. "Katy. What do you think Harry sent you over here for?"

"To get the head of course." Forbes moved in.

"The head has nothing to do with it. Harry was afraid the vaccine didn't take the first time. That was all. *You* have

137

nothing to do with the head. The whole trip has really nothing to do with the head. If you'll stop fighting for a minute you'll see what Harry meant."

She pulled back. "What Harry meant! You freak! Listen, that last night at Harry's was chemical. Purely chemical! I could have jumped into bed with the manager of the A&P!"

"Liar." His voice was gentle. "Harry told you what he was doing. You didn't pay any attention."

"He never told me anything of the kind."

"He said he would come to certain conclusions and then he would set the thing up himself, just like Rembrandt. He meant you. He meant me. He set you up."

"All he meant, I'm sure, was that he needed a curator and he applied for one."

"Listen, Harry saw you at the CAA meeting. Your Salviati paper. The whole thing was an inescapable conclusion. I'll admit it. I'm willing. I think he has good taste!"

She stared at him. "You're delirious." She threw the bathrobe on the chair and walked out. Mabel was waiting to hear about the party.

Chapter

10

Julia got him on the second try. Kate heard them from the cookhouse. Julia had been sitting on the patio, just waiting for someone to come around; preferably a man, preferably one with class, and one who could carry a bicycle up the hill with aplomb.

"Duncan! What luck! Georges is off down the hill with his new ruin."

"Is that a woman or a piece of land?"

"It's his new toy," she went on. "Some men buy trains and run them around the rug. He buys stones."

"And it's ruining your afternoon? Well now, uncle Forbes has a quick cure for that."

"Duncan, you're sweet. Would you like to look at my bike too?"

"Too? That's all I had in mind, little one."

"It's in trouble, I'm afraid, over on the path to the monastery. I can't carry it back and it won't go."

139

"Come on then, we'll have a look—Point me in the right direction."

"Wait till I get the stone out of my shoe. Let me sit a minute." Julia sat, and lost no time. "Do you really think that I'm too young for Georges? I look older in the city. If I had known I'd have bought an outfit suitable for older men. Tell me Duncan," and she became confidential, "are you really an electrician? You know, I doubt it somehow. The electricians at home aren't like you at all. Even the ones who own their own businesses. They drive in dirty panel trucks; their stomachs overlap."

"Those must be American electricians. Next question?"

"Next question is, what if you're not?"

"Not what?"

"Not an electrician." Julia must have slipped her shoe back on. "There, that's better." Kate heard her say. "Then I ask myself, what do you do? It's so . . . well, unelectric. You've been on the telephone all day."

"I was recuperating, my dear girl."

"You were asking for some information about something. I know you're going to meet someone on a train and that something happens with a boat. That much Greek I can figure out." Her voice jumped with anticipation. "I won't give you away! I was just sitting there, outside your window this morning, waiting for you to come and play. I'll be a spy with you. I can drink anyone under the table, and not get sick—almost not anyhow. If you help me with my bike, even better, if you help me with Georges, I'll be so grateful that I'll even chew up your secret documents and swallow them."

"Then I'd find you invaluable, wouldn't I? But if I'm not a spy, what can I use you for? Let's see—your Greek is limited, I'd say, if that's what you made out of my phone

140

call, and I can't have you eating up my mail just to prove something. Why don't you find some nice boy and make cookies for him. Someone less than twice your age."

"Oh, Duncan. It's 'grey eminences' now, not 'nice boys'; you *are* out of touch."

"Am I? Well, that shows what forty years will do. In another year Georges will be out of touch and what then? He'll stand on a street corner in his old age and pinch girls, and you'll have to come get him and lead him home. He'll still be handsome, of course, but drooling a bit maybe; eyes get rheumy, you know, little troubles pop up: unsteady gait, cataracts, catarrh, scaly skin . . ."

"Oh stop it! There aren't any young boys." A long period of silence while Julia pulled herself together—They were getting rather far away, too. "I *like* older men!"

"Well, uncle Forbes has a solution for that too."

"What?"

"You keep on lying in the sun all day and you'll get just as scaly as Georges. Only earlier, and then you'll both match."

Before she heard what Julia thought, the breeze came up again and their voices were lost to the other side. Mabel had left to take a nap. Kate went back to her cottage. She ate the last of the sandwiches. Then she ran a good hot bath. It took time to fill the tub half way, and one could hear the pump working in earnest down below the house foundation. She wondered idly how much trouble it had been to get all these cottages outfitted with luxuries like hot running water. She soaked for a while, refusing to think about Harry at all. 'Tomorrow, when I'm composed, all the way home . . .'' And then she toweled and crawled into bed for a quick nap. In spite of things she slept soundly until a tap on the door announced the dinner hour.

*　　　*　　　*

141

The gathering at the big cottage was cordial; it started out that way. John, Mabel, Julia and Georges, herself and Forbes. He was less bubonic looking, but ready to plague.

"Did you see the remains of the Temple of Apollo here?" It was John, being sweet.

"Not this time," she smiled. "I fell sound asleep."

"Of course you did, dear," said Mabel, fondly. "Can you imagine what's come over Harry? He wants Kate to come home right away. One afternoon in Greece? He's losing his grip."

"It doesn't sound like Harry, does it?"

"Well, yes it does." Mabel changed her mind. "It sounds exactly like him—somehow. Quirky. Remember that time in Scotland? Here we were north of Edinburgh somewhere, having lunch at a little inn. Out of the blue Harry goes to the phone, and comes back to say that he's just called Duncan Forbes and the plans have changed. We're all going up there for a visit—his northern place, you know. Well, we didn't know. Remember, John? Lawrence was driving. So then Harry says he knows the way. 'All you do is keep on the highway until you see the place, way off to the right through a gap in the hills.' We couldn't miss it he said. What he didn't say was that the road went all the way from Edinburgh to the North Sea. So then he tells Lawrence to wake him when he sees the place back there in the hills, and sweet old Lawrence drove on, hour after hour, all of us, in fact, except Harry, looking on our right hand side for the place. When we finally got there, Harry woke up fresh as a daisy and bounced out of the car, and the rest of us were half dead. That's the way it's going to be, Kate. Harry will be fresh as a daisy and you'll be dead!"

Kate kept quiet, feeling her way.

"How do you feel about it, Kate?" Georges was personal, gentle, selfless.

142

"Well, I don't have anything to say. This is just an assignment. There's always a reason behind Mr. Renshaw's decisions. But it's been a great afternoon in Greece." The strong, positive approach.

Mabel had other ideas just as positive. "Well, I'm going to say something to Harry about *this*. He always calls it 'cutting through complexities,' but if you ask me, he's just getting plain spoiled. No one needs Kate that badly."

Julia had on black, matronly black.

"Let's see the head, anyhow. Isn't that the reason Kate's here? She's taking the head back to Harry? Let's all take a last look. Poor Kate. I *know* how you feel. I'm afraid I'm just not up to these late nights and heavy schedules either. I'm settling down!"

Forbes looked over at Julia and raised an eyebrow. She had decided to take her chances with old age, and ignored him.

John got up. "I'll get the head out. Georges had a box made to hold it. Originally, I remember that Harry just had it sent around in a crate, with wood shavings. It seemed good enough then but I guess such simplicity is out of date. Maybe Harry was too casual. Nowadays there seems to be a regular rage for sculpture."

"They even found another Venus de Milo in a warehouse in Alexandria!" said Julia. "All set to go. It was cloned! I read about it . . . a perfect copy, but it was a fake. How exciting to make a perfect fake!" She looked past Forbes to Georges. "That's one thing, Georges, in my favor. You'll never find another me!"

"Julia," said Forbes "if they cloned you it would be one too many. Even one is almost overwhelming. And it wasn't in Alexandria. It was in Istanbul. If you're going to be middle-aged, then get your facts right. And it wasn't a perfect copy—it was mostly calcined marble, plastic and lead."

143

"How come you know so much? I just added Alexandria to make it sound romantic. I never even knew where it came from. The article didn't say. It just said Mediterranean, but that's so dull, everything around here is Mediterranean. Anyhow, the day that *I'm* heavy and filled with lead, Georges, beware."

Kate refused to flee where none pursued. "There's nothing so new in this. Even Greeks finally copied their own masterpieces, to say nothing of the Romans. It's just carrying on a tradition, I suppose."

"I agree," said Forbes, "unless they sell it at a Venus de Milo price. Only Americans would fall . . ."

"No, Forbes." Georges was gallant. "One can find fools in all nationalities. It's not fair to our hostess here because she'll be too polite to argue."

"Mabel won't be too polite at all, Georges," Forbes smiled an especially warm smile for Mabel. "I've never known anyone to get the best of Mabel."

"Only Harry," said Mabel, fondly. Then John came back with the box, carrying it carefully. He unsnapped the locks, and opened the cover. Everyone straightened up to look in. The head was there, nestled, swaddled in a satin quilted cradle, held by quilted satin straps. John undid these and took the head out, quite perfunctorily, and set it on the table.

There was a moment when no one said anything at all. Julia sat quietly, for once, looking. John and Mabel were more impressed now that it was leaving than they had been all the years before; Georges glistened in the reflected firelight. Forbes watched them all, expressionless. He even lit a cigarette and lounged back, uninterested to the point of being rude. Kate refused to look at him. She could feel his eyes, and he could tell from her astonished surprise what he had known all along.

144

For the sculpture was good. Terribly good. Unbeliev-able. The marble was creamy; the finish was so soft that it seemed like a kind of gauze—but without the hard polish of the Neoclassic. And it lived, with eager life. The curls of hair fell in tousled points around the face, a face that looked off into space, quivering with aliveness. One could almost see the open lips start to move. It was no copy, no copy of a copy, not Roman and certainly priceless. But it was too late to back down now. If Lysippos ever worked in marble, this was it.

"What do you think, Kate?" Georges was almost as quivering as Alexander the Great, or whoever it was. He was not intimidated by Forbes and his bored sophistication. "What do you really think?"

"Unbelievable," she said.

"I think so too!" he said unashamed.

John had seen the head on and off for years. He was more inclined to favor the box at this point.

"You did a marvelous piece of work here, Georges."

Georges demurred. "I didn't make it myself you know. A cabinet maker in Athens did. I just suggested the design and then a coffin supply store made the lining and straps. But it fits well in the space under the plane seat, so it should be equal to the trip."

Julia had been growing old for quite a while now, and suddenly she reverted. "I know where Georges got the idea for the cradle—from a urinal in the men's washroom at the airport. I've seen them."

Forbes groaned. "Julia, you don't have to display all your miscellaneous knowledge."

She didn't care. "I was curious, that's all. Everyone's curious. One day I had to wait for a late connection, and since it was evening, and no one was around, I went in, just to see how things were done on the other side of the wall.

145

I always wanted to know. No one saw me. I went right out again. If anyone had caught me I'd just have said I didn't speak Greek."

"Pictographs, Julia. Pictographs on the washroom doors indicating pointers and setters. No one could make a mistake."

Georges came to her rescue. "Never mind, Julia. There are worse things than that in Greece nowadays. If you can imagine, when I asked the coffin store to make a lining for a head and neck only, they expressed no surprise at all. Now that's what I call sinister. Little Julia here is being lively. There's a difference . . ."

Little Julia gazed at her elderly Greek with unconcealed admiration, and Georges cashed in before his star was in the descendant phase again.

"Julia, my pet, look at the head carefully. Note the early Lysippan qualities; see how he always gazes elsewhere. If you start with the neck, the head turns slightly; if you look at the face, the eyes look beyond you, and if you watch the eyes, they focus behind you somewhere, somewhere like distant India."

"I'm going to leave!" she shrieked, before he got to late Lysippan qualities. "I'm going to *leave* if you start in on Alexander the Great. Kate has just one night. We don't have time to get to India either, foot by foot. Thank God he died before he got all the way to China."

While Julia was throwing her gripes around, a houseboy knocked to call Forbes out, and in the flurry about Alexander no one noticed.

"Well I, for one," said John, "will be delighted to have Alexander go west. It's too much responsibility here for something this good. We try to live a simple life. It's time for Harry to decide what he wants to do with it. Let me get the key and we'll lock him up in the box."

146

Julia was practical. "It won't make any difference, will it? I mean, if a burglar wants it, he'll just take the whole box, lock and all."

Georges explained in a gentle way. "Julia, not burglars. No one wants to steal it from Kate. It's only that when she walks over the stone floors of the airports, if by chance a clasp is knocked, the box might open and the head would be delivered in 400 bits."

"Oh." Julia was disappointed. She enjoyed the chase. "I had thought that it might be stolen and copied, plastic, lead, and all."

John went out to get the key, and Mabel went off to see about the dinner. Julia left to put on more lipstick; maybe to try out another act on Forbes before she presented it to Georges. Georges moved over to Kate's side, to make her less lonely.

"By the way, did you ever hear what the natives tell about Mr. Renshaw?" She wondered if Georges were Athenian, to call his countrymen 'natives'.

"No. Tell me."

"A delightful story! Years ago, before all the loose sculpture around here had been plundered, Mr. Renshaw had anchored his yacht in the harbor. It drew quite a crowd, since everyone went to Rhodes in those days. Castellorizo was having its troubles, perennial troubles of course, no soil, little rain, nothing marketable." Kate winced at the word. "No tourism at the time. But one man here had discovered an interesting head in a cave over on the other side. He approached Harry's yacht in his fishing boat, and the two of them concluded a deal. Mr. Renshaw left with the head; the fisherman left with what he thought was a good price."

"But now, the essence of the story: later that summer Mr. Renshaw went on to an auction at the Hotel Drouet,

147

Paris, and saw what good Greek heads were auctioning off for, and he felt ashamed that he had had such an easy deal. He sent the man the difference . . ."

"Between the auction price and what he had paid?"

"Exactly. A saint."

'Harry was like that,' she thought. 'He would have called it good business.' Georges went on.

"It came out well for Mr. Renshaw, once the story became known. He was given preferred bargaining positions for his industry when they set up a plant in Athens."

"And the island? Did they profit?"

Georges passed her some anchovy hors d'oeuvres and shook his leonine head. "I am one who feels poetic about underdeveloped places. I like them underdeveloped. This part of the world was in ecological balance, as you say in your country, before the tourists arrived. Mr. Renshaw's money helped to start the tourist industry here. It set them on their feet for a time. But the reaction came, an imbalance you see . . ." He enumerated on his thin fingers. "Too many tourists, not enough water, wells ran dry, not enough drainage, hepatitis, typhoid."

"Why, I find that fascinating!" said Forbes at the threshold. The threshold of intoxication as well. "Got rid of the tourists, anyhow!" Cheerful now, as if civilization without them was just right for his pleasure. "How about another drink, Kate?"

"Let me get it," said Georges to her, jumping to his feet. "Sorry, I didn't notice your glass was empty."

"Thank you," she said. "An American martini, weak, please."

While the two men were mixing themselves replacements at the other end of the room, Kate held the head for a moment in her lap, and turned it over, just to see how it was finished on the base. On the bottom of the neck there

148

was a small blue-grey vein of imperfection in the marble, one that the sculptor had managed to place in an unseen spot. A row of little irregular holes that wandered about. A sudden impulse made her open her evening bag, and take out her gold pencil, and she stuck the point in the hole and broke a piece of lead off in it, fairly deep inside. It hardly showed. Then she put the head back on the table.

'There you are, Harry. No one's going to copy it and sell you a fake. Whether it's Lysippos or the son of Lysippos or the School of Lysippos.' and she felt like bursting into tears at that point. How miffed Harry would have been if his head were just labeled 'School of Lysippos' in some vague attribution.

Julia plopped down beside her. "What do you think, Kate?" she whispered. "If Georges would only stop teaching!"

"Maybe you should agree with him. Maybe he'll stop trying so hard." It was difficult to keep her voice that low. Georges was coming back.

"He might stop trying altogether." Julia whispered quickly. "I'd rather be thought dumb than abandoned."

"Is it Lysippos, do you think, Kate?" Georges was still eager.

"I have no idea. I thought Lysippos only did bronzes but I don't really have any idea. I'm completely out of my area here."

"Poor Greece." said Georges. "It's losing another fine piece."

"Down to your last plastic Parthenon, are you, Georges?" Forbes, drunk. He didn't seem to care what he said, and it was a relief to hear dinner announced, buffet style. Kate hoped they would sit far apart.

Dinner, however, was no better. Forbes seated himself carefully with his plate of food right next to Georges.

149

"Let's face it, Georges," he started in, "there's one rule to summarize all Greek temples—just so Kate doesn't have to travel thousands of miles again. They come in two varieties, temples do. The first is half ruined, and the second is completely ruined, and once that's understood everyone can go swimming instead."

"Jock," Kate muttered to him, completely put out. Georges looked irritated, but said nothing, so Forbes kept needling.

"I'm tired of looking at stones in the grass, even Georges' stones, trying to reconstruct buildings out of three lumps of limestone, holding onto endless maps that flap and tear in the wind, looking at them upside down by mistake, listening to guides explain in perfectly dreadful English that here is one corner, and over there another corner, and that there in that dirty area was where the sacred statue stood in a puddle of olive oil. Why don't they just get on with it and build themselves some new buildings."

"Well, Georges speaks flawless English, so you can't go around blaming him for the guides." Julia was piqued, too.

"And Forbes speaks fluent Greek, I'm afraid, so I can't complain about his complaints," said Georges with far more politeness than he needed. "He's right, of course. I'm afraid our day was over, a long time back."

"Oh Georges, never mind. I'm sure our day is just about over too." said Kate, trying to balance things as Harry would have done. "Do you remember in the *Iliad* where Hector says that he knows in his heart, and that his mind knows it too, that some day sacred Ilion will be no more? I think that's the saddest thing. I feel that way when I see the Jefferson Memorial in the rain at night."

"You don't even need the rain to think that," said the

150

barbarian in their midst. "Give the Russians twenty more years, the Chinese twenty-five maybe, Kate will have all her ruins right at home: pseudo-Greek, neo-Gothic, fake Renaissance, all the ruins right on the Mall. She can sit on the edge of the hole where the National Galleries used to be and quote Homer."

"Why Duncan, what a grisly thing to say!" Even Mabel felt that Forbes was becoming unnecessary.

'Damn Forbes,' thought Kate. 'He should have gone under.' But the man looked much better tonight, the flush of drink no doubt responsible.

Georges changed the subject. "You know, Kate, if you're nervous at all about the trip, I could fly back with you. I don't have to be in Paris until the middle of the week, and there would be plenty of time."

Julia saw her party, singular or collective, disappearing into the thin air above Greece, and she made a quick counter offer.

"I'll go too! Wait a minute! I have a great idea! Kate can stay here with Duncan, and I'll go with Georges. I'll pretend I'm pregnant: I'll stuff the head in a pillow under my dress. Why, I heard a woman say just the other day that she went to the hospital sitting on the baby's head. So there we are. I'll sit on Alexander, and Georges can rush me off the plane and into an ambulance, and we'll arrive at Harry's, flags flying, sirens screaming! What do you think of that?"

Forbes helped himself to more squid. "You, Julia, of all people, would give birth prematurely. In mid air, the head would roll out in the aisle, and people would wonder what happened to the rest of it. No, I'm going to take Kate to the plane myself tomorrow. Early."

"Don't bother," Kate said with a sugary smile. "Stay here, nurse your ills—"

151

Then Georges jumped in, offering once again to accompany her all the way, this time without a pregnant Julia, but the thought of Georges talking all the way back about archaeology and Lysippan qualities suddenly loomed too strong and she thanked him in what she hoped was a gracious but final tone. At this refusal the Scot took on new life. He leaned over, becoming more obnoxious and healthier by the glassful. She got up.

"Mabel, forgive me," she said, sidestepping the pest. "I've got to get to bed."

"I know you do. It's a terrible nuisance, New Hampshire. Why didn't Harry just stay in New York where the connections are good. What time is your plane?"

"I think it's around noon. It gets into New York at three something, then a shuttle to Boston."

"And then you still have that long drive? My God, Harry's out of his mind. Well you sleep late, and we'll see to it that the charter is delayed until the last minute. We'll keep feeding the pilot in the kitchen."

"You can feed me in the kitchen too," said Forbes. "Kate can sleep on the plane. She's going out with me early."

"Forget it," Kate said. "I thought the offer was that you would accompany me. The idea of my accompanying *you* isn't quite so gallant, is it. I'll stay and sleep. It's my choice."

"My dear, what makes you think you have a choice?"

Mabel broke in at that point. "Well, I think these children need to talk over this by themselves somewhere. Duncan, you and Kate take a drink outside and come to some conclusion before you go to sleep."

Duncan turned into Prince Charming himself at the suggestion. "Splendid idea, Mabel. You remind me of Harry, just now."

152

"Are you going, Duncan? Oh goodnight, sweet prince!" said Julia.

"Goodnight, lovely," he said. "Are you getting up to see me off?"

"At that hour? I wouldn't dream of getting up before noon! Georges would have me out on his dig by nine, sieving cups of Greek real estate, one by one, to look for God knows what. I *have* to stay in bed, don't you see?"

"Georges should look at you as the real estate," he said, patting her cheek. "Turn off his mind for a while."

Julia grabbed. "Oh Duncan! How about me as an investment. You appreciate my qualities. You can be my developer. I'm wasting time on Georges. Georges," she called to the other side of the table. "I will you to Kate. Duncan's going to subdivide me, not you."

Forbes grabbed Kate and pushed her out the door.

"I have a recurring nightmare," he said once outside, as if he hadn't a care in the world, "that I'll wake up all of a sudden and find myself married to that girl."

"She appreciates your rougher qualities, I'm sure. As for me, I thought you were completely revolting."

"Katy," he said, and his voice became sober, quiet. "All right. I agree: the head goes out tomorrow morning. I don't dare leave it here any longer."

They had arrived at her cottage. He didn't explain further. He didn't try to come in; he didn't even ask. He leaned down and his lips brushed her cheek. "You can save your revulsions," he said.

153

Chapter 11

The next morning at breakfast the hour was early; in fact the air was barely sunlit, and the breeze was chill. Mabel and John breakfasted with them; Julia and Georges were nowhere to be seen.

"I'm going to write to Harry! He's turning into a crank, getting you people up this early, taking away our fun. He's forgetting how he used to be himself. I think he needs straightening out before he sets in these new ways." Mabel was taking umbrage.

Forbes was taking orange pills. He tossed a number of them into his mouth, tossing with such accuracy that even John was impressed. John asked him if it was a daily diarrhea preventative. Even with their own wells they had trouble at times.

"Bombay Tummy!" said Forbes, full of energy at this hour, waving a plastic bottle toward John. Five hundred milligrams of something or other. Enough to kill a

155

horse. Good to have on hand."

"Especially if you're a horse," Kate said, feeling already exhausted with the day.

Forbes was attentive to the point where it seemed too much.

"Will we see you in Scotland this spring, Kate and I?" he asked Mabel, bending over her hand as he said goodbye.

'Don't mend your fences with me inside them' she thought bitterly.

Mabel cooed, and looked at John. "I knew these young people would straighten out their schedules. Of course! You say the word, we'll fly in."

Mabel hugged, John shook hands, joked about not taking any wooden heads, and they said goodbye at the low fence that separated Mabel from the rest of Castellorizo. Kate was sorry that Georges was not there. Forbes might have humbled himself just once. Homer's saffron dawn was spreading itself from east to west and she did look back as they started down the hill. Forbes gave her a whack on the rear. He was in a great good temper.

"Georges has other things to attend to this morning. Hurry up."

"Why should I rush. Your offer was to accompany me, wasn't it? Well I have five hours at least. Of course maybe you're trying to squeeze me into your schedule. Preserving you, spending me, as it were." She took her time.

He stopped, and waited for her to catch up, laughing at her. "Harry made a good choice, Katy. But if we had five hours I wouldn't spend it hiking. Come on." And he took her arm and steadied her over the ridges in the cobbles. In the early morning high heels were not the best. He said so.

"Stout oxfords, ribbed wool stockings, itchy shetlands," she said, expressionless. Harry may have made a good choice but it was not her conclusion. Forbes was just

156

having his own way. He was setting things up and squeezing her in to fit.

The plane was waiting, floating off the dock a ways. It taxied over. The porter passed in her two cases, Forbes' grip, and George's box with the head in it. Then they got in themselves. Fortunately, as the plane gathered altitude it was too noisy to talk, and she semi-slept most of the way to Athens.

In Athens he took the box. The porter took her two cases and Forbes' leather grip. Forbes spoke to the porter in Greek and the man nodded. They passed right through the airport to the taxi entrance.

"Explain to him, Duncan, that only yours are going on now." It was rather awkward while they stood there in the sun waiting for his taxi. "I'll say goodbye," she said. "I'm going out on the terrace and get a tan until my flight is called. I'll take good care of the head."

She thought he'd fuss some more about her taking the head at all, but he didn't. A taxi moved up to them and the driver opened the back door. The porter put Forbes' grip inside the trunk, then hers as well.

"No, no. Tell him, Duncan, the last two are mine."

He took the box from her hand and turned toward the porter with some money, saying something to the man, and then he shoved her into the back of the taxi and climbed in afterward.

Kate didn't make the decision fast enough. If she had been able to think things through with clarity she might have sat down on the sidewalk and refused to budge, she might have called for help; but the fact was that one simply didn't sit down on a sidewalk in the sunshine, nor did one call for help at 8:30 in the morning. One just didn't. And although the thought came to her that she might keep right on going out the other door of the car, she realized that

157

Forbes had the box. By the time all these thoughts were through, the taxi was pulling away from the entrance and around the dry circle of grass, onto the freeway in Athens. He pushed her well down, out of sight.

"What is this? I've got three hours, but I don't have to spend it hiding out on the floor of a taxi driving round and round, do I? For heaven's sake, Forbes, I'm going to get carsick."

"Get sick then, but don't fuss. I'm coming with you. That's what we agreed on last night."

"That just meant as far as the early plane."

"Early train follows early plane."

"Train!" She sat up. "What do you mean 'early train'? The one out of Greece? Listen, I've done that train. It takes twelve hours just to get to Igoumenitsa, and then two whole *days* to get through Europe. I did it once with Charles, just for fun. That's what it is, just fun. One can jog all the way beside the track and get there just as fast."

She tapped the driver on the shoulder. He looked around and she made a turnabout sign. Forbes shook his head, and after brief consideration, the men stuck together, and the taxi kept going. Coca-Cola plant, Fiat plant, Macaroni plant, suburbs, and she decided to jump out at the next light. Let him worry about the suitcases; she was going back to Harry the express way. But the timing was never right.

There was at least one traffic light by the big Temple of the Olympian Zeus, she was sure she remembered that, before they got too far into Athens. She took a strong grip on the handle of the box, and put her shoulder bag over her head this time. There was a stop light before then, and they slowed. But the timing wasn't right. Before she got organized the light had changed.

"Everything's going to be messed up," she whispered, furious with herself, with him. "Everything."

158

He guessed. "Better than being messed up by sudden death at an intersection, my dear," he answered equably. "Now you listen to me. I *know* you're going to be met at that plane. You're carrying at least a million dollars, and the box is too big to fit under the seat. I measured it. It doesn't matter because they'd get it anyhow, but you'd have to give it up to the steward and by the time he gave it back there would be a substitute head—or none at all. Catching that flight is handing it out for laughs. You've only got one chance, Kate, and that's to get out of Greece by some route that no one would think of . . . and there aren't many ways. By the time they find you're not on TWA we'll have three hours start."

"The mythical 'they' again! I don't believe you; and anyhow, in three hours we won't have gotten anywhere at all!

"Look, we'll be on the ferry to Brindisi. It doesn't leave Patras until two, but we'll give it a try. Train, taxi, and then out of sight on the boat. Once we're in Italy they can't be everywhere and the options are pretty good. Harry's head has one chance, and I'm giving you that chance. I don't want any lunatic behavior. All right?"

Since he had a terrible grip on her wrist, it seemed clear there was no alternative. And if it wasn't true, then there were no alternatives either. So she kept quiet.

"Let go. My hand is going to turn black."

"No. You'll just try some foolish stunt."

The taxi pulled up at the station, and the driver opened the back door; quarrelsome couple.

"Now put my raincoat on over that noisy pink coat."

"But that will look terrible, flapping in some outsize garment."

"My dear, no one will even notice." Then he pushed her in through the *Salle d'Attente* door. He was right. No

159

one who could do better ever went by train in Greece. The waiting room was full of military, of working people with string bags, of very old people managing somehow with black suitcases tied up with ropes and very young children, dark-smocked and well-behaved with black dressed mothers. No one noticed anything at all. The loudspeakers crackled something incoherent, even in Greek it would have been incoherent, and she followed Forbes, flapping along. By the central information desk he reached out as he passed and grabbed an envelope.

"What was that?"

"Travel agent," he said, without paying any attention. "There it is, down there." A porter trotted alongside with the suitcases. She trotted along too.

"For heaven's sake, how do you know he was an agent? He was a black-haired man with gold teeth and a toothpick. For all you know he just handed us a bomb in that envelope. He didn't look like a travel agent. He looked more like a terrorist. The IRA, the PLO. . . ."

"If we blow up, then he was a terrorist. Here's the gate," said Forbes, slitting open the envelope. The gate man checked the tickets and waved them down the platform.

The porter found their car and the right compartment. He placed the bags in the overhead string racks. Forbes tipped him, and after the man left, he locked the door, pulled down the window shades, and fastened the curtain snaps.

"Now, you can take a seasick pill."

"I don't get trainsick."

"You will on this run if you can't look out the window. I don't want to carry you off retching and vomiting and calling attention to yourself."

"You don't have to be rude all the time. This isn't my choice."

He gave her some Dramamine. She looked for a carafe of water. There wasn't one.

"There isn't any drinking water."

"Swallow it dry. I'll order you some tea when we get out of here."

She divided the pill in four, and put a piece on her tongue where it dissolved in a bitter yellow mess.

"My God. Take the whole thing."

"I can't; they're too strong. I'm not a horse. I'd pass out; that would draw even more attention, wouldn't it?"

He turned his attention to other things, checking the vents, prowling about the tiny space.

"What do you have that's heavy, smallish . . ."

"Two hardbacks—that's all."

"Good. Let's have them."

She stood up on the seat, unzipped the suitcase and felt around, pulled them out. Forbes unlocked the box, took out the head, handed it to her, and packed the books and two railroad towels that said SPAP in woven letters.

"It won't convince anyone for long, though it might buy us a few minutes. We'll put the head in your small case there. What's in it? Where's the key?"

"The key? I lost it years ago." He looked resigned, pained. She looked pained right back. "No one ever said I'd be carrying a marble head."

He opened up the case. "What have you got that we can pack around the head?" He pulled out some silky things, and looked at them as useless, tossing them aside. "Something more than this handful of nothing." He got to the bottom of the case and looked around elsewhere. "What have you got that's wool, strong."

"You're looking for goat's hair, stout corsets, I'm sure," she said with derision. "Strong, dull cotton stockings, suitable shoes, scratchy underwear. All those sensible

161

Scottish clothes with some body to them. Well, you won't find them here."

"Not some body *to* them; some body *under* them—I'd say. Not a skeleton with a skin on it," and he turned back to the matter at hand. "Sweaters, we need. Have you a couple?" The man didn't seem to volunteer any of his own clothes. She stood up on the seat again, and undid the zipper of her suitcase again, and pulled out a sweater and a mohair stole.

He nodded. "Just about do it, I think," and instead of letting her fit them around the marble nicely, he squashed them into a hundred wrinkles as he did the job. "Now, that's better, and if you had the key it would be better again . . ."

As if to emphasize the point, the train gave a jarring jump as though suddenly unstuck from the tracks, nearly knocking the case off the seat; and then they could feel the cars groping their way along the multiple sets of rails, groaning all the while. Over the next ten minutes the train established some sort of lumbering gait that had a four part rhythm with a lurch on the fourth beat. Kate shoved the case way back from the edge. As the pace quickened she went over to the window and opened the curtains to have a look. They were at a crossing in some random suburb of stucco buildings and telephone poles, and before anything became interesting she felt herself snapped backwards.

"Away from the window!"

"No one out there except two women in black with string shopping bags, no machine guns, no poison darts . . ."

"No bombs in envelopes? Be consistent at least. And in a country of black-haired people keep your bloody blonde head away from the window."

"You don't think of everything either. You could have

162

hired a car. We could have gotten much further, and then hired a boat."

"Cars can be run off the road anywhere along the line, no witnesses. Here, if there's a fight, it's going to be public, everyone leaning out the doors and windows to see, and they don't need that."

"A fight! So who's going to fight, for heaven's sake? You are, I can see that. And won't you look silly, fighting all alone."

"I'm saying 'if' there's a fight. And we won't know them, you can be sure of that, so you won't be able to wave out of the window to old friends. I think, however, my dear, that if you peel off the layers of hirelings, you'll find our quaint little Georges at the bottom of the pot."

"Georges?" she said. "Julia's Georges?"

"Julia's? Now that's debatable. I thought last night he was listing a little to the right."

Kate relaxed then, and leaned back against the seat.

"Oh for heaven's sake, Forbes. Neither he nor Julia could make it to breakfast. Julia says he's got so much money that he doesn't even work. He could buy the head." She looked up with a sudden idea. "Why, you're more interested in the head than he is. He likes Rhodian pots, actually. He told me so. The Wild Goat Style."

Forbes smiled. He settled himself comfortably. "Well, we'll just wait this one out. I think you'll be surprised." He glanced at his watch. "We have an hour."

Kate found her cigarettes and matches, and the Scot reached over and covered them with his hand. "I can think of better ways to use an hour."

She freed her hand and lit the cigarette, regardless, and tossed the match in the metal ashtray with astonishing accuracy for once.

"Forbes," she said as she took a deep drag and let it

out, "you have the instincts of a goat."

He grinned. "It's my Wild Goat Style." He wasn't pressed for time. "I'll go shave."

"That won't improve your status. Georges . . ."

"Georges would talk the whole time. He wouldn't know what to do with a woman if he got one." He reached up and pulled a kit out of his leather bag, shut it again, and disappeared into the lavatory closing the door behind him.

She finished her cigarette. Now that the books were gone there was nothing to read; with the shades drawn there was nothing to see. She checked things: passport, papers, money, driver's license, and then there was nothing left to check and she started to close her eyes. In fact, if the sweater hadn't been hanging out over the edge, there would have been time to think. She could see it, a rough brown shetland sweater, poking out of Forbes leather suitcase above; a fine, heavy piece of resilient wool for wrapping heads.

'Well, damn,' she thought, 'he could have donated that to pack Harry's head instead of using up mine' and it wasn't too late to change, either. She stood up and gave a short tug, just to see whether it would come down easily. It didn't. The suitcase was shut, that was why. Then she stood on the bed and gave the clasps a try. They snapped open. Even then she was too short to see anything, and she gave the wool another tug but it didn't move. Kate put her hand in the suitcase then and felt around to see what was holding it back. Something else was in there, something like a package; she pulled the whole thing to the front of the suitcase and lifted it out. 'Forbes, you're going to donate something of *yours* once in a while instead of mine. It's always mine that gets used: my sweater, my schedule, my reputation' and she was going to add 'my virtue' but then she realized

164

that the last she had given up quite willingly—no one could claim a rape.

She put the whole armful down on the bed and undid it. The sweater was wrapped around a package, the package then turned into a box, and when she saw what was in the box she just sat, sat down hard and said, "God damn," unable to decide what to think. She almost stopped breathing. It was a box, just like Georges' box, and then inside a head, just like Harry's head.

"Jesus Christ" she whispered, unable to contain her sudden fright. 'Julia's clones.' Her heart was pounding so heavily it sounded like the train on the tracks, and skipping every fourth beat. She took the head out of its straps with shaking hands and turned it upside down to see. If this was a fake, then the pencil point wouldn't be there. Forbes dealing in fakes?

But the pencil point was there, in that hole. This was the head she had held last night. This was Harry's! And the one Forbes had given her this morning was another; the one that had just been packed so carefully, doing it all himself, as if it were Harry's. He had somehow slipped her a fake. 'Well, goddamn you, Forbes.'

The train was lurching on, and she could hear the water turning on and off in the lavatory in sharp bursts. Forbes was rinsing the razor after each stroke. So why should he be putting two heads on the plane, and two heads on the train, no questions asked? Where did the second one come from? And what was she doing here in the first place or in the second place even? On some train in Greece, heading somewhere for a ferry. It was just as Julia had said about his telephone talk on the patio yesterday. Julia wasn't dumb; she was just like Mabel, in fact, and her Greek was pretty damn good. Forbes had been so disparaging about Julia's Greek.

And suddenly she saw herself the dumbest cluck of them all. Here she was, trapped on a train with Forbes, and there was nothing standing between him there in the lavatory, and Harry's head here, except herself—herself and a good long ferry ride over open water.

The train was moving along quickly now. The fourth beat was coming faster each time, picking up speed and the water in the lavatory was silent, as though Forbes had stopped shaving and was rinsing his face with a hot towel. The decision was like all the others: it had to be made at a moment's notice with one outstanding clarity, and that was to get some space between herself and him—and fast. The 'how' was pure conjecture.

'Oh God!' she thought, and grabbed her cosmetic case. She took out the fake and put Harry's head with the pencil point stuck in the hole in its place and then put the fake in Forbes' box, the box in his sweater and stuffed it all back up into the leather suitcase. She took the case and her purse and rushed out the door—and then tried to close it quietly behind her. Her big suitcase and her coat would have to stay behind, to buy time just as he had said. She ran down the corridor toward the exit.

With great good fortune the train was agonizing to a halt, maybe near Corinth. Kate just about fell off the platform right behind the conductor, and ran toward the exit sign. The *Wagon Lits* were already beyond this point; Forbes wouldn't be looking out of the corridor side, not yet. She rushed through the small station and out the front, looking for a fast miracle. Please God, right now. And it was there—in the form of one car of rentable aspect that stood on the empty parking lot gravel. She didn't wait for an introduction. She clambered in the back, head first, inelegant and hasty, and made herself so small that nothing would show through the window. The driver woke.

166

"Athens, airport," she gasped, leaning so far back he must have thought she was an addict in need of a fix. But the message was understood, and the car took off in a cloud of vapor. For the first time in her life it was a thrill to have a madman at the wheel. The gear shift was so loose it almost fell off at his touch, and the springs of the seats poked upwards in search of freedom at each swerve.

Kate tried to think as they were racing down the freeway, weaving around cars, cutting to the right and left with abandon. It did occur to her that Forbes would have produced a tidier end than being mashed here on an autoroute against the side of a cement truck.

After a while she quieted down. The traffic quieted down as well, and she tried to sort out things. The morning seemed like one of those three dimensional mosaics, where the pattern rose in one direction, then, with the blink of an eye, everything suddenly went in the other direction. Forbes on one side, and now maybe not on her side at all. There seemed to be no explanation other than to rethink the whole fall in a different perspective; quite different.

He could have ingratiated himself years ago with Harry. First putting in alarms where there had probably been no need, and setting them off himself maybe, or removing a print once in a while to make himself a hero in Harry's eyes. New Hampshire was a good place to hide out at any rate, if one had something like a messy bullet hole. A bullet hole from Kabul even. She had tossed it off at the time, but really, who ever needed to be taped up around the side unless they'd deliberately fallen on a spear. He never said. The man had never said one damn thing, as a matter of fact.

He could have picked up a cool million dismantling one alarm in Kabul for his group, hiding with Harry until the hole healed over, and then coming here, to pick up a second million from a dumb person like herself. It was no wonder the man had solid gold cufflinks. And later on he would be off again, picking apart Harry's collection by simply dismantling the alarms. He could be playing it all sorts of ways, backwards and forwards, up and down, just like a department store, glorifying himself in the process.

"Good men go into crime, "she remembered the words, "because crime is interesting, and life is not."

She thought about Georges then too. It couldn't have been Georges. He hadn't even come into the picture until yesterday. Forbes, on the other hand, was in all the exposures at once. Even Lawrence was a likelier suspect than Georges. He might have killed Harry. Maybe he and Forbes were connected: Lawrence with his slow, turtlelike movements and his disdain, Forbes with his lightning decisions and *his* disdain—both of them meeting once a year. And poor Harry, always keeping his respectful distance and never suspecting.

Then she thought further, and tossed that hypothesis out. It couldn't be Harry's staff. They would have moved long before thirty years had passed. So it was back to Duncan Forbes alone. He knew all about the head, even years back. He knew about her coming to pick it up. Harry must have told him. Harry and his conclusions. Well, Kate faced the fact that unless she thought about things as they were, there would neither be thoughts about the Renaissance, nor about Rembrandt, ever again.

The heavy, chrome-plated car streaked around the curved approach to the airport that she had just left a couple of hours ago, and stopped in some sort of epileptic fit. The young man jumped out and wrote "$50" with a pencil stub on the back of a greasy *Guide to Athens.* There was no way of judging whether that was outrageous or fair, for Kate had not had the time to decipher the name of the town where she had jumped ship, and didn't know about the price of train tickets either. There was no time to waste in any event, and she pulled out two American twenties and three red bills that she once figured to be ten dollars—although whether that instinct dated from Charles' time or more recently she didn't know. The amount must have been sufficient for the boy smiled broadly and folded the bills into a limp wallet.

Kate grabbed the overnight case, the purse, and fled through the door marked DEPARTURES. Thank God the airport was not Kennedy, with fifteen planes lined up in a slow waddle to the takeoff. By now the implacable man would be off the train too, and heading back, maybe less than fifteen minutes behind. She looked around. The departures list. The flight to New York was no longer on the screen. Kate got to the Olympic desk out of breath with fright.

"When is your next flight?"

"To where, Madame?"

Now that had been a foolish thing for her to ask. She must collect her wits.

"Any flights to the States, or one that will connect. There's been a death . . ."

The agent checked. He was sympathetic to upset travellers.

"We have nothing for one hour, but Sabena leaves in ten minutes for Paris and Brussels. You would have a very good chance from there, and while you are in flight they will check. Shall I inquire if they have room?" He was so leisurely. He picked up the telephone.

"Yes, please. Brussels." She would go on to Brussels, for Forbes would think she might try Paris. Maybe that would split the trail in two parts.

"Yes, Madame. There is space. They will rewrite your

169

ticket downstairs." He bestowed a benign smile.

She grabbed her case again and would have liked to glance quickly toward the door, just for reassurance that the dreadful fiend was not close behind, but she was afraid he might be so she ran downstairs without looking left or right.

Sabena was closing down the departure gate, but the agent was in no hurry. No hurry at all. He wrote out a new ticket, her complete name, word by word, form by form, adding taxes, origin, destination, fare basis, allowable kilos, carrier, flight, date, the time . . . Jesus.

"Can't you just add a sticker to the old one?" she asked, quivering.

"You will have to carry your luggage, I'm afraid," the agent said, as he ripped off the intermediate flimsy. At the gate itself they stopped to ask her what choice of seats she would prefer. They turned the chart around; there was one on the aisle in the smoker, or a middle seat in the non-smoker toward the front, or one near the tail.

"Anything," she said, and the man shrugged his shoulders and chose the nonsmoker in the middle. And then she was allowed to leave, with the case, the ticket, the boarding pass, her purse; she tried to walk with cool, with savoir faire. A ground man stood at the stairs, waiting to roll them back, and she had an excuse to run the last hundred feet and scramble aboard. The door was then closed, locked with a comforting thunk as the wheel and bolt did some clever thing, and no one ran out at the last minute, waving a piece of paper.

She walked to the middle section, and the stewardess took the case. "You'll have to put this in our closet, I'm afraid. It's too wide, I think, to fit under the seat."

Kate never moved a muscle. "Just my ski boots," she said, in a voice loud enough for any pursuers left; she sank into her seat and did up the belt.

170

The plane taxied to the end of the runway, gathered speed as it turned around and took off into the wind.

On her left side, an older woman took off her glasses and looked up from the December issue of *Vogue*.

"My, you must be pleased to catch your flight."

Kate nodded. "I certainly am . . ."

After the first hour had passed Kate asked for some airmail paper. She wrote a long, detailed letter, addressed to the trustees of Harry's estate, in care of the Boston office. That way it could circumvent everyone, even Lawrence, just in case. She put it all down: theories, the knowns, the unknowns, and she left a short note about her boys. The stewardess had a stamp; the steward took the letter. Kate felt that she had done all she could. She ordered a double martini, American, and read *Réalités*.

Chapter 12

It was raining in Paris and raining in Brussels. Simple, really, even in the rain. All one had to do was put one foot in front of the other and keep going: one eye on hotel posters, the other eye open for trouble, wall-eyed as it were, walking down the airport corridors. In spite of a bright pink suit in a land of dark blue raincoats it would perhaps be possible to disappear into the Metropole, the Grand, or the Carleton, to make a reservation for the next flight over the telephone and never show one's self at all. Without baggage the comings and goings were greased. Well, relatively speaking.

At the Passport Control, Immigration, Emigration, Declaration, Customs, one of them, she could never sort out which, there were two men at the end of the big *salle.* One stood storklike, with a heel planted against the wall; the other on two legs. Both watching. They could have been almost anything: narcotics agents, enemy agents, double agents, reporters waiting for the Shah of Iran, South Americans waiting to assassinate each other, advertising executives counting the number of blue jeans per hundred people. She had just never seen anyone watching before, nor had she looked. They were not after anyone, they just stood, inanimate, like umbrellas. She kept going.

The Belgians had no heat. They probably had all the windows and doors open. She felt cold without her coat. She would have been cold probably even with her coat. It was the color. There was no trick to find the only woman in Europe wearing pink. But the men against the wall didn't seem to care. Neither one brightened up and said, "Ah!"

"Passport, Madame." The man in the glass box was holding out his hand. She grappled fiercely with the inner zipper compartment that ripped off her nails like coupons. "Please have your papers ready, Madame," he whined in a tired monotone. He looked from her to the photo to the list of suspects without any comment. He stamped, he held out his hand for the next passport.

"Declaration," said the next man in a tired voice. "You have something to declare." The men were there still.

"I haven't filled out my card. I need to see someone in private."

"You are staying here?"

"I'm passing through."

"You are in the wrong line, Madame. Please read the signs."

"But I need to see a customs official," she said. The man right there had on an official uniform. "Can I talk to you in private?"

He looked at her. She was holding things up. The man behind her had a briefcase and a raincoat over his arm, an

174

umbrella, and he was glancing at his watch. The customs man, or whatever, growled something over his shoulder. A man looked up. *"Eh, Jacques. Tu parles donc à cette dame?"* He jerked his head toward the back, toward Jacques, and Jacques took over, borrowed from the next section. The line shuffled forward. The man with the briefcase, raincoat, umbrella had his papers in order.

It did no good to smile and thank the official. He wouldn't have smiled back. He wouldn't have encouraged her, or taken her arm to show her where to go. They all had worms, these northern civil servants; circles under the eyes, irritable, pale; Jacques was pale too. A stringy man with a life spent burrowing into dirty laundry, damp plastic makeup cases with eroded aspirin at the bottom, glittering ladies with glittering poodles, sallow men with briefcases, campers with damp backpacks tied together with knots that never undid; parcels, bags, cases, boxes, and a gaggle of single women.

"On peut parler quelquepart?"

He shrugged. He was hardly impressed, but he gestured toward a small, frosted glass room on the side. Another man with a green eyeshade was there at a desk. He looked on, bored.

"Do you speak English?" It had to be in English. She would never understand technicalities, explanations, in French.

The second one, the green eyeshade, nodded, neither pleasant nor assiduous, just tired. She put the case on the desk and tried to use clear words.

"I have here a valuable piece of sculpture. The papers are in order. I am on my way from Athens to Boston, but there was some trouble in Athens. There may be trouble here. Could I leave it with you to be locked up until tomorrow when I fly on. Is that possible?"

175

"Take it out of the case, Madame. May I see the papers, please."

They looked at the head: they gave a perfunctory glance at the papers. The second man, Giguère by his label, whistled softly to himself and rubbed the back of his prematurely wrinkled neck as if he were tense with the sheer weight of passengers carrying heads that week. Then he hunched his shoulders and stuck out his neck. Like a goose swallowing.

"Unfortunately, Madame," and he made the swallowing motions again, "we have no facilities for your request. This is something for the police maybe, or to be locked up in a hotel safety vault. Your papers are in order. We do not concern ourselves with travellers whose papers are in order. Here, in the airport, I can only suggest the storage units in each section."

There was no way of telling where the men against the wall were now, or even if they were after anyone at all. There was no way of telling anything, but in a few minutes, maybe, Forbes would arrive on another plane.

"I don't want the police. It becomes so complicated. I just hoped that you might have a small cage where you lock up heroin or firearms or something, where this piece could remain a few hours."

He made a dubious face. "Ah, yes, if you had heroin we could help you, but we are not a checkstand, Madame. You can imagine what it would be like. Within a few days we would be getting necklaces, rare books, paintings, poodles."

"I know." She put the head back in her case; put the sweater and the stole around it carefully. It was a try, and she had lost a few minutes, that was all.

"*Mais enfin, Giguère, cette tête: elle a une certaine valeur. Pour une nuit seulement.*" The little man with pale skin stood

176

up for her. Giguère swallowed again, and then scratched his chin while the lines of people outside shuffled by with their dirty socks and tubes of Prell.

"On peut faire semblant qu'il y a quelquechose. Les papiers sont douteux; pas en ordre? Une nuit. C'est tout."

Giguère considered and then he nodded at her. *"Bon.* For one night only. Tomorrow, you know, we must find those papers in order and you must remove your sculpture. Do you understand our position? We are not a . . ."

She nodded. Not a dumping ground for nervous ladies. "Yes, indeed. And thank you very much for your help." She turned to leave.

"A receipt, Madame," the tired voice reproved. "You need a receipt. One must be businesslike. Tomorrow one cannot tell. One of us may be sick. You need authorization. One moment please." He looked at her sternly as if she were hardly fit to carry any item of value—or even fit to be travelling alone. He pulled out the forms and wrote a receipt. "Here you are, Madame."

"Thank you." She stuffed it in her purse and once beyond the glass cage and through the doors she found herself suddenly catapulted to the sidewalk with a wave of travellers. They were packed in so tightly that the suit was buried. A few more steps and she would be free. Taxis gulped a few passengers each minute and the crowd lurched forward in rhythmic pulses, but it was slow. People were irritable. A man behind pushed her into a man in front who carried five or six parcels. He dropped one on account of her and he turned around.

"Enfin, Madame!"

"I'm sorry. I was pushed into you."

"Oh." He tried to tip his hat holding on to everything and he explained. *"C'est la police,* ahead. The police. They are checking *cartes d'identités* and *passeports.* I can see them

177

down at the edge of the *trottoir*. They get *nerveux*, periodically. They check on *communistes*, agitators, terrorists, moving in and out. It slows everything."

Kate got her passport ready this time. The minutes were ticking by. The man in front of her got waved through. A young officer took her papers, looked at the photograph and back to her face. He checked a list of names and gave her a nod. The man with the parcels climbed into a taxi and a lady with three children pushed by into the next one; the car that opened its door beside her was a police car that had slipped in between. A man got out and tipped his hat.

"If you would be so kind. We see by our list that there is a *confusion*, Madame. Do you have a moment?"

She glanced behind but it was a solid wall of people—all in dark blue raincoats, none in pink suits.

"The use of your name by someone else? Are your credit cards with you? Sometimes these names are for stolen cards that have been found."

"All right," she said nervously. "I'll wait here if you want to call and check. My only credit card is right here. A VISA card. That's all."

"Madame," he explained, as if to a simpleton, "our records are not here on the sidewalk. They are at *rue Josef II*. We must check there. If you would take a moment, we will then drop you at your hotel."

The man held the door of the police car open for her, showing polite concern. It would be easier to be jailed as a communist than dumped somewhere with her hands turning black. Jail at *rue Josef II* might be the safest place yet to spend the night, and she climbed in. It was too bad she had left the head—it would have been safer with her.

The men got in the front; the other police were still checking names on the sidewalk, and the black car turned

178

slowly through the lines of taxis onto the airport cloverleaf. One of the officers lit a cigarette as soon as they were in the clear, and tossed the match out the window. Slob.

They drove onto 'E' something, then exited on a beltway, and then she lost count. Grey cities were grey; intersections looked the same. They wound in and out. At some point, a very small inch of worry made an appearance in her mind, and it grew some more. The crime rate in Brussels couldn't be this low; police stations in Belgium were closer to each other than that. If they were police, that was—and she finally admitted the doubt to herself as the worry grew larger.

"You haven't lost your way?" she asked from a very small reserve of breath, because of the tight feeling inside.

"Nous y sommes, Madame," one of them said. He had a superior air. Belgians seemed born with a superior air.

The black car slowed along the heavily traveled street and then turned through an archway into a dark, cobbled courtyard. Broad daylight in there looked like dusk. Five-storied walls, shuttered ground floor windows, and one lone lightbulb burning in a metal cage at the door, looking as if it had been turned on ten years before and then forgotten. The cobbles had moss growing in the cracks.

The door of the car was opened. They waited for her, prompted her. *"Madame?"*

Kate had seen police stations before in vicarious ways. They were always the same: people waited about, cars were parked at angles that indicated the speed with which they had pulled up to the door, officers pushed drunks in ahead of them, disorderly arrest cases shuffled forward, lawyers ran up the steps to spring wealthy clients that remained forever anonymous, papers were typed up in triplicate by beefy, ordinary types seated at mammoth black typewriters. On the whole, police sta-

179

tions were interesting places, like hospital waiting rooms.

"*Madame,*" the man repeated. "You are requested to come upstairs." He pointed to a third floor room.

Kate had no coat on, and a wet cold seeped into the car, licking at her legs, chilling her neck; the two men stood by the car door becoming restless. Perhaps they were hungry as the hour was getting on. It was quiet in the courtyard there, not even pigeons intruded. Kate thought about it, twisting her hands nervously around the strap of her shoulder bag. One could refuse, naturally; just sit in the car and catch pneumonia. Or one could catch pneumonia first and then be dragged out, getting clobbered twice, as it were. Perhaps the unseen sign was just be on the other side of the building, through another arch somewhere, with comforting letters that said POLICE on a large lighted globe.

So she left the car with the two men and walked past the 25 watt bulb into the building, dark cream colored walls inside, grey painted baseboards, an open cage elevator that groaned upwards and to another long hall.

'My God.' she thought, sinking fast. It had taken so much effort today to get this far, and now everything had unravelled all the way back to the difficult part, like sweaters she used to knit when she was young that always had to be taken out several times.

The men stopped at number 211, chicken wire in the glass of the door. They opened it with a key, and stood aside for her to enter. Actually, the moment one is wheeled into the delivery room is not the propitious time to discuss the pros and cons of having a family. One man was using an official stance, the other blocked the escape route back down the hall.

'Jesus Christ,' she thought again, as she went in, 'if it were only going to be rape.'

It was an office. Empty; empty of clutter, of office work,

180

of workers. Disinfected sawdust on the floor, wastebaskets and chairs piled on the desks in dull attitudes, bits of the green sawdust plopped here and there by a mop. Windows with bars.

The two men started taking down the chairs—not well organized. *"Il n'est pas encore arrivé,"* said one.

"Who isn't?" she asked, coming to her senses. "I should like to use the telephone right now, please." The telephone was still hooked up. She could see that. Its wire ran along the edge of the floor and up over the baseboard where it had been painted to match, then it disappeared into a hole in the wall.

The taller of the two men shook his head. "We regret. We are requested for you not to use the telephone."

"Nonsense! Any American may call his Embassy."

The man lifted his palms in a whining attitude of supplication. Imbecile gesture. "These are orders. You are requested to wait. You may use the inner room. There are restroom facilities."

She had an impulse to laugh. He sounded just like a Berlitz recording. "Where are the washrooms, please? I should like to try a larger pair of gloves. The bird is sitting in the tree, is it not?"

He opened the next door. A smaller office off the first one, with a 'facility' at the far end. "Be comfortable please." No more English came to his mind so once she was inside he closed the door between them.

Before all the dreadful drabness carried any real conviction of hands turning black, bladder and so forth, the telephone in the outer room gave a discreet jangle. Kate went to the door to listen but nothing much could be made out. Mostly orders, for the man answered *"Oui, monsieur"* a few times, and then *"Tout de suite, monsieur,"* and hung up. The 'tout de suite' was the sound of his steps coming closer.

181

She backed off in fright behind a lamp, but the man never came in. There was the sound of a key turning in the lock of her door, then shuffles and then a key turning in the outer door, and then nothing. Nothing at all. The men had gone.

Kate stood there, five minutes, maybe longer. Then she tried the door handle. It turned, but to no effect, of course; she had heard it right the first time. Locked. She kneeled down to look through the keyhole, but the key was in it on the other side. She thought then about pounding on the door, calling for help, but all that noise would give the impression of someone out of control, and hearing herself screaming would certainly *send* her out of control. Kate sat down on a dismal chair to think, to snatch at her wits as they flew out was more like it, and she tried to take stock of the situation.

The room was small. It had a steel cot with a utility grey cotton cover, two oak chairs with leather cushions, one strong table, a cupboard against the wall, and one standing lamp of mammoth ugliness. On the outer wall, the single huge window was shuttered and padlocked; the other wall had a varnished oak door leading to the facilities. That year must have been the one for varnished yellow oak. In the bathroom the toilet had a varnished yellow oak toilet seat, there was a shower *à l'improviste,* meaning a slope in the floor cum drain, a wrinkled grey cotton utility curtain hanging in a circle around it. The usual black and white tiles, a medicine chest holding a bottle of green disinfectant soap, and a clean towel that did not say 'Stolen from the Police'. Beyond that, there was a far door that must have led back to the hall. Locked, probably locked from the time they had installed the W.C.

In the other room Kate checked under the bed. Nothing. Then the cupboard, top and bottom. The top section held four glasses, thick and functional, down below, a case

182

of whiskey. Even in the shuttered light one could read the smug Scottish label burned into the wood of the case, just like a brand.

He couldn't have! Not that fast. Forbes might be in Paris, perhaps. But not here. Yet there it was, name on the wooden crate, on the bottle labels even, splatted all over the place, *D. Forbes and Sons, Edinburgh.* No one else in France had ever heard of it she was sure. Kate felt a steam of indignation building up that she knew she should have felt last September.

Those peasants! Throwing their cigarettes and matches around—not police at all but hired for the day, hired uniforms, hired car, probably a hired building about to be torn down.

'I'm going to be killed all over again' she thought in a rage. He missed on the train, the ferry, and now there's no place. She looked wildly about for some air vent or chimney that clever people in movies discover at the last moment; finding nothing, she sat down and lit a cigarette. The chances of death from lung cancer were becoming relatively insignificant today, and one might as well exit smoking. 'And pulled together,' she added *sotto voce* as she went to the bathroom to do her hair and put on fresh makeup.

The liquid soap in the bathroom did give her one idea. She went back with it to the outer door and poured it over the floor and under the crack. Then she took one of the glasses from the cupboard, filled it with hot water and slopped it over the soap on the floor to make it spread. Then the soap bottle itself—she poured out the rest of the soap and, covering her face with the shower curtain, whacked the bottle hard in the basin until it broke off at the neck; she rinsed that off and put it in her pocket as a last resort.

183

"This isn't going to be the cheapest head you ever got, Forbes."

The lamp. She took off the yellow tasseled silk shade, Scottish Victorian no doubt, and unscrewed the wire thing on top, and then the bulb. It took a moment to arrange these in a fine High Renaissance triangle on the table, and then she put the pseudo-Corinthian stem by the door.

It did seem inadequate. Especially if all he did was to open the door and shoot. He might never slip, or come close enough to be hit by the lamp, gouged by glass. The cupboard, massive and weighty as a barricade wouldn't budge. Not very good odds.

She had a swallow of *D. Forbes* as she cast about for more ideas, and she lit a cigarette while looking. The windows had heavy inner shutters, locked, and on the outside they had bars. One could see that the success rate of murderers was high because people like herself were ineffective; they sat in dead-end rooms and became dead in short order.

An alternate was to get out, and at this stage there was not that much to lose. She took the lamp back beyond the shower curtain and smashed its base into the thinnest panel of the hall door.

The first bash made a frightful noise. Everything had been so quiet until then. Kate listened for a second, but there was no answering sound. By the third crack the panel was splintered right through, and the next made a good hole. Not big enough to climb through and she had to swing again. God, that door was resistant. Twice more, and the splintery opening was almost right, and it was when she raised the lamp to whack off the splinters that she saw the shadow of a man.

He was silhouetted on the wall a little way up from her door so he must be standing by the outer office. He didn't move and she didn't either. Forbes never wore a hat; this man had a hat and a wide-shouldered coat—she stared at the shape in a kind of semi-paralysis. To squeeze herself through that splintered hole would take more than a minute, long enough for him to take casual aim and shoot, leaving her hanging there half in, half out, bleeding onto the hall floor. Useless now, this escape, she thought, frantic, and then she heard the slow whine of the elevator, creaking upward until it stopped. She heard the cage door open, close, and then footsteps coming down her way, and she retreated, back to the dead-end room.

Chapter

13

The footsteps and the shadow got together.

"Elle est folle, celle-la?" said one. She didn't hear the reply. They assessed her insanity, the situation.

"Attends." said the other. *"Tu restes ici."* One of them left the other in the hall, and there was the sound of a door being unlocked, probably to the outer office, and a second later the turn of a key in the door to her room. Kate tightened her grip on the lamp.

"You come in here and I'll kill you." she said to the man. A rash statement.

"Katy, stop that nonsense."

The sound of the once-familiar voice released an enormous rage of resentment and she gave the inner door a great smash with the lamp to punctuate her feelings.

"Those were your lines in the last act weren't they? Always picking on someone, always superior. You and your greasy peasants out there, your little tin soldiers . . . Those

187

pitiful acts resembling Heathcliff on the moors, the tragic widower, rootless and disconnected, roaming about the world in search of significance. How Gothic can one get? You and your butter-on-oatmeal, your burned scones."

"I'm coming in. Put down that lamp."

"Try. Just try. Bring your hired hand. Finish the job and you can move on to some Flemish primitives, and some primitive woman to match. It shouldn't be too hard: you've got such a cast-iron alibi. It won't be as tidy here as on a ferry of course, and you won't find the head either so don't get your hopes up. There's just me."

"I know there's just you." Forbes answered, from the other side of the door. "Georges, precious Georges has got the head."

"He does not."

"Yes he does. Now I'm coming through so put down that lamp. What's this stuff all over the floor? *Attention au plancher,*" she heard him say to the other one.

He came through faster than she expected, and he twisted the lamp out of her hands and threw it across the room. It hit the wall beside the cupboard and cracked the plaster right down to the lath.

"I have a mind to smack you good and hard." For once the burr was very audible. "A one woman brawl in a bar-room?"

Calm descended on her then, a kind of euphoria of the doomed it was. She shrugged. "It was not my first choice," she said, haughty. "I found it dull. Terribly dull."

Forbes looked over to the man who stood in the door-way. He nodded. The man retired. He shut the door behind him, and she could hear sounds as he made himself comfortable out there, settling down for the night, no doubt.

"Have a drink," she said, waving her hand at the cup-

188

board. "Some unknown brand in there. Do it like you do in Scotland, right out of the bottle. I did. Don't give yourself airs."

Forbes took off his raincoat. He tossed it onto a hook behind the door in a gesture that implied a certain familiarity. Then he went to the cupboard, took out one of the tumblers and poured himself a shot and drank it straight. Then another shot, and he went to the bathroom to add water.

"Jesus. Another mess in here? You'd better start talking, young lady."

Kate sat down on one of the two leather chairs, pulled her skirt up quite high, took a cigarette out of her purse, lit it, and threw the match into the ooze on the floor. She inhaled, blew out the smoke slowly, examined her stocking for runs. Cool, collected now.

"All right. Let's! Let's talk. Let's talk about Georges," she said brightly. "Why don't you run after him? Why run after me? Let's ask ourselves all sorts of 'why' questions. Like 'Why don't you go to the police?' Why? I'll tell you why! Because you've had one bullet hole in your back at Harry's, and you don't want to get caught with two, do you! It would be embarrassing to be so *riddled!* It would seem, somehow, so *active,* so *hyperactive,* wouldn't it! If you were really in with the police you'd take me to the police station. After all, anyone with gold cufflinks as collateral can hire two goons and a black car, bribe a night watchman in an empty building . . ." Her foot began to tap nervously, like a cat switching its tail. "I imagine that if the head *really* had been stolen by Georges the news would be all over Brussels. The Embassy would know, wouldn't they—Let's give them a call." She said this last with a smirk. "Let's see if you have the guts." She sank further back in the chair.

He sat himself in the chair across. "The news of the

189

head is being witheld." He didn't smile.

"I'll *bet* it is." She straightened one stocking while her leg was in the air, checking for recent snags from that dreadful oak furniture, and then she put her leg down and looked up. "Lisas has nothing to gain. I told you so on the train. Sculpture doesn't interest him."

"No? Well then it must be just the money . . ."

"Don't give me that. The only interested party is you. Georges didn't even know that I missed the first flight. I imagine he was bedded down with Julia."

"Georges wasn't bedded down with anyone last night. He left well before dawn, in his own plane."

"And you left with the head! Both heads, as a matter of fact. Aren't the two of you sweet! Each with his *own* thing!"

"We picked up Georges' copy, if that's what you mean."

"Never mind whose copy it was," she snapped. "The point was that Harry and I were stuck with the fake, and you were left to make money on the real one."

"That's not true. The risk was less if he got hold of you."

"Forget it. Never mind your true blue statements. When the chips were down I was left with the wrong bag. And don't give me that 'Georges' business ever again. If he flew off, he was just doing whatever he was going to do in Paris. He had no way of knowing I was even coming here."

"For God's sake, Kate, you put your own name down on the Sabena-Brussels list. All he had to do was ask."

"Just like you, I suppose."

"Just like me."

"Well then," she said brightly, "here I am! You haven't got the head, and neither do I!"

He grinned. "Drink?"

190

"So I'll get dead drunk and tell you where it is?"

"So you'll bloody well calm down."

"Well, I'll tell you what'll calm *you* down. Before I got off that plane, I wrote a detailed letter to the executor of Harry's estate, care of the Boston office, outlining all my suspicions, all the known facts from September on; I added my personal conclusions and I mailed it. If you yourself pick up this head you're going to find that your own head goes with it. And if you kill me this is going to become the most public deserted building you ever shot anyone in."

He went to the bathroom and mixed her a drink, keeping an eye on her in the cabinet mirror. "Deserted? Don't be so dramatic. It's late Saturday afternoon, that's why it's 'deserted'. And from the look of things, it's just as well." He came back and handed her the glass.

She put it down without touching it, and shoved the ultimate question. "All right. So it's Saturday and everyone goes home. You've had your little say and I've had mine. I haven't got it. You haven't got it. Stalemate. So we can go, can't we?"

"Sorry," he said, settling himself down in a chair and pulling a cigarette out of its pack with his mouth. "Other plans."

"Listen, staying with all you boors would drive me out of my mind!"

"Your mind, Kate, has never entered into any of these decisions." He lit the cigarette and tossed the match to the floor. "Just consider yourself better locked in here with me than going out on the town for a last ride with Lisas."

"I doubt *that,*" she said, suddenly afraid again. He was playing for time—waiting for her to soften. "I doubt it would be a last ride. I doubt that Georges is in Brussels; I doubt that Harry's head is gone. You're just trying to get me to say where it is. I doubt every damn thing you've said.

191

And contrary to what you think, I'll have you know that Georges is one of the nicest, most sensitive, most well-bred men I've ever met."

"Then you haven't met enough men, my dear."

"No need to be rude." She stood up.

He pushed her back down in the chair, rough. "I'm beginning to feel like being rude. Look at the mess! Do you know how much the average policeman like Boisvert in there makes?"

"Police!" She felt mad all over, and hungry, and half dead. "Police indeed. I'd like to see some real police and I'd tell them who you are—you and your low risk ventures, Kabul, Cornish, Castellorizo, low risk ventures, all of them, no doubt, with a splendid price-earnings ratio, preying on old men and unsure women."

"The only unsure thing about you, Kate, is your brain."

"Why, you're no more a police officer than your fumbling, weak-witted man out there . . ."

"Boisvert is neither fumbling nor weak-witted, and his salary is considerably less than one of your American charwomen."

"Charwomen! No wonder Scotland isn't out of the Bronze age."

"And you don't suppose you're mucking things up by breaking perfectly good doors and throwing stuff around. Who pays for that? And why should we have to take three men off their regular jobs just to keep Hollywood types like you from smashing an office."

"Oh come off it, Forbes! Don't muddy the waters. You're the only key that fits all the puzzles: Kabul, Cornish, Castellorizo. Listen, if you'd stayed back in Scotland Harry would have been better off."

At the mention of Harry there was an ominous silence.

192

She had gone too far. She knew it. Like the silence on the stove just before the pressure cooker blows. He got up and came over and pulled her out of the chair by the neck of her jacket.

"Listen, you spoiled brat. I'm fed up with your cheap insinuations. Now you shut up and listen. Lisas, your pretty Lisas, has been in on every big haul for the last four years. Yes, your sensitive, poetic well-bred Greek. Yes, and his men were in on the Kabul manuscripts last summer. One of them was shot, died. I was shot and didn't. Lisas was in on the Scottish Cross, Venus de Milo, he's been in on all the major Italian substitutions; not only in on it, he directs it. All for the benefit of himself and you fool Americans, willing to buy anything that looks like culture."

She was about to counterattack, but he shook her.

"We're nearly on top of him now, with his shipping operations right here in Brussels, and I'm not going to have any American halfwit ruin our plans. He needs you now, sweetheart. You'll be the lever that springs him free if something goes wrong. So you're staying here in this room. Somewhere in Brussels his stuff is being shipped out tonight, every night, and once he picks you up—and believe me, he's looking—once he picks you up he's got us over a barrel. We'll have to let him go to get you back, and a bloody poor exchange that would be!" She was dropped back into the chair.

"Well, I find it bloody poor just as it is."

He couldn't have cared less. "Lisas had one of my men killed last week right here in Brussels. A good man named Jouvet. Jouvet was trying to telephone something after he had reconnoitered an antique market. He was shot in a phone booth not far from the Royal Museum. He died there, and he tried to scribble a message on the wall before he bled to death. Tonight you're going to stay in this room,

193

and tomorrow you're going over to the Sablon and you're going to look around there with me and see if you can spot whatever it was he saw. Maybe you can be of some use after all. Then we're going to put you on a plane for Boston, and the state police are going to meet you and get you to where you're going. And that's the end. The *finish.*" He left her and went to wash his hands and face, amidst the broken bottle pieces and green soap splatters. He called back—

"Your fastidious Georges would hate this, wouldn't he! He's such a sensitive type!" Forbes cleared out the big pieces of bottle and dropped them in the wastebasket under the sink. "He's so well educated; he's so gentle; he's so precise—let's bet he hangs up his toothbrush—hates dogs, hates children, has only one plant in his house, guaranteed not to grow. No unpruned habits about him!" He dried his hands and face. "Doesn't do his own killing either," he called, from the depths of the towel. "It isn't the idea of death that bothers him so much as the idea of a mess he has to see."

"He isn't here to defend himself."

"By God, he'd better not be. I'd take him apart. I suppose you can remember back to those two accommodating customs men this afternoon."

"Bribed them, did you? Hoping they'd know something? Paid out thousands?" She hoped it sounded loose, relaxed. He was trying to find out.

"Critical list—hospital."

She refused to get involved. "Critical list? Took them apart, did you? Are you bragging or complaining. Of course you're probably like me: I always say if you want them well done you take them apart yourself." She refused to panic. Maybe he had the head. Maybe not. He was waiting for the night? Less traffic on the road? She could hear the cars faintly as they swished on the boulevard outside the courtyard.

194

"They were shot, Kate." It had an ominous sound. A threat?

"So if I don't tell, you're going to shoot *me?* Don't throw your weight around! You expect me to grovel. Well blow, mister. You'll get nowhere."

"*Before* I landed. Alain Giguère and Jacques Rolland. Not shot by me. By two of Lisas' boys."

She looked up then, confused, unable to decide. He pushed the facts.

"When Rolland tried to reach an alarm button. The men shot them both, took the head and left."

"But you can't shoot people in glass rooms—the noise . . . everyone can see."

"Not with silencers, and it's only glass from half way up. Those men were still sitting at their desks, before Rolland had even locked up your head—which, by the way, you had no right to ask him to do." He looked at her, accusing now, and angry. "I was pulling three men off their jobs just to find you. To keep you out of trouble. I should have protected them instead. I never thought you'd be so dumb."

She sat there, horrified. The implications. "I saw those men against a wall. I thought that they were yours, waiting to get the head from *me.* I tried to get it locked up where no one could get at it. I mean, there was no way . . . I didn't know that people just went in and shot other people." Her voice trailed off. She looked at the floor—the bits of sawdust, the broken glass, the liquid soap mixed with water. When they cleaned it up, the varnish was sure to be eaten away underneath, right down to the raw wood. Her fault, then, and her fault now.

"Why didn't you say so at the start," she said, her voice low, needing that drink.

"Say what? That they were shot?"

"That you were the police, from the very beginning."

195

"I'm not with the police. I can call on them when I need them. Period."

" 'Period' is no answer. What are you?"

There was no reply. He took a gun out of a shoulder holster, broke it open to check whatever one checked, and put it on the table; then he loosened the leather strap: Julia's bubonic plague—swollen glands under the arm—as big as oranges. "I was Harry's friend," he said, finally. "I've told you the truth all along."

The gun was lying on the low table, within her reach. Forbes got up and hung his sportscoat on the hook, over the raincoat. He turned his back. She could have grabbed the gun. But, somehow the act was over. She felt cheap now, cheap and gritty, and two men were almost dead because she had missed the plot.

"Why didn't you tell me about the customs men?" she asked, wearily again. "Why didn't you tell me, right at the start?"

"I was about to tell you. You kept carrying on and on. I would have told you about switching the heads, on the train. You never gave me a chance. I took the real one because I had to extend the odds. Both you and the head were paramount to Georges—and to me. One could be used to get the other. If he got you, I could have used Harry's head to get you back. We knew he had a fake, ready to go. One of my men found it while we had Georges holed up at Mabel's: second head, second box, good for a switch any moment, or to be peddled."

"Your men. The police?"

"One carrying your stuff up the hill in a cart; one on the other side watching Lisas. One piloting our plane. You're a damned expensive toy, you know."

Outside, through the locked shutters, she could hear tires on wet roads. People going home to supper on a

196

Saturday night. Nice, normal people going home. Not herself. She sat. Then finally she said it. "All right. Why don't you come right out and say so?"

"I'm not going to say anything at all."

"That's even *worse!* Why don't you just haul off and get it out of your system; out of *my* system. Say that I'm silly; say that I'm unreliable and arrogant. Say that you told the truth and that I didn't believe you. Why don't you add something cutting about Rembrandt and the Renaissance, about conclusions." She could feel herself getting maudlin and out of hand, and she almost burst into tears, but the thing had to be finished. "I'm glad that Harry died. I'm glad he didn't have to see this. I've lost his head; I've almost killed two people. His trust in me was completely betrayed. It's selfish, I know," she blew her nose on a Kleenex from her purse, "but I wouldn't have wanted him to know I was no good."

Forbes got impatient. "I didn't say you weren't any good. You aren't any good against Lisas, that's all." He spotted the bulge in her pocket and came over and pulled the jagged bottle neck out, disgusted. "Another stupid idea, for Christ's sake! Look. You hold it; Lisas grabs your wrist and turns the edge into your own face." He tossed it in the corner. "You didn't 'kill' Giguère and Rolland. You were used. But you're holding things up with your refusal to do what I say. You can't figure Lisas. You're just not operating on that wavelength. You *or* Harry. The only truth you really care about is whether Salviati was influenced by some North Italian trip in 1539. My God, any other kind of truth you wouldn't know what to do with. And Harry never thought you'd be up against this."

The Kleenex was in shreds now. He handed her a clean handkerchief. She blew her nose again.

"Then you really came to Castellorizo to get Lisas? Not to see me?"

197

"Katy." He was gentle now. "The minute I heard that Harry had been fool enough to send you I came. I would have come from anywhere. He knew that. He let me know in plenty of time. And that's *all* that Harry had in mind. That's all."

Outside, the tires kept swishing softly on wet streets, and once in a while she could hear a muted car horn.

"So what's the next step now, to undo what's been done."

He smiled at that and went over to the door, sidestepping the soap. "Boisvert, is the telephone working?"

"Oui."

"Call out for two dinners, two coffees, a double martini. Bring up the suitcases and the coat in the car. Then you can go for the night."

"Oui, monsieur."

Kate felt her cheeks grow red. "Forbes, what does Boisvert think about all this. Dear God."

"He isn't paid to think. He does what I say."

Chapter

14

The next morning was Sunday. About eleven Forbes lifted the telephone. "Boisvert. On your way over here pick up some coffee and rolls; also a dark raincoat, size small. All right. Thanks."

"Where's he going to get a dark raincoat on a Sunday?" Kate came out of the shower stepping gingerly among the potsherds.

"He can get one anywhere he likes; I didn't specify."

"Well, I suppose you have your own way of doing things."

"We don't sit around and twitter, if that's what you mean. There's a murderer running loose."

Kate thought about things for a few moments, not the murderer, but the ambiance. "Would you mind, maybe, just meeting Boisvert at the door?"

"And keep him standing there in the hall? Nowhere to sit? I can't do that. What's the matter?"

"The circumstances," she said, subdued; "they seem a bit bald right now." Even with the furniture straightened up and the grey cotton cover prim on the iron cot, the present surroundings appeared somewhat equivocal. On one side wall plaster was cracked and had fallen off, revealing the wooden lath; the varnish had been eaten away under the middle door, exposing bare oak beneath that; then, the hot water and the soap had run under the baseboards along part of the outside wall, probably dripping green stains down the wall of the office below, and there had been no way of sweeping up anything. The only source of light in the shuttered room was an overhead bulb since the standing lamp was bent at an unusable angle from the strain of the day before, and the skeleton of the previous night's dinner was stacked on the cupboard along with a glass containing two olive pits. "It looks a bit depraved."

"That's just what came into my mind when I walked in yesterday," Forbes said comfortably. "Don't let it bother you. Boisvert twitches at nothing."

"But *I* twitch . . ."

"Well, you should have thought of that long ago, shouldn't you. It's too late now; so just act as if this were an everyday affair. After all, as you said once, emotions have no place in art history."

Boisvert arrived before she could think of a rebuttal and Forbes was right. Boisvert twitched at nothing. He brought hard rolls, butter, jam, coffee with hot milk, and a dark raincoat, size small.

"Here, take a look at these;" Forbes handed her a number of Xeroxed pages from the Brussels telephone book. There were four columns to a page, starting with the capital letter *D*, then capital *DEM,* then small *dem,* right through to *Des.*

"What does this prove?"

200

"Just a wild guess. Jouvet died in the phone booth, you know, after he'd fallen, he scribbled something on the wall, way down low. It was in his typical, crabbed handwriting, so we know it was his, and the pencil stub was in his hand. He wrote 'A de M,' and the letters after the M were indecipherable. It was just a wavy line. He couldn't do any more I guess. So we're left with the name of someone—maybe an artist? 'A de' and then 'M something'. Whatever he found at the Sablon antique market that Sunday was so important that he was shot. Or else it was the name of someone living in Brussels and these are the pages of those names.

"Or else Alfred de Musset?"

"Don't think so. Jouvet never read a book I'm sure. No sensitivities, no twitches." He looked at her. "He was a pragmatic, dogged, careful man."

Kate looked at the pages, feeling apologetic. The letters combined and recombined in infinities of names, none of them meant anything at all. After half an hour she shook her head.

"Did Lisas ever mention anyone with those initials?

"Why, I never saw him except at the main house. He couldn't have said anything everyone else didn't hear."

"Walking up the path. The man carrying the suitcases said that Lisas and you sat down and talked for a while."

"I guess we did. But I don't remember what about . . . about Charles, I think."

"The perfect gentleman! I wouldn't spend my few hours with you learning about Charles." He brushed the last crumbs of the rolls onto the plate and finished his coffee. "Boisvert, is the car ready?"

"Oui. Le Citroen."

"All right, we'll go. Get someone to clean this place up: new door, new lamp. Have the cupboard put in front of the plaster for now."

201

The impassive man nodded, and they left.

The Citroen was waiting in the courtyard, its engine running obediently and its exhaust making little chortles. Forbes slipped the car into the traffic. The rain had stopped, and the grey city showed patches of color here and there, as flower vendors sold their roses and pots of chrysanthemums. They drove through a park and around traffic circles, through two tunnels and out again at high speed, then turned right by the Royal Museum of Fine Arts. The car screeched to a halt underneath a statue of someone. "Here we are," he said. "Now listen as we walk. This is what I want you to do."

Kate was subdued. They got out of the car and walked. She kept thinking about Harry and other things, and Forbes was talking on in a completely offhand way, as if he were ordering off a menu. He stopped talking. He stopped completely.

"Katy?"

"Yes."

"Are you listening?"

"No," she answered, "I'm not. I was just thinking about Harry and wondering what I was doing way off here in Brussels. I was hired to look at some prints and drawings. I should be back there now. I don't know how it ever got to this," she waved her hand at the little churchyard where the striped tents of the dealers were set up, in layers, going down the slope, and where the people were beginning to gather. "I feel as if I'd been hit on the head about a month ago; nothing's been right since. I don't understand anything. Who you are; what my part in this is; why I agreed to get the head in the first place. It's a terrible mess, and I don't feel good about it. What have I got to do with Georges Lisas anyhow? Why am I being used to trap him?"

He didn't explain; he didn't clarify; he just repeated

202

very patiently what he had just said: That the stuff was being shipped from somewhere in Brussels, maybe taken to Antwerp; that Jouvet was working on exactly that theory when he had scribbled those initials and died, shot by one of Lisas's men.

"All right," she said, dull and dispirited. "It doesn't have to be Georges Lisas though, does it? Jouvet was shot by 'someone.' Leave it at that."

"Are you still on that Lisas kick? After last night?"

The emphasis was wrong. The whole idea. "I'm not hunting anyone, Forbes. I'm trying to redeem myself in Harry's eyes. I know, I know, you're going to say that Harry doesn't care, that he's dead. But I care. I'm here because I feel about Harry, and Jouvet, and the customs men. I can't sort anything else out. Yesterday it was you, the missing piece of the puzzle. All day."

"Not all night."

"I can't sort that out either. But I can't hunt Lisas down like a killer."

"You were ready to hunt *me* down."

"Well," she sighed, "somehow you can always take care of yourself. Georges is different. He's . . . he's pitiful. There's no nobility when you're strong and successful. I think the nobility only comes when you're a failure."

"Christ! Georges is being canonized right before my eyes!" He glanced at his watch. "Look, let's call him 'X.' All right? We haven't got all day. Your plane leaves at four. Keep your mind on Jouvet then."

They crossed the square. The Sunday antiquities were set up inside the low, iron fence of the churchyard. A sample of everything since Imperial Rome or before was there, either lying on tables or sitting on the ground or simply leaning: bronzes, kettles, cauldrons, candleholders, pitchers, bowls, parts of columns, stained glass windows, coins,

203

clocks, vases, door knockers, mirrors, combs, stilettos, ink-wells, paperweights, paintings, lithographs, etchings, en-gravings. 'I'm going to be sick,' she thought, but she kept on going. Books, frames, glasses, plates, soup tureens, celtic horse bits, and some just plain junk.

The dealers were muffled against the damp: big black rubbers, long dark coats, and they were warmed, in addition, by a surly distrust of all oncoming buyers. Kate pushed her hands into the pockets of the raincoat and kept on going: umbrella stands, trivets, wine glasses, pocket watches, salt cellars, spoons. She tried to put herself in Jouvet's shoes. Forbes was off, two or three stalls further down, hunched over some dreadful allegorical paintings.

The sun tried. It came through the clouds for one minute only, which might have been an all-time record for that date, and it highlighted two plaster casts that leaned drunkenly against the diminishing Empire legs of a table. They were just two plaster reproductions, probably of a Hellenistic frieze on a sarcophagus, maybe Roman. One of them was cracked on the side, which ruined it for hanging, but the other was intact. She took a minute off the search to inspect them more closely. The first had a beautiful swing to it, a marvelous design. Yet the better cast had its trouble too, as it was badly stained on the far side. Tricky dealers. Worth a question though.

"Where does one get those reproductions?" she asked the man in the back. He wasn't interested enough to speak English. It wasn't a sale.

"Bah, je ne sais pas. L'Atelier des Moulages, peutêtre," and he turned away, swinging his arms, stamping his feet to get them warm. She went back to the plaster casts and looked at them once more. Fighting men with circular shields, swinging gestures. She wrote it down, that name: 'Atelier des Moulages' and then it struck her, looking at the letters.

204

Her mouth fell open as she picked up a silver-backed brush and looked at the plaster cast again and tried to think what Jouvet had thought. She put down the brush and picked up a silver plated mirror next. Jouvet had been working on the shipment angle, and she tried to see the plaster from his point of view. In a moment the solution came to her. The back had an edge on it, an edge that would hold a panel. Most plaster casts just ended at the sides. The bulging front relief of the figures and their shields would make hollows on the reverse side. Hollows that could be packed with things, and then the whole could be sealed over by a panel sliding into those curious L shaped edges. In fact they allowed about an inch more than was usual. Plenty of room for a straight piece of canvas even, if the canvas was covered with plastic wrap and placed in the mould before the wet plaster was poured in. She put down the mirror at this point because her hands didn't hold it very well, and asked one more question.

"C'est où, l'Atelier des Moulages?"

The man looked out from the back of the tent while he lit his pipe. He guessed it was where it had always been, in the Cinquantenaire, and since he had no sale he went to talk with a fellow dealer.

Forbes was down further. He had progressed from the allegories to a series of badly framed pious prints after Greuze. A sufficient punishment, the pastoral visit, and more like that, and she walked down to where he stood. She picked up the print and rubbed the dust off.

"Can we talk here?" she said, out of breath with nerves.

"You have something to talk about?"

"Yes." She traced a line on the glass with her finger, held it up to a raking light. "Three stalls back, a plaster cast . . ."

205

"Right." He followed her finger line on the glass.

"It's a cast of some Hellenistic frieze, lots of depth, relatively speaking, room in the back of the heads and thighs and shields. Do you follow me?" She turned the print over and looked minutely at the nails holding in the backing.

"And?"

"The cast has an edge in back. Makes it deeper still. The edge would hold a panel. Casts don't usually come with panels or edges. They hang on the wall, flush."

She put that print down and picked up another.

"Go on," he said, taking it from her.

"I asked where one could find a fresh cast and was told the Atelier des Moulages, up by the Cinquantenaire."

It only took him a second. "Right. Let's go."

She put down the Greuze, and shook her head at the dealer.

"Too badly foxed, I'm sorry," she said.

Forbes took her arm and they threaded their way back up past the stalls. He never looked over at the casts. The square had filled with cars, and a policeman was there directing the parking and the traffic.

"Slow down," Forbes said to her, as they crossed the square. "You want them to see a sequel to Jouvet?"

"What's the Cinquantenaire?" she asked, as they reached the car.

"A kind of Brandenburg Gate. You know the type: triumphal arches down below, horses galloping on top, with a museum tacked on where they stuff everything that's been donated unwisely. The workshop must be part of it." He fiddled with the knobs on the two-way radio.

"Boisvert? What time does Mrs. Gordon's plane leave? Four? All right. Get Nicholas on the phone; arrange a diversion at the Cinquantenaire this afternoon. A good

206

one. Reroute traffic off on the other side. The side opposite the Atelier des Moulages. Then get me four men. Thanks."

"What are you going to do? Peer in the windows with your Keystone Cops? Arrange a high-speed chase to keep the place clear? Smoke everyone out?"

"We'll set up a collision, I think. That's the easiest." His plan was moving quietly on, and Kate became just another piece of equipment.

"Easiest for whom? For the people who get smashed?"

"A setup," he said, absentminded. "Arranged beforehand. Loose fenders, loose bumpers, loose doors, broken glass. You'd enjoy it, now that you're over the hump."

"Over what hump?"

"Loosened up a bit, not quite so encased in solid gold."

"Oh?"

"Get the map out of the door pocket and tell me what avenue runs along the Cinquantenaire, going out of town. I think that's the side. It slopes there, with room for a basement operation above ground."

The map unfolded in all directions, falling down to her ankles, and she was still struggling with it when they pulled into the courtyard and parked. He took the map from her.

"There it is. Maybe Avenue des Nerviens. We'll give it a try anyway. Boisvert will put you on the plane."

"Oh." Her answer was getting repetitious.

"There'll be two men on the plane."

"Come on, Forbes, this is overdoing it. They've got the head. What more can they want?"

"If your guess is right, they've got nothing to lose. You might find the most astonishing behavior."

"What does that mean?"

"When Mr. X loses his cool I want you out of the way."

207

Kate began to be 'nerveuse' herself. "Well, what about you? I'd just as soon you weren't there when X loses his cool either."

He shrugged, leaning back against the door of the car. "Difference of temperament, that's all. If I get Georges, I'll hack him to death little by little, and I'll enjoy every minute. I'm a northerner. If Georges gets me, he'll kill you and let me go. And he'll enjoy every minute of my remaining life. He's a southerner. All right?"

By the time they got upstairs, the cleanup crew was in high gear. Forbes picked up the telephone in the outer office as he walked in and he never got off. Boisvert remained at his side, taking down orders, making himself useful. No use pretending she had just dropped in for a chat, since her suitcase was on the cot, so she made herself small. By the time the drab official layer had been restored it was time to leave. Forbes took time, five minutes, to say goodbye, and he did it right. That helped.

"All right now?" A nice smile for the uncertainties.

"The action is very compressed, isn't it," she said. "I mean, there hasn't been enough time . . ." He was quiet, smelling of comforting shaving soap and tobacco, and then Boisvert appeared and she left with him, powerless to stop the machinery of inexorable progressions.

Chapter 15

In Boston some snow had come and gone, leaving the streets with a pewter bloom of salt that had dried in light, uneven layers. From under the footmarked ice one could see little moist edges of melt coming out, even though cigarette wrappers and crushed aluminum beer cans still lay trapped in the gutters and along the sides of the streets where they had been pushed by the snow plow. It was ugly; it was frightfully ugly, but Kate had come to a small conclusion on the plane home to Boston: that being out of print, and being dead were two different things. Never mind the ugliness, it was significant just to be alive.

The ride from the airport to New Hampshire had been uneventful; the police had never blinked an eye. Escorting women from a plane to some place in the trees upcountry was nothing new to them. They even changed their gambit when she discovered the lower gate locked, and had to find the key on her key ring.

"You going to be a witness on some case?" said the more talkative of the two. "Being hassled? Kept under wraps?"

The house was warm and polished as she walked in, smelling faintly of lemon oil and floor wax like always. The prints gleamed cream-colored in the evening light as they had before, and Lawrence and Mrs. Oliphant stood in the hall. After the big door closed behind the men and the car had gone back down the driveway there was an awful moment. Kate burst into tears.

Mrs. Oliphant folded her in her capacious arms, and Lawrence patted her on the shoulder. She ate a bite in the kitchen, and heard about how Harry died.

It was exactly as Forbes had said, and Lawrence had already explained it to so many relatives over the past few days, before and after the funeral.

"It happened just after he finished the big brown legal envelopes, Mrs. Gordon. He spent all his time on those piles of papers, you remember, and he called me in to get them off his feet because they were heavy. Before I got to him, why he just started to slide over, like his envelopes. He was gone. I mean, we had thought he might get real chest trouble these winters or have a heart attack, but never just slide off the bed like that. Oh, I'm telling you, it was a terrible shock. Mr. Forbes asked me to delay the announcement and we did, but only for a day, and it didn't help much. One of the prints went the night we announced his death, and another one the night of the funeral."

"What?" Kate jerked up. "The prints?"

Mrs. Oliphant shook her head, more depressed than if the freezers had gone off. "One of us has been awake most every night since, get some sleep during the day. It doesn't do any good, I can tell you that, Mrs. Gordon. Poor Mr. Renshaw, fresh in his grave out there."

210

"That isn't possible." she said. "What about the alarms?"

"Turned off," said Lawrence gloomily. "Both nights, the alarms turned off. The first night, Mrs. Oliphant and I made a little joke about it, just to relieve the tension you know. The relatives had begun coming in and the funeral was to be right away the next day. Mr. Renshaw left strict instructions about not 'lying around.' He said to get the box closed up and him laid in the ground. So that first time, after it was discovered, the day was so busy anyhow we had no time. We thought it was one of Mr. Renshaw's cousins. The one he didn't like too much. Maybe he'd told him to choose one, or maybe he decided himself to select one from the walls. We told Mr. Klein right away. And the police. But they were busy."

"We sure were awful busy for a couple of days." Mrs. Oliphant was kindly, and she pushed some more salad and cold cuts onto Kate's plate.

"Mr. Klein said he'd have the collection reappraised and the insurance raised and he'd send someone out, but that Boston office is too busy right now to concern themselves with Mr. Renshaw's hobby."

"They just got time to get him buried and all that business divided up. No time for what he liked best. I'd have done things the other way . . . done what Mr. Renshaw liked best first." Mrs. Oliphant shifted in her chair to ease her back.

"Where is he buried?" Kate asked.

"Out in back where Turner had planned a real good rose garden for next spring. Lucky too; he was able to dig the ground because it was so heavily composted, he could get the shovel in there. It snowed and froze pretty bad last week—ground was already cold except there; melted some since."

211

"No headstone," said Lawrence, sadly. But the sadness was almost more like exhaustion. It was no wonder they looked as if their flywheels were broken, trying to keep going night and day. No wonder they hadn't unlocked the gate either. "Mr. Renshaw wanted the collection to be his grave marker." Lawrence shifted about in the kitchen chair. It was a yellow varnished oak chair, just like the office chairs in Brussels, and the toilet seat, in fact. "Looks like Mr. Renshaw would have done better to have a headstone if the prints are all going to disappear."

"Maybe they won't go anymore," she said, brisk, trying to put some order in the situation. "Maybe it was just a two-time snatch. People coming in and out. I think professional burglars watch for that sort of thing. Unlocked doors, gates, everyone at a funeral."

"We did lock the gate for the first time," Lawrence said. "But that didn't keep the man out, Mrs. Gordon. It just kept him from bringing his car and loading the whole thing with prints. But it didn't make any difference at all: the second print went too, right through the locked gate and the alarms and the locked door, and locked windows too."

"Which ones?"

"One was Dürer's *Knight, Death, and the Devil.* Mr. Renshaw liked that one a lot. We were waiting for you because you have the chart."

"Dürer's *Knight?* That was in his own apartment."

"Yes. Both from there."

Kate was too tired to go see. "I'll look tomorrow," she said. The cook and Lawrence were sitting there, like tired lumps, and it was up to her now, fresh from a holiday in Greece, to do something. Mrs. Oliphant was tending to the kitchen, Lawrence had everything he could do, and her province was prints and drawings.

212

"Who's here now? Is Turner?"

"No Ma'am. Turner wasn't none too happy. Of course he stayed to dig the grave, but he counted on getting south before the cold weather got too bad on his shoulder. It's real bad in changeable times. Then we got a wind, and it blew out some of the west gallery panes. Mr. Lawrence asked him to stay to put those back in. He did, and then he left. There's nobody but us."

"Tomorrow I'll call Mr. Klein and ask him to send us someone.

Lawrence drew some air into his chest with an effort and then slumped and sighed it out. "Well, I'm telling you, Mrs. Gordon, that's an eerie feeling, going in there into that empty apartment. Mrs. Oliphant won't go in at all now. She thinks it's Mr. Renshaw's ghost, coming back to get his favorite prints."

The cook was timid and apologetic, wiping her hands over and over on the black and white print apron. "You know, Mr. Renshaw had always said that we should stay on, Mr. Lawrence and me; he was going to keep the house open for people who liked looking at his prints, poor man. But now, I dunno." She wiped her forehead with the edge of the apron. "Don't know as I could round a corner each day without worrying about meeting up with something."

"What did the police say?" Kate asked. It was her last question. She had finished her tea and felt as though she were becoming insulated in cotton wool.

"They weren't none too pleased neither."

"It appeared that they had a series of car thefts to attend to, Mrs. Gordon. They implied that they could better use their talents in that direction. They felt that Mr. Renshaw had had an untrustworthy alarm system put in by foreigners, that he had not spent his money wisely. I'm afraid that they don't have the same qualities that Mr. Ren-

213

shaw required in all of us." Lawrence, dear Lawrence, was at his best. She could see those patrolmen in her mind right now. Pulling up their belts around their stomachs, tucking in their shirts, hitching up their britches, swaggering down to investigate stolen cars—of more concern to Sullivan county than a New Yorker's pretty pictures. Kate had already decided not to call them anyhow. All in all, except for breeding purposes, women didn't stand too high on their totem poles. Rural New England and rural Scotland probably had a lot in common.

Back in her apartment, she thought about those prints. They were just pin money; nothing compared to the head she had lost. As far as she could recall, the last time the *Knight* had changed hands at Christie's it went for around ten thousand. A good price, but it would hardly interest Lisas and his department store boys. She called her sons to chat; then she turned out the light and slept right through the next burglary: the first and seventh states of *Christ Presented to the People,* Rembrandt.

Lawrence had discovered it on his morning check. After breakfast there was another round of panic. Mrs. Oliphant hovered. She went on about Renshaw's spirit until Kate finally excused herself and took her last cup of coffee to the living room to think. If Forbes had once said that Harry was out of his mind to send her for the head, no one was going to repeat that he had been out of his mind to leave her in charge of the prints.

Coming to conclusions was not difficult. Turner, the only man who could handle a rifle was gone and the three of them were easy prey. The light-fingered visitor must know that.

So after lunch she drove to Concord. An advertisement in the Yellow Pages said "Come in and Browse" and in addition they also "bought, sold, traded, appraised, refin-

214

ished, customized and repaired" guns, so they must have seen more than deer hunters in their day. The salesman was genial, and it bothered him not at all when she explained: unfailing, small, accurate, easy to work and safe. He raised no eyebrows, asked no questions. He wrote down the serial number of the two-inch barrel revolver along with her name, and looked at her driver's license.

"D.C., huh," he finally said. "Fust time I saw one of those. Git a lot of Bostonians here. Got to file a permit down'n Boston." He wrapped the gun and washed his hands of responsibility. "Survey shows half New Hampshire killins done with knives."

She thanked him and left. Crimes of emotion were things of the past; this was more an intellectual problem. Scissors or a knife would be too—she tried to think of the right adjective—too 'fleshy' she decided, as her car picked its way over icy patches in the road. If "improving the conditions" of Harry's collection, to use the Director's words, meant shooting the opposition, it had better be done in the abstract, not in the flesh, and guns kept one at a distance.

She saw young Richard at the gas pumps in Plainfield. He remembered her.

"Hello, lady," he said. "You was going up to the Renshaw place once, remember?"

"And you were juggling two apples and a walnut. How did that go?"

"Pretty good." He filled the tank to the very top. "You going back up there now? Old man died, you know. We got cars here all day long last week. I work here nights, after school."

"That's fine, Richard. Good for you. Yes, I'm going back. I live there."

"Gee," he said. "I thought there'd be nothin' left." He

215

wiped his nose as he took her money.

"Oh yes, there are three of us left. And Mr. Turner makes four." She was going to add that he dug them out after the winter, but Richard, with his sense of the macabre, might have misinterpreted.

"I know Turner. He got gas here yesterday morning."

"Maybe that was his brother. He takes over sometimes. Tell your mother to come and pick apples with you next summer. We've got so many now, and there's no one to harvest them."

"Thanks lady. I'll tell her."

Immediately after she got back she asked Lawrence to move her things into Harry's apartment. She didn't call Mr. Klein to ask. She didn't write to the Board to ask. She just told Lawrence what to do. It was useless to defend Harry's collection from the other side of the house, and Harry himself would have hated a stranger coming in to poke about, bothering Lawrence, as he had once said.

Lawrence gave in. It was a temporary arrangement anyhow. Mr. Klein had increased the insurance on the collection and was busy with things of greater moment. Lawrence and Mrs. Oliphant were too undone by the third incident to argue.

In fact, Harry's apartment looked better after Kate moved in. It lost that half frozen-in-place look. If the siege continued until spring, Kate decided she could move up some of her things from Washington and even settle for a while. There was no sense in losing one's cool; it might go on for some time.

It did go on for some time, or rather the waiting did. Whoever or whatever ghosts took their time. She tucked the gun under her pillow nights, and learned to fall into an uneasy sleep, always uneasy—and not always sleep. Partly the new location and partly, one night, the wind.

216

The wind that night screamed, moaned, shrieked through a loose window in the hall. Something to get used to, that's all. But then it was partly the new revolver: she was afraid she'd forget to slip off the safety catch and the thing would click stupidly without firing. She would go through the motions the salesman had showed her; as she tried to get in the swing of grabbing the gun. Forbes must have practiced in his early days.

In the morning Kate tried to fasten the hall window somewhat better to stop the whining. She undid the catch on the inside, lifted and slammed the frame down again to close the gap. This wasn't necessary. The window was well greased apparently, unlike the others, and it hit the bottom sill with such force that a pane dropped out at the top.

"Well, so much for today's improvements." The wind came through the empty pane even louder now, so she simply shut the door. Win a few, lose a few.

"Why does that window slide so well, Lawrence? The one in Harry's hall." Lunch time in the dining room, alone.

"Mr. Renshaw used the one without a storm as a fire escape," he said. "The others all have doors nearby, and Mr. Renshaw didn't want people to fight their way back to him. Forbes told him, later, that it was silly to keep his hall freezing cold and to put a storm window there; so he did. But only after the sprinkler system was installed."

Kate wandered about that day, checking the windows inside and out. They all had locks. The storms had locks on the inside, according to Forbes, and yet she could hear the Director's voice saying "Even the storm windows clip on from the outside." Suddenly she decided to look once more at that hall window. She ran out and around to the south side. There was still snow so she kept to the walk. There should be no footprints to show a burglar that someone had been checking. It took but a second to see that Harry's hall

217

had the one storm window of the old kind which clipped on the outside with small screw clips that had been painted over to match the new ones—and it took only another second to see that the paint was worn off these threads. The man must have unscrewed them and then quietly lifted off the storm. When he knocked out that upper pane on the inside window, he held it with a suction cup and reset the lock. The apartment had been empty. No one heard.

Kate ran back to the front door before Lawrence caught her in the act and removed the cigarette package from the latch. She then tried to chart some sort of clear future action. There was the gun and there was the window. She could hear Forbes, his bossy voice: "Obviously, if the house is tight everywhere else, you get the gun out and wait." All very well; he enjoyed playing cat and mouse, but he was always the cat. She doubted the mouse enjoyed the game as much. To shoot at someone coming in a window or silhouetted in a door, just pointblank—well, to begin with, it would make such a noise, and it might hurt them, even kill. So about an hour later, she got a hammer and some nails from the garage, and nailed the storm window instead. She did it from the outside while Mrs. Oliphant was off and Lawrence down getting the mail. It wasn't a good job: two of the nails bent, and one broke while she was trying to straighten it, but the burglar would have a terrible time removing that storm window even with a crowbar, and she could think further about shooting him then.

Several nights passed without incident. Lawrence assumed some of his old assurance, and Kate bought herself some pots of flowers, ones that didn't look like memorial wreaths. In fact, if it had not been for a yeasty rise in temperature and the unfamiliarity of Harry's bed, Kate would have slept right through the next night. It was one of those heavy, liquid winds that blew an unseasonal

218

warmth, upsetting people's equilibrium, and bringing South Carolina to northern New Hampshire in about twenty minutes. She awoke in the pitch dark drenched in perspiration under three blankets and inclined to get a fresh nightgown out of the chest.

There was a chewing noise in the wall, however, and Kate had no wish to step on a mouse as she stepped out of bed. Mrs. Oliphant had tried to stem this mouse population with all kinds of products, but contrary to the manufacturer's claims, they did not run out into the night seeking water; they ran in between the walls instead, and died there, making dreadful odors, while hundreds more took their place. She thought about it. But after a minute more of listening, the dreadful truth seeped into her consciousness: not mice; the hall storm window screws were being quietly undone, turn by turn. The man must be standing there, just ten feet away. He would try her window next, after the hall storm was found to be immovable, or else he would take a chance and break the glass.

Kate reached for the gun under her pillow. Harry's bed was a double, fortunately, and the gun was under the other pillow, otherwise she would have knocked it to the floor, her hands were shaking so.

The turning noise must almost be at an end—twenty turns by now she guessed. And the man was deliberate. He had to be putting each screw on the ground. She heard a slight adjusting sound, as if he were tugging without result, and then a creak as the wood was strained. Her heart was making so much noise that she could hardly be sure.

There was a pause. The man must be thinking things over, and then there was the sound of the screws being replaced, squeak and scratch, over and over.

'Now it'll be my window,' she thought—and the moment to summon up a Forbes-like approach to problems

219

that simply arise from time to time. For her, however, it was a terrified paralysis, waiting for that instant when she must shoot a person she had never seen. If he was too tall, she would hit his intestines; if he was too short it would go through the base of his neck. At such short range she could hardly miss. Disemboweling someone, loudly, in the middle of the night. Did being a curator actually entail all this?

She pushed back the safety, and lay down on the bed in a position where she could steady the gun and either aim at the middle of the window or switch to the open door of the hall. Her gun hand grew prickly as it grew tired, and the moment never came. She heard nothing more, and she saw nothing at all, and by the time the morning light greyed the outside, she had half fallen asleep, still holding the gun, and kinked almost beyond repair.

When the sun was well up, Kate slipped the safety back on, feeling almost silly. She then locked the gun in her drawer—Harry's drawer—as she had done every morning, and took an hot extra-long shower. Breakfast was the same, Lawrence was the same, Mrs. Oliphant was the same. The sunlight struck the rug at the same moment and there was a letter from her boys.

At ten o'clock Kate took a moment off to circle the house, as if she might be looking for Christmas roses in sunny spots. Under Harry's hall window the leftover snow had been scuffed around, mussed to remove any trace of prints. Nothing else was wrong.

Chapter 16

Babysitting a collection at night was a good way to lose weight: babysitting at night, and moving along with the print room during the day and trying to figure out what the man would think of next in between times. Kate grew thin and jumpy. She decided the thing she should have done was to have shot him that night as he put back the screws—have it done with. This was too hard.

So when the alarm rang outside her door early one morning she nearly dropped her coffee cup onto the muffins. Kate ran to the alarm panel, but she didn't know which switch was which. Lawrence arrived on the double and threw the right one. It stopped the noise.

"The gate alarm, Mrs. Gordon."

'Jesus Christ,' she thought to herself, 'in broad daylight.'

They looked at each other. Then she straightened. It might be any number of things, she reminded him. A teenager, trying to turn around on the narrow road; a drunk, tossing out his beer cans; a new parcel post man; the telephone company checking their new number; the county engineer inspecting septic tanks; the Cancer Crusade looking for volunteers. She finally stopped. Burglars didn't arrive after breakfast. Bright sun forecast.

"Let's reset it and see if it starts up again."

Lawrence reset the alarm, and it did start up again.

"All right," she said, "I'll walk down to the gate and check. When Turner gets back he can see if there's something wrong." It was a brisk thing to say.

Lawrence disapproved of her going. He wanted to call the police instead, but Kate waved him off with a story about deer and the apple tree. After he had left, she went back to the bedroom and put the gun in her coat pocket. It was a big Loden coat with huge pockets. One could shoot right through the coat, for that matter.

From the front door Kate could see a car down there, right in plain sight, and a prickle of annoyance arose. People were always stopping to toss out their containers after drinking all night in Claremont. Once they got enough booze in them they seemed to gravitate upward, and since the Squaw Hill Road was the highest road that had any paved look to it, they often turned around there and got sick, fell asleep, made love or abandoned their old cars, too lazy or drunk to look for the dump. But why always pick Harry's gate?

Actually, it wasn't very smart to walk all the way down in full sight. A bit silly, really, since all these people had to do was to wait for her to arrive, giving them all kinds of time to think excuses.

It wasn't, however, a question of derelicts. For she saw a familiar outline down there, leaning against the wall, and the sun lit up his grey-brown hair.

222

"Forbes!" she called out as she ran the last hundred yards, with the gun banging around so wildly that it might have slipped its catch and shot off her leg.

"Oh, Forbes, I'm *glad* to see you," she said, and his face felt rough and scratchy against hers.

"You look like a scarecrow," he said, starting right in.

"You don't look so suave yourself." He had been travelling all night, maybe? She refused to sink into a curtsey. He took the keys from her and unlocked the gate. Quiet. He pulled the jeep through and then locked the gate again. He had never locked the gate before.

"Something's going on," she said then, "or you wouldn't bother."

"Right. Get in. And watch the gun in your pocket before you shoot both of us by mistake. What are you doing with a gun anyway?"

"I bought one." Saving her questions. Saving her answers.

"I can see that," he said as he roared the jeep up the drive and into the garage beside her car. He switched off the engine and helped her down. "Didn't anyone ever tell you not to let it bump around in your pocket while you're running?"

"Well I don't run usually," she said lamely, always in the wrong.

"The first rule is not to carry it where it can blow you apart; the second rule is to keep it out of sight, not in an outside pocket; and thirdly, stay out of sight yourself. I mean, Lisas could polish you off while you wandered down your Renaissance fields, picking all those flowers, checking all those facts." He kept his voice light, as if he had dropped in for coffee.

"Lisas?"

"Right."

223

She stopped on the steps. How much more trouble did she need? "But he's got the head. What more could he want?"

"*I've* got the head. That's what he wants."

"You do?" Kate slumped against him with relief. One thing resolved. One right thing. "I'm so glad for Harry. Thank you, Forbes."

"It isn't here. Harry left it in his will to the Metropolitan. I had it sent there. Lisas doesn't know that. He's coming here, and he thinks you have it. I'm just one minute ahead of him, so let's move."

He pulled her up the steps and inside the door. "Where's everyone?"

Lawrence was around the corner. He had seen them coming. He was pleased and assured to the point of being his old self again. "I should have known you'd be testing your equipment, sir. Would you care to have Mrs. Oliphant bring you some breakfast, sir. She'll be so pleased. We're both so pleased. Let me have your coat."

"Hang it in the closet, Lawrence, out of sight, and call everyone in. Who's here?"

"Yes, sir. Delighted. Mrs. Oliphant is in the kitchen, and Turner got in this morning. He's having a cup of coffee. You'll be wanting to see Mr. Renshaw's grave, I'm sure. It's out in . . ."

"Not this morning, Lawrence. Get everyone in here fast."

Lawrence stopped talking abruptly. Something serious. He went out to the kitchen, and Forbes turned to her again.

"Katy."

"Yes?"

"Say the word if you want Georges alive. Just say the word and I'll try harder." He smiled in a crooked sort of

224

way, but his eyes were serious.

"For me? Georges? You've always misunderstood. He was nothing to me. Just an acquaintance."

"A noble acquaintance?"

She smiled back. "No. Not even a noble acquaintance anymore, if what you say is true." She tried to keep it light. "I'm probably the northern type."

His eyes, catching this, picked her up. For a moment everything stopped. Then Lawrence came in with the others. Mrs. Oliphant sat down on the Flemish bench. She reacted quickly to crises of any kind and today she looked more uncertain than usual. Lawrence and Turner stood.

Forbes shook hands, summarizing the situation in a quiet, grave manner, thinking as he talked, passing his hand over a stubbled jaw, looking tired.

". . . a man named Lisas. He's going to make a try for Mr. Renshaw's Greek head, the one that's been with Mabel and John Houseman. It isn't here, of course. He left it to the Metropolitan; it's there now as a matter of fact but Lisas doesn't know that. You can tell him, but he'll think you're lying." He walked over to where one could see down the driveway, looked out. "We'll try to get him before he tears the place apart." Forbes moved to the back gallery and stopped to scan the slopes behind the house and then returned. "He's after Mrs. Gordon too, as a hostage, and after the collection, in a spiteful sort of way; very dangerous, really. A good shot, so I'd like to plan this right. It would be just his bent to put a bullet through every print, if he had the time, or through every drawer in the print room." He kept looking out, one window then another. "I've put in for some police, but they're out on some other chase. Turner?"

"Yes." The man looked good: spare, unruffled, steady.

"You can handle a rifle?"

"There's one in the garage. Ammo."

225

"Good. Lawrence?"

"Yes, sir."

"Lawrence, you and I are going to cover the front and back. Mrs. Oliphant is going to act normal in the kitchen. If she gets into a commotion we'll help her out. Now, I have an idea that might work in the west gallery."

The two walked to the other side. Lawrence seemed bothered, but he was reliable, and Forbes explained the only plan that had come to mind.

"Harry's clock it will have to be. From behind it you can get a view of both ends of this hall."

The grandfather clock stood with its back to the inner wall, among a flurry of large, potted plants—Harry's only concession to Mother Nature. Forbes made his way among them, and opened the clock.

"The plants grow almost to the ceiling here Lawrence, and if Lisas comes through the back I don't think he'll see you. He doesn't know he's expected; he won't be looking for people behind plants. So if you see him before I do, pull this lever out and down. That starts the clock running through its chime. It's an hourly one, and if it rings off the hour I'll be there." As Forbes climbed back out, looking like a tweedy husband trying to escape his wife's garden club, Kate had to stiffle a giggle in spite of circumstances.

Forbes helped Lawrence through the pots. "Blood will pool in your legs. I know what it's like. Don't let yourself get numb. And don't come out unless I call, even if you hear trouble. All right?"

Lawrence nodded.

"Now then, Mrs. Oliphant." He found her standing in the back hall entry, large but timid. Forbes smiled encouragement. "Yours will be the hardest job, you know. You have to act normal or Lisas will think something's wrong. Make some of your delicious burned scones. Bang things.

226

Slam the oven door. Sing. If he shows up tell him everyone's out. Tell him you're the head cook. Scold. Pretend he's the delivery man and late with the delivery. Pretend he's me. I'll hear you; I can hear you all the way to Europe, you know: 'Forbes! Get this freezer fixed or get out!' " He patted her on the shoulder and gave her a comforting push toward the kitchen.

She nodded, red and flustered, and fled.

"Now, Turner."

Turner was there, ready.

"I'm going to give you Mrs. Gordon. If Lisas gets her, he's got us all. Both of you go to the garage and stay put. There are small windows onto the driveway. You'll have front and rear exits. Make sure before you shoot. Watch for any friends he might bring along. And Kate, for God's sake stay down, out of sight. No windows this time. Is that clear?"

"Yes."

He walked over to the front window again. "And Turner, if you hear shooting or any other commotion, don't come out. Stay with Mrs. Gordon until one of us comes to get you. I'm counting on that."

Turner nodded, grizzled and competent. "Right."

"Fine." He moved toward the door to get them going.

"Why don't you just lock Georges out? We'll all stay with you." It was a clumsy maneuver; she was being propelled out anyhow.

"We'll concentrate the field of action, Katy. Otherwise he'll be behind every tree. It's time now; get down there."

He opened the door and motioned them through, but she stopped him.

"Where will you be?"

"In the receiving line." He motioned to Turner and Turner took her by the arm, so she went.

227

In the garage they heard the shots. Not just shots, but shooting.

Kate was huddled at the top of the stairs in the loft. She would like to have been right at the window, but this was an alternate spot, back from the front with a view out the driveway. She sat on a storage box, surrounded by more storage boxes and old leather harnesses, extra tractor parts, oil cans, drive shaft belts hanging on hooks, oddments of all sorts.

Turner had stayed down below, across from her. He had unhooked the rifle from two large nails on the side of the far stall, and then returned in that rangy, stringy way of his to station himself.

For about thirty minutes they stayed like that, listening and watching.

Then they saw him, Lisas, going up to the house. It was Georges all right, with a dark blue European overcoat, his skin looking yellow between his dark hair and the dark blue coat. It was hard to tell because of the tree branches and the sunlight that intervened. He looked 'foreign' today; not like the man she had met once before, tan and in a continental linen suit. It looked as if he had a gun in his hand, but the terrace was far away; maybe it was just a dark glove. He moved up the steps, stopping, then going on to the big door; he pushed it open and went in.

They waited about four minutes in silence, and then the shots: first one, and another, then about four in succession, a pause and several more that sounded like fire and answering fire. Then nothing. The blood was pounding in her ears from fright. There were two more shots and again a silence.

The garage roof was warming up by creaks and groans and slight shiftings of weight as they watched together, eyes

228

glued to the terrace and the front door.

It was freezing cold, sitting in thirty degree temperature doing nothing. Even Turner hadn't moved; he just shifted the position of the rifle slightly when he saw Lisas go inside. At length the front door opened; they stiffened.

A man came out, rust color he was, not dark blue. He walked slowly down the drive. Even through the fly-specked window she could tell it was Forbes.

"Thank *God!*" she whispered to Turner. "Thank *God.*"

Turner didn't answer. He just kept up his vigil. When Forbes was close enough she stood up, ready to fly down the stairs and out the door.

"Sit down, Mrs. Gordon, just like he told you," said Turner in his cold, nasal way. "Don't move."

It was true. Forbes had said to stay put until he came. So she sat down again on the storage chest, wild to have the whole thing over and done with.

Turner raised his rifle then, ever so slowly, as Kate watched, horrified. Someone was coming down after him, someone Turner had seen somewhere along the driveway. She tightened up inside again. Lucky that she hadn't run out to complicate matters.

The loft window was dusty but clear enough to see Forbes. He kept on coming. There was no one else that she could actually see, but there were trees of all shapes to conceal someone. Forbes kept walking, unaware, and Turner tucked his chin up against the rifle stock in a businesslike way.

"Turner! Do you see someone else?" she whispered.

The man was preoccupied. He didn't answer. Forbes was almost down to them, and Kate saw quite clearly that Turner was going to shoot. Shoot Forbes? Kate somehow managed to get the little revolver out of her floppy coat pocket. She slipped back the safety, aimed and fired.

229

It made a terrible noise. The older man spun slowly around, and sank down on the floor clutching his shoulder, trying to figure out what had happened.

Then Forbes burst in through the door, gun in hand. "Good God! Who else is in here? Turner?"

He saw Turner on the floor. "Where is he? Where did the shot come from?"

Turner looked up, slow, with a kind of dull surprise. "Nowhere." He held his shoulder; the blood was beginning to drip off his fingers. "Nobody here but us."

Forbes kneeled down and pulled the coat back, undid his shirt.

"Mrs. Gordon's got a gun, I reckon," said Turner. "Musta gone off by mistake." He faded a bit after that.

Forbes said nothing. He was looking at the flow of blood. He got out a clean handkerchief from an inner pocket and made a pressure pad. Turner held his fingers over it.

Forbes stood up, and got Turner to his feet. "Steady. All right? Good clean hole, missed the artery. I've called for an ambulance. They'll take care of it at the house."

Turner lurched away from him. "Reckon I'm okay." Forbes opened the door, watched, as Turner started up the drive alone. He waited to make sure. Then he turned back toward the loft.

"Kate? Where are you?"

She was in the same place she'd been all along; the gun was still in her hand. He ran up the narrow wooden stairs, took the gun from her, unloaded it and slipped it in his pocket. "Come on."

She just sat, oblivious, staring down at where Turner had been. He pulled her up, and she sat down again.

"Come on, Katy. You're going to chill."

She felt nothing, dulled. "No. I don't think so."

230

"What do you mean 'no'?" You've got to move. Georges isn't dead. He may make it."

"Leave me. I have to think."

"You can think later. If you're worried about Turner, forget it. Your hand just convulsed, that's all. Now get up."

"I don't think so," she said in a monotone. "I meant to kill him." She didn't look up.

That stopped him. "Wait a bit now. Go back to the beginning. What happened in here?"

"I've forgotten," she said. "It's a blur."

"What started you thinking that Turner had to be shot?"

She looked at him. "When you came down the driveway."

"And?"

"He was watching. He had the rifle. I asked him if he saw someone because he raised the rifle. He didn't answer, and I thought . . ." She gave an involuntary shudder and her teeth began to chatter, almost biting her tongue. She put her knuckle against them to stop it.

"So you asked Turner if he saw someone behind me. And then?" he prompted.

"Then? I couldn't see. They might have been behind." Kate took a deep breath and the shivery feeling receded. "So I saw you still walking. And Turner I'm sure, was aiming at you." She looked up at him in surprise, as if she saw Forbes for the first time. "You were coming on so fast. I didn't dare wait. I had to make a decision!" She tore her eyes away from his face. "You see, it isn't so good. I've shot Turner, one of Harry's oldest friends. It's . . . it's like all the other times," she added, dull and confused now. "The customs men, even jumping off the train. And now I've murdered someone. Between breakfast and lunch. Another wrong person."

231

He pulled her up then. "Come on. Get out of this icebox. There's nothing wrong with your mind, if that's what you're worried about. Nothing."

The sound of a car roaring up the hill sent some adrenalin into her system and she pulled back. "I can't. Don't ask me to go up there, Duncan, and face them. Mrs. Oliphant, Lawrence, all staring. It's like having shot Harry; don't you see? I can't support anything I did."

He dragged her down the stairs and up the driveway, oblivious of the ambulance.

"Rubbish. There's nothing wrong with your conclusions. Turner's never surfaced before, in all these years. Think of that, Kate. Good old Turner. Come on, now, walk like a queen."

She held back. "All very well for you to say. I can't support my . . ."

He pushed her in the door. *"I'll* support your facts." He led her past Turner, past a figure covered by a blanket, and on to Mrs. Oliphant.

"Hot coffee right away, Mrs. Oliphant, and bring another blanket."

As Kate sat in a chair and watched, the men trooped in like a show on television. Unreal. Even the sound had gone off. Nothing registered, the murmurs of the medics who crawled around Lisas, or Lisas himself. His body faced away from her, his face a dirty greyish color, like old gym socks. Turner was grey too.

Mrs. Oliphant clucked over with the blanket and the coffee. Kate was shaking so badly that half the coffee slopped on the saucer.

In about fifteen minutes the medics were through with Georges. One went back for a stretcher and together they rolled his unresponsive body on it. Lawrence held the door; they eased the stretcher out and into the ambulance.

One came back to attend to Turner. He did something, and then helped him walk out. Lawrence closed the door again.

"Turner looks poorly, don't he," said Mrs. Oliphant softly to Lawrence, as they both watched the red car pull away.

"Not as poorly as he's going to," said Forbes, clear and grim, coming from another part of the house.

Kate didn't move. Not even at the sound of the police car screeching to its halt and scattering Harry's gravel. She just watched the spot where Turner had been, on the Flemish bench in the hall. Forbes went out to meet the police and Mrs. Oliphant took the cup and saucer from her cold hands.

Chapter 17

They were in all stages. Forbes still functioned, of course. He always did. But Lawrence seemed to be fading. He wandered about the north room, starting to pick up bits of plaster, pieces of chair stuffing, broken glass, only to be told by the younger of the two police officers to leave everything where it was. He would put the pieces down and then in a moment he would absentmindedly start picking up again. Mrs. Oliphant kept clearing her throat as if she were about to make a speech. Kate was inert on her chair, and Forbes was anxious about her pallor.

"If you good gentlemen don't mind," he was saying, "we'll wait for a few minutes until Mrs. Gordon warms. She's been sitting in that cold garage all morning and she's caught a chill. I know Mrs. Oliphant has been making buns, haven't you, Mrs. Oliphant. And some coffee?" Voice hearty, almost overdone. Forbes followed the three as far as the butler's pantry where he poked about in cupboards,

235

whistling through his teeth, and then heated up a mixture of brandy and coffee whose fumes alone would have made a mule fly. Returning to the front room, he pushed the mug into Kate's hands.

"Start drinking and keep on."

Every time she came up for a breath he pushed her face back into it.

It was warming, no doubt about that. Within four minutes it was down to her feet; a moment later it practically blew her head off.

"My word." She sat for a few minutes more, percolating. Then she staggered to her feet. "I think I'll go wash my face with cold water." She managed to get to her room, and it helped some to rinse her face, but returning to the living room she had to run her hand along the walls for balance.

The small company was assembling in the south room. The older policeman scratched his head and said he always thought someone would go after Harry Renshaw one day, but not after he was already dead.

And Mrs. Gordon there, sitting quiet in a cold loft could leave a body with a real chill. Lots of people picked up pneumonia like that, even out duck hunting they did. Now did she mind if they started with her? One thing at a time of course. They'd like to start with the first shooting, the man called Lisas.

Kate had little to say, since she and Turner had been in the garage. The police assistant wrote slowly on his triplicate forms with a ballpoint pen. It was warm, and Kate hoped she wouldn't fall asleep with her mouth open.

Lawrence told about being behind the clock. He had heard the shots and the furniture fall.

The cook had been in the kitchen, shaping bun after bun. She had heard the shots too.

236

Forbes gave his version then, answering in such a docile and agreeable manner that Kate opened her eyes once to see who it was. She remembered that what he was saying had once seemed very important, but now it rolled around in her head without coming to roost.

"Just where did you wait for this Lisas, Mr. Forbes?" the older policeman was saying.

"In a closet in the hall."

"The one with all the bullet holes in it? Musta known you were there."

"I told him to drop his gun. The closet door was ajar; I could see him."

"Pretty foolhardy wasn't that?"

"No more so than being behind a wall where you can't see."

"What happened then, Mr. Forbes?"

"He was in the room across the hall. The doors are double. I kicked one open and came out the other. I got to the side of the arch; he went behind that red chair by those books. He couldn't move without my seeing him; yet I couldn't enter without being seen. Actually I planned to keep him holed up there until you arrived, but then I began to worry as to what he might be planning."

"So you moved in and shot him?"

"Not precisely. I managed to get my hand behind one of the bookcases by the arch—one that he couldn't see from where he was—and to knock it over, as a diversion. At that point he moved and must have tripped on one of Harry's rings in the floor. Before he could recover I was able to get him."

"Did you check Lisas right away, Mr. Forbes, give him what help you could?"

"I certainly did not." Forbes gave a short laugh. "I waited. I thought he was setting a trap."

"What made you change your mind then?"

"The blood. He was bleeding profusely. Lawrence called the ambulance."

"Self defense I'd say," said the senior officer. He looked around, on the defensive himself. "Anyone care if I smoke in here?"

"I'll get an ashtray, sir," said Lawrence.

"The lady's looking better," said the second policeman.

"Lost that drawn look; looks more relaxed now, don't she," Mrs. Oliphant commented softly, and Forbes defined her still further: "Not so much 'relaxed' as 'vacant'," he said, sounding quite pleased with himself.

Then, having disposed of the unfamiliar, the police turned to the familiar. After all, who cared if some Greek had been shot by another foreigner, but locals, now, that was something else.

When Mrs. Oliphant was called, Forbes excused himself for a few moments. After a timid start, the cook volunteered some assorted facts. Turner had been here as long as Mr. Renshaw. Everyone in Plainfield knew the Turners; they were a huge clan, maybe two hundred in all. This one came part-time winters, full-time other seasons. If one Turner was too busy there were other Turners who helped. The family had a hand in everything, from dumps to snowplows. This particular Turner went south sometimes, because his back got real bad in the cold weather.

The older policeman nodded. He knew it all anyway. Then Lawrence gave a few more facts, mournfully, as if he were clearing a neutral path between Kate and the gardener. Mr. Pelham had sold his house to Renshaw; Turner was already here then. Renshaw had kept Turner on. He did the heavy things and the lighter ones as well, like the gardens. He even stayed on after the fu-

238

neral to fix some loose panes in the gallery.

The assistant wrote on. Forbes returned. He had an encouraging smile for Kate, but it went unnoticed. Kate had fallen silent, partly because no one had asked her anything, but mostly because she was dead drunk. An hour had passed since she had downed the brandy on an empty stomach and she no longer needed an encouraging smile. At best she would be able to answer the questions put to her in but one or two words.

"Well now, Mrs. Gordon, I guess you should tell us your side of the story. Why don't you begin by telling us what you do here." The policeman was genial. The signal honor before the axe.

His assistant looked up in alarm at the broad question. Paper was running short.

"I'm the curator."

"And how long have you been in this position?"

Kate tried to count from September to December, but lost track. "Since September."

"Hmm. That's about four months. Not very long, is it, to start doing away with the old time residents. Did you see Mr. Turner often?"

"Yes."

"Now then, did Turner ever act peculiar, Mrs. Gordon, during the times you saw him? As if he were turning a mite queer?"

"No."

"Then what made you think that he was going to shoot Mr. Forbes?"

Kate thought about this, trying to unmuddle her mind. It was an important point, and hard to remember. She looked over at Forbes in confusion, but he seemed to be watching a fly on the ceiling. Everyone else was watching her. So she began to feel her way.

239

"I remember that Mr. Forbes was walking down to us. Mr. Turner picked up his rifle," she paused, "then aimed it at Mr. Forbes. Right at him." She thought some more. "I cleaned the window to make sure."

"To make sure of what?" The thread was becoming lost.

"To make sure there was no one else to shoot at, I guess."

"And then."

"There wasn't," she said.

"Wasn't what?"

"Wasn't anyone else."

"So you shot Turner."

"Yes. To keep him from shooting Forbes."

"How long have you known this Mr. Forbes?"

"Four months." She remembered the number.

"Mr. Forbes. You got anything to add?" He hoped not; the forms were used up. "You weren't actually involved."

Forbes looked straight at him. "I certainly do. We'll use Harry's tape recorder here and you may do what you like with the evidence." As he said this he pushed the *record* lever down. The elder man shrugged. He wasn't that much impressed with fancy stuff.

"I have a certain interest in all this, naturally, because I'm alive," said Forbes, spinning it out, expansive even. "It's a pleasant feeling, I find. I'm also interested because I'm chairman of the Board of Trustees of this estate, and I'm also on the Board of Trustees of the Renshaw Corporation."

Kate opened her eyes at that. She looked over at him, and thought about the letter she had written on the plane. He nodded, a significant smile, and continued.

"I have to deal with thefts as well. I can't go into it

240

right now, but Harry had asked me, as a friend, to burglar-proof his collection a few years back after a whole rash of troubles, none of them very well explained. He didn't want a stranger. Mr. Renshaw was rather definite on some things." Forbes lit a cigarette. "First, I put in a gate alarm, so whole rooms of prints wouldn't be carried off in a truck. Second, I put in a complete system on the bulk of his collection that was stored in one room, and finally, for the rest, I experimented with different kinds of devices: vibrators, suction, pressure pads, as well as one that you have at your station. I tried everything except proximity detectors and radar microwave because they are much too limiting for a private house.

"The switches for the alarms were in Renshaw's apartment. By themselves, gentlemen, they should have trapped any outsider who came around. But they didn't seem to, did they?" He looked up with an innocent expression of pained surprise. "Or else, of course," and his voice became very soft, "it wasn't an outsider at all. Harry was fortunate, you see, in that the permanent personnel never changed. Very loyal, for one reason or another, weren't they?"

"Now you men know the rest. This fall you were in on one alarm: the man must have been surprised by Harry's guests leaving early in the morning. Nothing was taken. Then just recently three more attempts, when things were upset by Renshaw's death. The alarms had been turned off each time. Your men came up on two of those."

"Four attempts," said Kate, still talking thickly, but she could now count up to four. "He tried again, after I nailed the storm window shut, but went away."

"Right. Mrs. Gordon, I believe, discovered Harry's old fire escape route. She became suspicious and nailed it shut. At least I think that was her handiwork, from the looks of it."

She nodded.

The older policeman intervened. "This is all very interesting—all these stories about alarms and prints and storm windows, but where does Turner fit into all this, Mr. Forbes? We're investigating attempted murder, not theft."

"He fits, I'm afraid." Forbes looked at them quietly and nothing was said for a few seconds.

The older policeman tucked his shirt into his belt. "Now then, Mr. Forbes, let's have some plain talk. I don't rightly like the idea of you folks coming in and throwing ideas around without saying what they mean and how you get there. Are you meaning to say that Turner here, after thirty years, is stealing Mr. Renshaw's pictures? Turner went south you know."

"No, he didn't." Kate lifted her head off the chair. "Richard saw him. You know—little Richard at the gas station in Plainfield?"

Forbes shook his head. "Little Richard's too small for evidence, Kate, but there's a man in Boston who's been seeing some of Turner these days. Turner got as far south as Boston, anyhow."

"We're still talking about the garage, I reckon? Got the garage fitted into the yarn, Mr. Forbes?"

"Quite. Sensible idea, isn't it, to connect these things. Mrs. Gordon herself discovered an oversight on Turner's part back last fall, but she never connected it. As a matter of fact, she tried to connect it to me—a label. That morning Mr. Renshaw's guests left unexpectedly early and disturbed Turner's nice plan. Turner got fussed, and forgot to pick up the mess, the one label. Little things like that trip us all, don't they, gentlemen. He did trip the gate alarm, however, to confuse things. At any rate, Turner realized that the golden days might be coming to an end, and today he found a fine way to extend them."

242

"Riddles, Mr. Forbes. Talk plain."

"All right. I was Turner's greatest stumbling block. My alarm systems. He had hoped to move in after Harry was gone, but then he found I was still Chairman of the Board. He had nothing against Lisas. Never met the man. Never even heard of him. But here was a splendid opportunity right this morning. If Lisas came out the front door, Turner could shoot him from the garage and become a hero. His reputation was safe. On the other hand, if he saw *me* coming out, there was the sun in his eyes and he could shoot me with impunity, and say that he thought I was Lisas. That's just manslaughter: not too bad. Turner could appear upset and that would be the end of it." Forbes was finished, almost.

"You see, Mrs. Gordon had to make an important decision in that garage. She had no facts to go on. It was just Turner's bad luck that she wasted no time in making up her mind—in coming to the right conclusion."

Forbes looked over to see if Kate was conscious now. He saw her take a deep breath and smile for some reason. This satisfied him and he turned to the police again.

"There you are, gentlemen. Very brief for now, but I'm at your disposal for details anytime after today. And I must add that I think you have all done well. Covered things absolutely splendidly! I thank you."

The men took it rather well, considering. There was a scraping of chairs, an assembling of papers; some cursory politenesses, and they were shown to the door by Lawrence. The sound of their car on the gravel faded into the distance, and the great house lay just as quiet as it had the day she arrived, four months ago.

From the driveway now the Renshaw house appeared as immutable as the great pines that stood in its icy mead-

243

ows, as ordered as the edges of the flower beds and the flowers that would be blooming there the next summer. And from the terrace, the sunlight that poured through the French doors lit up the parquet floors and the cream-colored prints on the walls, the huge oriental rugs. Nothing moved.

However, just for this particular day, there was a difference. The difference was not so much in the quiet within these front rooms as in the quality of that quiet: The butler lay back in one chair; the cook slumped in another. The curator seemed to be in an alcoholic daze, and at the far end of the room, a man wrote things in his little notebook. Except for some fat flies that had survived the winter thus far, nothing moved. *Nature morte* on this side of the great hall or maybe only half *morte.*

On the other side the scene was frankly a shambles. Plaster lay about from the energetic bullets which seemed to have traversed the whole room, chairs, books, prints in their paths, and then gone on into the basement below. Chairs had burst into bloom where their long-repressed kapok had been unleashed. Glass, frames, books, a bookcase strewn about in the quiet, and even the oriental rug had declared its independence of the time-honored Anatolian geometric and formed a new free-form red design all its own.

It might have even been reproduced, this quaint tableau vivant, on a milk calendar series, showing scenes in rural New England—this one titled "The Police Inspector Comes to Call." It brought the Greuze pastoral visit more up-to-date. For about a quarter of an hour things remained this way. Then Kate sat up with a dreadful premonition.

"Lawrence. Don't we have guests coming today? Relatives of Mr. Renshaw? I remember something."

"Not any more, Mrs. Gordon," said Lawrence. "I can-

244

celled them at the first shooting. Also the maids."

"Thank you, Lawrence. That was most foresighted of you. For some reason it completely slipped my mind." She lay back again.

Encouraged by his own foresight, Lawrence began to straighten a few tables and chairs. Mrs. Oliphant pushed her hair into a better shape and walked off to the kitchen with a "Well, well" to herself. Finally, Kate got up, testing her balance first, and then slowly gaining control.

"We'll close the house for a couple of days, I think. I'll cancel whatever was on the agenda."

"That's a wise idea, Mrs. Gordon," Lawrence agreed. "I was feeling rather old this morning and I've aged a little since." He started to pick up the books from the rug, and then put them back down and announced he would take in the matinée at the Bijou instead. He smiled somewhat as Harry used to smile.

Mrs. Oliphant was in the kitchen, staring at all the buns she had made during the morning's diversions. "Well, well" was all she could answer when Kate announced the two-day recess. Beyond those two words lay the nervous collapse of her entire inner dam. She gestured mutely to the refrigerators and the sandwiches, and after a wordless hug for Kate, she sniffed and put on her coat, print scarf, and plastic overshoes, and took some buns in a paper bag for her grandchildren.

Kate was feeling the detente as well—something tight behind the eyes—but maybe hangover was the word. She brought some ham sandwiches and a pitcher of plain, old-fashioned milk out to the living room and put them in front of Forbes. He closed his notebook and regarded the milk with suspicion.

"I gave that up at age two. You Americans love to keep on growing, don't you?" Nonetheless, he helped himself to

245

the sandwiches, finishing the first in one bite, and going on to the second without noticeable pause. Then he stopped to pour himself, and her, a glass of milk.

"Cheers," he said. "Can't really remember when I ate last. Some place called Hanscomb Field, coaxing a plastic chocolate bar out of a machine." He finished the milk.

She offered some more.

"Sorry. It would give me an ulcer."

"Would you like something more substantial? An egg?"

"*An* egg? In Scotland, my dear, *an* egg sits beside seven or eight other eggs on the plate. Life goes on with vigor, not a thin, exhausted trickle."

"It wasn't the 'one egg' that weakened me this morning, it was the five brandies or whatever that was. You deliberately undermined me. They must have thought I was a halfwit."

"Well, I couldn't have you crying and blubbering all over your testimony. It would have given the police the idea that you didn't know what you were doing. I thought you replied just splendidly." He passed the plate back. "Have another." She did.

"I don't usually eat this many," she said. "Mrs. Oliphant gives a couple to the cardinals."

"Is that a bird?" he said, not too interested.

"And you a birdwatcher? Cardinals are quite rare this far north."

"I've never looked at a bird in my life."

"You haven't?" She thought about this. "What were you doing with binoculars that first day back in September? You were coming up from the meadows to a parking lot on the Interstate. I thought you were looking for hawks."

"Unwarranted conclusions," he said, "from your earlier days," he added, smiling. "Binoculars, my dear, were

246

not invented for the Audubon ladies that come tramping through my lands each year searching for great crested this and that. Binoculars were made for war."

"A private war? On the Interstate?"

"I was simply trying to see if Harry's house showed from points along that route. Especially the skylight of the print room. Any more untidy areas? I can't have you making the next decision with a mess in the corners like Rembrandt." A bantering voice that hardly matched his eyes. "It has to be clear, this decision."

She smiled then. The corners were almost all clear anyhow, but it was nice to have the tactical advantage, just once. "Tell me about Brussels. Did it work, the diversion with the cars that came apart?"

"Quite well, actually. We caught them as they were moving. They were in a bit of a rush: casts, molds, paintings and objects all wrapped in plastic, ready to be sealed into those reliefs and shipped out of the country. Art school furnishings, I suppose, private collections of various kinds. It was a handsome operation, well thought out. Hated to spoil it—something so adventuresome in free enterprise."

"But wait a minute" she said, swallowing her last sandwich and almost choking. "So they send these reliefs to other countries, what happens then? They rush in and say 'sorry, we forgot something' and hack out the loot?"

"No, my dear, Georges left no untidy ends, like hacking heads out of friezes in Walla Walla. They had an agreement, you see, that said they would unpack and deliver from port of entry to the purchaser . . . and *voilà!* Goodness knows what goes on in trucks."

He shifted in his chair, to scrutinize her face, and it flustered her, this direct approach. There were a couple more questions remaining.

247

"But how did you know Georges was suddenly coming here?"

"Let's see." He remembered back. "We got the head that night." A pause. "Of course Georges had left the underlings holding the bag. He had gone to Rome. I found out just by chance then, through Julia. She was apparently in Rome, too, and feeling desperately unloved. She had been cancelled by Georges, I gather, whose secretary told her that he had left for Montreal. And here was Julia who had bought four outfits suitable for older men! Though she confided that much, I hesitated to inquire what those outfits consisted of."

"Sweet Julia! She's so transparently charming."

"I'm sure the garments were as well."

"Poor Georges. He escaped Julia, but not to much." For Kate, Georges was still an abstract, noble virtue. She could never bring herself to change.

"He damn near made it, you know. If there hadn't been an ice storm in Burlington, he'd have arrived here first." Forbes was serious for once. "Katy," he started—

"No," she interrupted. "There *is* a next question. I . . . well, since I saved your life this morning I don't feel as timid about asking once again. I feel as if I owned you."

"Oh?" He smiled. "So what now?"

"Well, what do you really do that you can get flown to Hanscomb field at the drop of a hat . . . that's military, you know. That you can call police—you were rather evasive before."

He lit a cigarette, and watched the tip of it for awhile. "Katy, I'm going to have to be evasive again. I *can't* say anything. You're just not going to be a party to some facts in life, ever."

That was all. She looked up to see if he was being sarcastic, if he was partly joking, but he looked sober, miserable even. The voice was light.

"Whole empires have fallen because of a Helen, a Cleopatra."

She expected more. He went on, not explaining, just talking laterally.

"Scotland, you know, isn't a matriarchal society, like America. You'll have to take things as they are."

"What does that mean?"

"It means that I had really made up my mind, if we got out of things alive today, to go back to Edinburgh, back to law. Give up this unsettled part. That is, if you'd come."

She was quiet, and he went on. "You know it works a little better if I own you, rather than you owning me." He passed her the remaining sandwiches.

She looked up to find him watching her with amusement, and when their eyes met it was like being lifted up once again by that Pacific wave, and the sandwiches started to slide off the plate.

This was Harry's decision of course. He had planned it from the start, even before her arrival the first day. Harry and Rembrandt, trying this and that, pushing their conclusions. Forbes had caught on early in the game, and Kate was the last to know.